Unhooking the Moon

Unhooking the Moon

Gregory Hughes

Quercus

New York • London

Excerpt on p. 196 from "A Dream Deferred," by Langston Hughes (*Collected Poems of Langston Hughes*, Alfred A. Knopf/Vintage).

ISBN 978-1-62365-020-9

Library of Congress Control Number: 2013937924

Distributed in the United States and Canada by Random House Publisher Services
c/o Random House, 1745 Broadway
New York, NY 10019

Manufactured in the United States of America

2 4 6 8 10 9 7 5 3 1

www.quercus.com

For Stephanie and her kids Kyle,
Russell, Amber, and Taija

One

Marymount Manhattan is a small, cozy college on the East Side of New York. It was a women's college at one time. It's not now of course, because I wouldn't be here. And I like being here. The girls are pretty and the teachers are pretty cool. And I tend to enjoy my classes now that I can choose what subjects I take. But they're finished for today and so I'm writing in the library. I'm writing a story in the greatest city in the world. But my story does not begin here. It begins in the wonderful city of Winnipeg, or rather the prairies of that city. A land so flat you can watch your dog run away for three days.

I was almost thirteen years old at the time. An unlucky number in some people's minds but I wouldn't have to wait until thirteen for bad luck. It was already on its way. I could sense it coming on that summer's evening, standing outside our farmhouse. I was watching the Rat dribble a soccer ball in and out of the orange cones. When she came to the end of the cones she would blast the ball into the goal my father had bought her in town. Then she would retrieve the ball from the back of the net and start over.

The Rat was happy when she played soccer, but I wasn't happy with the Rat. Only a few days to go before summer vacation and she had spoiled it already. "I think Dad's going to die soon." That's what she had said on the way home from school, as calmly as if she had asked you to pass her the milk. So I suppose I never sensed there was bad luck coming—I had been told.

You may think it was just the ramblings of a ten-year-old, but the Rat was strange. She said things that came true, like the time our dog ran away. I threw him a ball and he ran after it. "You'll never see that dog again," said the Rat. He ran past the ball and kept on going. He ran off into the sunset, a little trail of dust kicking up behind him. We watched until he was out of sight, and I never saw him again. "He wasn't happy here," said the Rat. "Don't take it personally."

Or what about the time she woke me up in the middle of the night to tell me that something bad had happened to Felicia? Felicia was the Rat's best friend; they went everywhere together. But when her parents split up Felicia moved back to Chicago. "You've had a bad dream," I told her. "Go back to bed." The Rat was always having dreams, good and bad, and although she had the biggest dream catcher in Canada they still got through. But the next day at school we found out that Felicia had been murdered. A madman had strangled her to death. The Rat was devastated. Me too. She was a really nice kid. The Rat brooded over it for days. "Maybe the Windigo got her," she said.

The Windigo was a monster from Native folklore. It was a giant that lived in the forest. It had blood-red eyes and claws for hands, and it preyed on little children to satisfy its insatiable lust for human flesh. And the Rat was very fond of it.

That's when Dad sat her down and told her that there were monsters that hurt children, but these monsters were human and they were called pedophiles. The Rat developed an instant hatred for these creeps, and she kept on the lookout for them in every nook and cranny of her life.

"Hey Bob. You wanna play soccer?" shouted the Rat.

I ignored her.

"I'm going in then," she said.

That was the Rat for you: Dad's going to die and I'm going in.

I looked straight ahead and turned 360 degrees. All you could see was sky. Winnipeg really was flat, but there was beauty in the flatness, especially when the sun set. You could watch the whole thing sink into the horizon, which I did before following her inside. The mosquitoes would be out soon. Winnipeg mosquitoes are as vicious as they come. There's no need for mosquitoes to exist as far as I'm concerned, and I'm always getting bit. Unlike the Rat, who seems to be immune.

When I entered the living room she was dancing in front of the television to the latest thing in rap: the Iceman. She had her baseball cap turned around and she was shaking her nonexistent butt in time to the music. The Iceman cursed and swore when he rapped, but the Rat never swore because Dad didn't like it. She bleeped instead.

"I blew his bleeping head off and bleeped his bleeping Ho,
And all his bleeping crew has no place to go,
Tomorrow I'll hunt them down and you will see,
That any mother-bleeper that bleeps with me,
Will be buried in the same bleeping grave!"

The Rat bleeped a lot when she listened to the Iceman.

"Supper's ready," said Dad, entering with a tray. He was already kind of soused. Normally he never started drinking until we were in bed, or close to it, but tonight he had started early. But he was a good dad; he'd do anything for us. And drunk or sober, he was a great cook. I suppose he picked it up from Mom. She died in a car crash when I was a kid. I don't remember much about her except she was French. Winnipeg has an old French community, but she wasn't Winnipeg French—she was proper French from France. And her father was a famous Parisian chef.

Whichever way it happened, Dad could cook, and tonight was his French onion soup and olive bread, which he baked himself. I looked at him as he handed me the bowl. There were no signs of death about him, no signs of sickness for that matter.

The Rat switched off the TV and dropped down on the couch. "Soup, my good man, when you are ready," she said, speaking like an aristocrat.

"Of course, my lady," said Dad, putting a napkin over his arm.

"These days one must be careful whom one talks to," said the Rat. "The muck one meets at the mall are quite despicable."

The Rat could do various accents. But this one, her aristocratic English accent, was her best. She sounded like a snob on the BBC. She could do other accents too. Her Irish accent was quite good, and so was her Southern drawl. But her Indian and Jamaican accents sounded the same, and her Russian accent sounded like Dracula with a cold.

"Would my lady like bread?"

"Bread, yes—one must have bread. Let the peasants eat cake."

"Anything else, my lady?"

"That's all, babe, take the rest of the night off."

"Marie Claire! You can't call the help *babe*!" Dad slumped down next to her. "A lady would never speak to her butler in that casual manner. How do you expect to make your fame and fortune on the silver screen with slipups like that?"

Oh yeah, the Rat wanted to be an actress.

"Sorry, Dad," said the Rat.

"So you should be. Now eat your soup. There's a good girl."

When she had finished, the Rat walked up and down with a book on her head. "Ms. Mountshaft said a book is good for balance. She said it helps posture as well."

That's all you got out of the Rat some days. Ms. Mountshaft said this and Ms. Mountshaft said that. Ms. Mountshaft was in charge of Drama and English, the Queen's English as she called it. And with the Rat wanting to be an actress, they got on like beavers building a dam. Ms. Mountshaft was from England and she spoke all hoity-toity like she had Prince Charles and the lads around on a regular basis. The Rat would mind her Ps and Qs when talking to old Fergy Mountshaft. She would even straighten her back and elevate her chin like a little English princess.

"Being Ms. Mountshaft's protégée is very prestigious," said the Rat aristocratically. "She could have chosen anyone to star in the school play, but she chose me. And I alone will go to the world-famous Winnipeg Ballet this summer. I could be on the brink of brilliance."

"Well, Ms. Mountshaft is a very intelligent woman," said the Old Man.

"Well spoken, Father!" said the Rat. "It's a matter of breeding, you see. And you played your part in my upbringing: good taste and what not."

But then the Iceman came on MTV and the Rat's good taste went out the window. She dropped the book, turned up the sound, and started bleeping all over the place.

"Don't let Ms. Mountshaft catch you bleeping like that," I told her. But she ignored me.

When the rap was over, the Rat read to Dad from the paper. She was a good reader. She would read various articles and then they'd discuss them, commenting on the ongoing wars or famines or the names of the latest hurricanes, and whether they liked them or not. Then the Rat pondered over the paper a while longer. "All these wars. Why don't the people who want war go fight with each other and leave the rest of us to live in peace?" The Rat was big on world events. "The world should be more like Winnipeg," said the Rat. "Winnipeg is the way the world is meant to be."

She would often turn into Little Miss Winnipeg when she read the paper, although some of the kids in school said we weren't real Winnipeggers and that we were just prairie kids. But I was born in the St. Boniface General Hospital in downtown Winnipeg, so I was as much a Winnipegger as anyone. Unlike the Rat. She was born on the Broken Head Reservation. My mother was visiting her friend Mary White Cloud when she was caught off guard. And, being born on a reservation, the Rat was given a Native name. They meant to name her Wazhushk, which means Muskrat. But somehow things got turned around and she ended up being named Wazhashnoons, which means Little Rat. And if that doesn't make her enough of a Rat, she was born in the Chinese Year of the Rat. The Chinese are a clever people. She wouldn't have been born under that star sign if there was no Rat in her. And anyway, it's on her birth certificate. So, old Marie Claire Wazhashnoons DeBillier will be a Little Rat forever.

Although I have to admit, she doesn't look like a rat. She has blue eyes that are large and clear like a Japanese cartoon, and her face, while being far from cute, has nothing rattish about it. But her ears are pointy and she does have mousy blond hair, so there's definitely some rat in her. And, as I've found out on more than one occasion, her teeth are as sharp as a rat's.

"Forget about it, Marie Claire," said Dad, pouring himself a drink. "Guess what I've got for the evening's entertainment? Only the original *King Kong*."

"Great," said the Rat.

The Old Man and the Rat were regular movie buffs. They watched movies nearly every night of the week.

They'd watch anything. They watched black and white movies and movies with subtitles. They even watched silent movies with slapstick comedy and a piano blazing away in the background.

I was into poetry myself. Someone had to have a little culture, and that chore fell to me. I was just about to go up and get started on my new book when dramatic music blasted around the living room. Dad turned off the lights and since it felt cozy on the couch I decided to give *King Kong* ten minutes of my time, even if it was in black and white. Well, I ended up watching it right through to the end. And I don't mind saying I felt more than a little emotional when they shot him down.

Dad went outside when the movie had finished, and we followed him. He walked away from thc houselights and, taking a drink, he stared up at the starry sky. "If you ever have trouble believing in heaven, kids, just look at the stars and you'll see it for yourself."

Me and the Rat stared up at them.

"If people looked at the stars more often they'd see how big the universe is and how small we are in it, and then their troubles wouldn't seem so large. Anyway, it's getting late. You kids better hit the hay."

"See you in the morning, Dad," said the Rat.

"Good night, Dad," I said. And kissing him good night, we climbed the stairs.

"'Twas beauty killed the beast," said the Rat. "The beast was killed by beauty. Beauty and the beast killed Bob—hey, Bob, you know what I don't understand? If they built a wall to keep King Kong out, how come they built a gate to let him in?"

"You think too much," I told her. I still wasn't speaking to her, not really.

I went in my room, got into bed, and opened my book. I hadn't been reading for more than ten minutes when the Rat knocked on my door. She sat on the bed waiting for me to put the book down. I never stopped reading but I could feel her eyes burrowing through the paperback. "What?" I asked.

"Nothing."

"You should be ashamed after what you said!"

"I don't want him to die. I just think he will."

She could get on my nerves sometimes. "You're just a dumb kid! What do you know?" But any time I shouted at her I felt guilty, and then I felt sorry for her. The Rat could do that. She could get you feeling sorry for her. She was quite manipulative in that way. "He's not even sixty," I said. "He's got years to go."

"I'd do anything for my dear Papa," she said aristocratically. "I love him dearly."

"Stop talking like that," I told her. But she *did* love him and she *would* do anything for him.

Not so long back, Dad got beat up. He got drunk and played poker in some bar with this piece of white trash named Pluto. The next day Pluto came to the house and demanded that Dad pay him the $10,000 he'd lost. Dad never had the money and he wouldn't have paid him if he did, and so Pluto beat him up. Dad's kind of skinny.

He'd never stand a chance against a brute like Pluto. And the way I heard it, Pluto tricked Dad by telling him they weren't playing for real stakes. When we got home from school Dad told us he'd fallen down the stairs. He tried to make light of it, but I could see that his pride was hurt.

When I found out what really happened, I told the Rat and she went ballistic. She ran around the house slamming doors and shouting in French. The Rat always spoke French when she was angry; she thought it was more dramatic.

"I'm gonna take care of that creep!" she said. And she said it in such a bitter tone I half believed her.

"What are you going to do?" I asked.

"I don't know, but he'll never hit my father again!"

Well, the next day wc were cycling to school and we passed by the Pluto place. And there he was sitting on his porch, all the debris of a junkyard decorating his lawn.

"Tell your pa I want my money," he shouted. "And he'll pay me if he knows what's good for him."

The Rat stopped her bike. "And you'd stay away from my father if you knew what was good for you!"

Well, that pig Pluto was up and off his porch. "What did you say?"

"Come on. Let's go!" I said.

But the Rat put her bike on the ground and folded her arms. "You heard me."

Pluto stopped in front of her and lowered the top half of his body like an ogre from a bedtime story.

"Listen, little girl. If I don't get my money, there'll be trouble."

I hated that Pluto for hitting Dad. But I was so scared, I was on the verge of apologizing for her. But the Rat put her hands on her hips, looked up into that big ugly face, and said, "If you go near my father again, I'll go to the cops and tell them you put your hand up my dress."

I near fell off the goddamn bike!

"That's not true!" said Pluto, taking a step back.

"So what!" said the Rat, taking a step forward. "Who are the cops going to believe? Me or an ex-con like you?"

Pluto began to walk backwards.

"And you know what happens to pedophiles in prison, don't you? They'll put a dress on you and they'll all have a dance!"

Pluto ran for his front door. "You lying little witch! You stay away from me!"

"Go on, you goddamn creep! You big white-trash bully! You're gonna get yours! You're not getting away with hitting my dad!" When Pluto's front door banged shut she picked up her bike. "I'm gonna make a doll of that bleeping pig and stick pins in it!" I was kind of speechless, so I never said anything. But then the anger left her face, and she smiled. "Told you I'd take care of him." Then she rode away like nothing had happened.

When I tell you the Rat could be scary I'm not even joking. As for Pluto, he must have gone in his house, packed a suitcase, and dropped off the edge of the world because he was never seen again.

"What do you think happened to that creep Pluto?" I asked.

"Maybe the Windigo got him," said the Rat.

"You got him more likely."

"Ah bleep him. He hit my dad. Goddamn pedophile!"

"Just because he hit Dad that doesn't make him a pedophile."

"Yeah, well, he looks like one."

"You can't tell what they look like."

The Rat gave me her scary kid look. "Sure I can, Bob. They can't hide from me."

I never said anything then. She was starting to freak me out.

"And even if that creep Pluto wasn't a goddamn pedophile he hit my dad. And that puts him down there with them."

The Rat could be stubborn at times, and she could be really irritating, but she was right. Anybody who hit our dad was a goddamn pedophile. And that's all there was to it.

Two

THE NEXT MORNING I AWOKE TO THE ONE AND only Frank Sinatra singing "Mack the Knife," accompanied by my dad, of course. Dad's a big Sinatra fan and that's how he got us up in the morning. There was no shouting up the stairs or banging on doors. There was only Frank singing as loud as the sound system would let him. And no matter how much Dad drank the night before, no matter how late he went to bed, he always got up on schooldays to cook us breakfast. He must have been really soused last night because today was Saturday.

The Rat rolled her eyes on her way to the bathroom and I trotted downstairs to tell the Old Man he could go back to bed.

"Dad, it's Saturday," I shouted.

"And a beautiful Saturday it is too," he shouted back.

I was annoyed at being woken so early, and for no reason! But the smell of Dad's blueberry pancakes wafted around the kitchen, and since I was out of bed anyway I took a seat and waited to be served. Dad came toward me doing this shifty little dance, as if to imitate old Mack the Knife himself. You could never stay mad with the Old Man. He was too nice. But I could see where the Rat got her craziness from. Then she came in and sat herself down at the table. "It's Saturday, Dad."

"I know it's Saturday," said Dad, slapping a wad of cash on the table. "I want you kids to go to town and treat yourselves."

It was the surplus from the Old Man's welfare check. You see, Dad used to be a farmer, and quite often the government would subsidize him not to grow certain things. Now they gave him a welfare check, which was like subsidizing him not to grow anything at all, which he didn't, not unless you count the secret garden. It was just a few acres where he grew fruit and vegetables. He sold them around town or at the side of the road; did pretty good at it too. And so he didn't really need the welfare money. But rather than going to all the trouble of giving it back to the government, who probably didn't need it either, he gave it to us kids. I have to say that me and the Rat lived pretty well on welfare.

"Try buying some clothes this time," said the Old Man, sliding the pancakes onto the table. "I don't want people calling my kids white trash."

The Rat mouthed the word *cell phone.* She'd been after one for some time.

"We'll never be white trash," said the Rat, dividing the money. "We don't curse or swear and we're far too sophisticated."

"Of course. What was I thinking?" said Dad. "Well, you kids eat up and head to town."

He never had to tell us twice. We swallowed breakfast, showered, and we were outside on our BMXs before the sun had a chance to turn yellow.

The Old Man came out to see us off. "Look after your sister, Bob."

"I will," I said, riding away.

"Try and be back for lunch. And watch out for pedophiles."

"If I find any, I'll let you know," shouted the Rat over her shoulder.

The Old Man was always telling us to watch out for pedophiles. But I don't think there were any in Winnipeg, not as far as I knew. But the Rat was always on the lookout for them. She's a little strange, like I said.

We rode off our land and onto the dirt road that ran to the train tracks. Far in the distance a 4X4 cut a trail of dust across the horizon, and way beyond that we could see the trees that grew along the riverbank. We passed various fields, brown with wheat or yellow with sunflowers, and then we bumped over the train tracks, which marked the halfway point between our farm and the river. From then on the road turned to tarmac and we covered the same distance in half the time.

The sun was golden when we reached the trees. Its rays were warm and mild for now, but later it would dry the ground to a crisp. Believe me, Winnipeg's as hot as the Sahara in the summertime.

Dismounting our bikes, we made our way down the slope to the river and our beloved *Marlin*. It was a long, lightweight canoe with a square back and an outboard motor, and it went like the wind. But we never used the motor on the weekend; we paddled downriver to save fuel. I positioned the bikes in the boat, the Rat cast off, and we pushed ourselves away from the bank.

I like the morning time; it's special, but it's made more special by the river. The Assiniboine River was our Amazon. It even looked like it in parts, with tall trees blocking out the sun and bright beams of light blasting through for the butterflies to play in. The silence was broken every now and again by the shrieking of an almost-exotic bird or the swish of a catfish's tail. Apart from that there was only the rippling of the oars.

Not wanting to disturb the tranquility, I paddled smoothly. But then the Rat sang "La Vie en Rose" as loud as she could, in French, her voice echoing around the river. All of a sudden the butterflies left, the birds flew away, and the catfish sank to the riverbed. I turned to see her small face straining with the notes, but I said nothing. I wouldn't give her the satisfaction. Every time we paddled downriver she sang that same damn song, and what got me was that the Rat knew the words to every song ever written. She was only doing it to wind me up. And she was worse when she was with the Old Man. They both fancied themselves as a couple of crooners and doubled up every chance they got. The Rat, the Old Man, and Frank Sinatra, it was as much as a twelve-year-old boy could take.

She didn't stop singing until we reached the Forks. The Forks is the place where the Assiniboine and Red Rivers meet. If the Assiniboine was our Amazon, the Red River was our Mississippi. Later it would bustle with paddle steamers, water taxis, and tourists strolling along the riverbanks. But for now it was quiet, except for the few families having breakfast in the riverside restaurants.

"I want a mocha," said the Rat. "Keep paddling."

What that meant was she wanted to hang around the French Quarter. I didn't mind because it was still early, but even if I did mind I'd have no choice. Whether it was that thing with Felicia I don't know, but the Old Man never liked me to let her out of my sight. She was ten and tough and could look after herself, but he worried. So what could I do?

She guided the *Marlin* to the opposite bank and we docked at the jetty below the St. Boniface Cathedral. I jumped out and tied the *Marlin* fast. "Lock the bikes to the boat," I told her. You can't be too careful. There's a lot of petty crime on the mean streets of Winnipeg.

We ran up the stairs to street level and looked across the river toward the downtown skyscrapers, not a single cloud above them. In the center stood the Fort Garry Hotel, quite famous in these parts, and just upriver stood the Esplanade Riel; a splendid name for a very splendid bridge. It mightn't have been the biggest bridge in the world, but it's white and pretty and it gleams in the sunshine. And we're very proud of it here in Winnipeg. I met some people from Saskatoon who said it looked shabby. I'm not going to be childish and say something bad about Saskatoon. There's no need. And if you ever go there you'll see why.

Entering the green graveyard, we made our way toward the St. Boniface Cathedral and the gaping circular hole that hovers in its center. The cathedral burned down long before I was born, but nothing could destroy the stone walls. The hole is from where the stained glass used to be, of course, and above the hole sits a bishop. He looks like a piece missing from a chessboard. Me and the Rat like to position ourselves until all we can see through the hole is sky. It's just something we do. The Rat said it could be a portal to another world. She's crazy, but I've always thought of the cathedral as being a magical place.

I walked up the cathedral steps but the Rat stayed where she was. She was one of those kids who always lingered behind, and I'd always have to tell her to catch up. When I turned around she was staring at the gravestones like a scary kid. "Come on," I said.

She ran toward me. "Guess what I've just seen?"

"I don't want to know!" And I didn't want to know. Last Halloween she had told me she could see the ghosts of the Grey Nuns of Montreal hovering around the graveyard. I bet she only said it to freak me out. But it worked, and so I never let her tell me anything else.

We made our way into the roofless interior of the cathedral and out back. Then we passed the St. Boniface University, where local kids like me and the Rat go when they're older. It's a sophisticated university with a huge silver dome you could see for miles. I really liked it. And I really wanted to go there. The only thing I didn't like was the statue of Louis Riel.

Louis Riel is buried in the St. Boniface graveyard and he's a real Winnipeg hero. You see, he stood up for the Métis, who were the French-speaking descendants of European men and Native women. When the government tried to install English-speaking settlers on their land, old Louis Riel wasn't having any of it, and he led the Métis in rebellion. To cut a long story short, they captured, tried, and executed him. But old Louis Riel would be up and out of his grave to start another uprising if he could see this statue of himself. It is, beyond a shadow of a doubt, the ugliest, scariest statue you'll ever see in your life! It's even concealed in a concrete partition so it doesn't frighten the kids on their way to school. And to give you an idea of how deranged my little rodent sister is, she thinks it's cute.

You know you're in the French Quarter when "streets" turn to "rues," and this is where the Rat liked to hang out. We headed to the stores and cafés that line Provencher Avenue, and all the proprietors greeted the Rat like she was a relation. She bought a magazine from La Page bookshop so she could catch up on celebrity life, and she bought candy from Chocolate Affair. Then we sat outside Le Garage Café where she dons dark sunglasses and orders a mocha. The Rat likes mocha. Then she sat cross-legged in the sunshine and watched the people go by like a Parisian on the Champs-Elysées. And of course the Rat would only drink mocha in the French Quarter because she thinks it's more sophisticated. You see, at heart the Rat is a little French snob, even though she's eating candy out of her pocket because she's too cheap to buy a cake from the café. I said nothing because she had bought me a hot chocolate and was passing me some of the candy. And doesn't everyone who wanders by stop to talk to her, and isn't she on her high horse speaking French? You see, I speak a little French but the Rat speaks French like a Frenchman. And here's old mademoiselle what's-her-name who can speak English but never speaks it to me.

"Bonjour, Marie Claire, comment vas-tu?"

"Bien, merci," said the Rat.

"Et comment va ton frère?"

"Il boude parce qu'il ne peut pas parler français."

And when there were no passersby she flipped carelessly through her magazine, and there was no way she could see anything through those blacked-out sunglasses that make her look like a fly. But I said nothing.

Eventually she finished showing off and we made our way to the Forks.

It's a nice place to escape from the bustle of busy Winnipeg. There's an amphitheater and a podium. And there's always some sort of entertainment around there: a comedian or a clown, or someone collapsing in the heat.

Me and the Rat made our way toward the Forks Market. It sells a lot of cool stuff, most of which we don't need but always seem to buy. And as we did so, a large Native man came toward us.

"Aniish na Wazhashnoons?" he asked.

"Giiuk Miigwech," said the Rat.

The Native laughed and patted her on the head.

"Who's that?" I asked.

"That's Mike. He works on the Hawks Head Reservation."

That was another thing I could never understand. I never let her out of my sight but the Rat knew everybody and everybody knew the Rat. She knew all the vendors who worked in the Forks Market and the boatmen along the river. She knew the immigrants who hung around Tim Hortons, and she knew all the guys who wiped windscreens on Portage Avenue. She knew strange people like Mad Mike the biker, who was the head of one of the biggest bike gangs in Manitoba. He called her his Little Indigo, and he was always polite to her, which was strange because Mad Mike wasn't polite to anyone, not even the other members of his gang. And you'd think she was an informant the way the Winnipeg cops pulled up and talked to her. Sometimes their conversations became really intense. Maybe she was a Rat: ratting people out all over the city.

The only person the Rat didn't get along with was Running Elk, who was walking toward us with my best friend in the world, Little Joe. They called him Little Joe because that was his name, but there was nothing little about him. For a twelve-year-old kid, Joe was built like a sumo wrestler, looked like one too. And his sister Running Elk was no small size. She was a year older and a good deal heavier, and she went to a school for Native kids. I don't know what they taught her there but she was always on the warpath about something.

"Hey, Bob," shouted Joe.

"Hey, Little Joe, Running Elk."

"Hey, Marie Claire," said Joe.

The Rat and the Elk just looked at one another.

"Good news, brother," said Joe. "We're going to meet up with the other guys at the zoo. My grandfather's waiting to give us a ride."

"Great," I said.

The Rat folded her arms. "I don't want to see animals in cages."

"I knew she'd cause trouble!" said Running Elk. "Daddy's little Rat always has to have her own way!"

The Rat clenched her fists. "Listen, Running Buffalo!"

"Okay! Okay!" Joe stepped in between them. "Let's try and behave in a mature manner. Running Elk, why don't you go and wait by the river?"

"Or preferably in it," said the Rat.

"I'll squash you, you little rodent!"

"Enough!" said Little Joe.

Running Elk walked off toward the river, and the Rat walked off toward the park.

"The Rat and the Elk," said Little Joe. "It'll become a Native legend. You see if it doesn't."

"I thought you were First Nations people."

"First Nations, Natives, Indians. Who cares?" He touched my shoulder. "It's not happening, brother. But you'll see. We'll have a great summer—last day of school Monday."

"Okay, Joe, I'll see you at school."

We did our funny handshake, and I watched him walk away. I was angry then and I went to find the Rat to give her grief. "You better watch what you say to Running Elk. She'd eat you for breakfast."

The Rat kicked at the ground in front of her. "Ah bleep her. She thinks her poo don't pong."

"Well I wanted to be with Joe and the other guys. Now I'm stuck with you all morning."

"If you'd sooner be with them you can go. I'm only your sister."

She got me with that one. I felt kind of bad then. "Well, what do you wanna do?"

"Well, we can buy the cell phones and then we can do some stunts on our bikes. If you want to hang out with me, that is."

The Rat liked doing stunts. She had the reputation as the best stunt girl in Winnipeg. She was a real tomboy, but she was nowhere near as good as me. "Come on then," I said. And having gotten her own way, she returned to her ratty self.

First we went to the Bay, which is one of Canada's most popular stores, and there we bought the cell phones. The salesmen wouldn't give us any free call-time and so the Rat kept going on about how much they cost, and how we were just kids, and how she wasn't sure if we could really afford them. In the end he gave us fifty text messages each so she'd go away. The Rat's irritating attitude could pay off at times.

We sent text messages to our friends, so they would have our new numbers, and then we headed to the State Legislative Building. It looks like any other big-domed building, found in most big cities, but it has lots of stone and stairs, and we did some great stunts around there. It's always more fun doing stunts where you're not supposed to. We skidded on the smooth floor until the security guard chased us, and then we cycled around the flowerbed until we were dizzy, and he chased us again. But we came back and encircled it some more because he wasn't nice, and then we rode on to Broadway.

Broadway is one of Winnipeg's best streets and all along it are life-size statues of polar bears. There was a bear with wings like an angel, a bear on a motorbike, and a bear reading a book. There was a bear painted with the Northern Lights and another showing the prairies in full bloom. They're called Bears on Broadway, and they're really cool. Winnipeg is always doing arty things like this. But the Rat started placing her pointy ears against the bears, as though listening to their hearts. "I have to find out if they have a happy spirit." Turns out they all did because they were raising money for cancer, but of course the Rat had to check them all.

When we got home the Rat ran upstairs and I went into the kitchen to see the Old Man. He looked really sad. He got that way sometimes. "You okay, Dad?"

He looked up at me and tried to smile. "Hey, Bob, you hungry?"

"Are you okay?"

"Sure, son, I was just thinking about things. Go tell your sister lunch is ready."

I never knew what caused his sadness and he never talked about it. All I knew was that something pained him and he drank to drown the pain. I shouted to the Rat that lunch was ready. If the Rat had only one usefulness, it was that she put a smile on Dad's face, and in that she never failed.

We ate tomato and ham sandwiches with hot tea, and then we wandered outside where the midday sun was blazing. Dad followed with a bottle and a glass and, sitting on the porch, he poured himself a drink. The Rat shaded her eyes and looked into the horizon. "Dad, Harold's coming."

Dad was just about to take a drink but he stopped himself. "Oh, sorry, Marie Claire."

"It's okay, Dad."

Dad poured the whisky back into the bottle. "I'll go make you kids some lemonade."

Harold was the Rat's boyfriend and a nicer kid you'll never meet. Unfortunately he had something wrong with his legs and no matter how many operations he had, he still needed crutches to walk on. But you never heard a single complaint from old Harold, not about his disability, not about anything.

He lived with his mother in a small shack on the other side of the tracks. She was a hard-bitten woman if ever there was one. She had nothing, and she took nothing from nobody. "You can be whatever you want to be, Harold!" she would tell him. "And I'll have words with anyone who says different!" But no one did say different. Everybody liked Harold.

I remember the day Harold's father left Winnipeg for work. Harold and his mother went to the train station to see him off. He was only supposed to be gone a few weeks, but that was two years ago and they haven't seen him since. When the Rat got the Red Cross to provide Harold with a driver he took up train spotting. The Rat said he did it in the hope of seeing his father come home, but he doesn't talk about it much.

The Rat sat on the back porch swing-chair and read her magazine until Harold was panting in front of her. "Hey, Harold!" she said as though she'd only just seen him.

"Hey, Marie Claire. Hey, Bob."

No matter how hot it was Harold always wore a clean shirt and a tie, and his hair was always neatly combed in a side parting. He was the tidiest kid I ever saw.

"Come sit next to me, Harold."

Harold struggled up the steps and placed himself slowly in the swing-chair. When he got settled I took his crutches and put them within easy reach.

"How are you, Harold?" asked the Rat, handing him a glass of lemonade.

"Fine, thank you."

But it was plain to see that Harold wasn't fine. He looked exhausted to the point of pain, and sweat was pouring down his face.

The Rat put her hand on his shoulder. "Just rest, Harold, it'll pass."

She fetched a damp washcloth from the bathroom and wiped his face and forehead. The Rat rarely helped Harold. Even at school he would struggle to his feet to give her his chair, and she would always take it. I thought it was pretty mean at first. But she told me that all Harold wanted was to be treated as though he could run around the block. So that's what she did.

"Why don't you loosen your tie, Harold?" asked the Rat.

"I'm fine, thank you."

"Honestly, Harold, you can be so difficult," said the Rat and, reaching over, she undid his tie and top button.

Harold never liked to be helped. But a little fussing from his girlfriend always brought a smile to his face.

Leaving them alone, I walked over to Dad's prairie garden to putter around. It was really nice. It had a small gravel path and an old tree trunk that we used for a bench. And Mom's remains were buried here. There was a plaque with her name and dates written on it and under the plaque was a stone jar containing her ashes. Dad said he kept the garden to show us how the prairies would have looked had they not been cultivated into farmland, but really it was dedicated to her. She loved prairie plants, and the garden was full of them. There was the fiery Red Gaillardia with its yellow border and the Stiff Goldenrod with its sticky buds. And the Purple Coneflower, which was the Rat's favorite, grew in abundance. I took a seat on the bench and stretched out. It was so silent you could almost hear the grass drying in the heat. That's the great thing about the prairies, there's plenty of peace and quiet when you want it.

Harold must have recovered from his walk because he and the Rat followed me to the garden. I got up and let them have the bench.

"Thanks, Bob," said Harold, taking a seat. "It's such a beautiful garden. And look at those butterflies. I've heard people call them floating flowers and I can see why."

"Did I ever tell you the Native legend of how butterflies came to be?" asked the Rat.

"No, but I'd like you to."

The Rat knew more of those Native legends than the Natives themselves.

"Well, there were human twins born to the Spirit Woman. And all the animals looked after them. The wolf hunted for them, the birds sang to them, and the bear protected them. They wanted for nothing. But in time the animals saw that the twins never crawled or walked the way their young ones did, and they never reached for anything. This concerned the animals, and so one day they sent the dog to the top of the mountain to see the Great Spirit. 'Go to the edge of the river,' said the Great Spirit. 'There you will find multicolored stones. Collect them and place them at the feet of the children.' The dog obeyed these words, but it had no effect on the children. In frustration, the dog picked up the stones and threw them in the air. To his surprise, they never fell to the ground. Instead, they floated and fluttered and turned into butterflies. Then, the children reached and crawled for them. And, in time, they waddled after them. But the butterflies always stayed just out of reach. And that's how butterflies came to be. And the moral of the story is, don't pamper your children."

"I like that story, Marie Claire. You know so much."

"You do as well, Harold . . . Bob, would you like to get me and Harold more lemonade?"

"Sure," I said. Normally I would tell the Rat to go jump in the river, but she knew I wouldn't say anything in front of Harold. But as I took the Rat's glass from her she began to sway. I knew it was coming. "Dad!" I shouted. She went to stand up but collapsed. "Dad!" Her teeth clenched and she began to shake uncontrollably. I pinned her shoulders to the ground before the spasms grew too violent. Her face cringed with pain and saliva ran from her mouth. I heard a shutter crack and the Old Man's feet swishing through the grass.

"She can't breathe!" shouted Harold.

I tried to unlock her jaw but I couldn't. Suddenly dad was kneeling next to me.

"Daddy's here, sweetheart! You're going to be okay!" His face was hard and serious. "Can you hear me, sweetheart? Daddy's here." She began to make a strange gagging sound. "Try and relax! Breathe normal now, there's a good girl!" Her hands tightened into fists and shuddered back and forth. Her heels ripped at the grass. Dad threw his arms around her and held her tight. "Come on, sweetheart! Let it go!"

I didn't know what to do and so I took hold of her hand. I turned to see Harold. He looked terrified. "She'll be okay, Harold." Just as I said it, the spasms became less violent. Her eyes opened and her jaw unlocked.

"Come on, sweetheart. Take a deep breath." She was still shaking slightly but she took a breath. Dad held her until the pain left her face and then he held her some more. "It's all over now, sweetheart," he said, kissing her on the side of the head. "And you were such a brave girl."

She blinked as she tried to refocus, and tears ran down her cheeks. "I'm surrounded by monsters. But a warrior in black comes to my rescue. He has silver swords and he fights to protect me."

"You've had too much sun," I said. But it's not the sun. It's whatever plagues her. They're like fits and when they happen she says the spookiest things. The doctor said she's not epileptic and he couldn't find anything else wrong with her. He wanted her to see a specialist in Vancouver, but she wouldn't go. The Rat hates hospitals.

"What about me?" asked Dad. "Don't I fight for you?"

Her face was pale but her eyes returned to near normal. "You always fight for me, Dad."

"And I always will," said the Old Man, smoothing his hand over her forehead. She tried to sit up. "Slowly, Marie Claire." Dad helped her sit on the bench by Harold; sitting next to her he held her close.

Harold took hold of her hand. "You were really brave, Marie Claire."

Dad kissed her again. "Wasn't she, Harold? She's always been a brave girl."

We were quiet for a time, nothing but the buzzing bugs to disturb the silence. I stood there feeling awkward. I felt bad for her, but there wasn't much we could do except wait for her to recover. She laid her head against Dad's chest like a child who had just woken up. "Them Gaillardia's are coming up nice," she said.

"Not as nice as you," said Dad. "You're nicer than any flower that's ever lived."

After a few minutes she pulled away from Dad and sat up. Then she stood up. "I'm fine now. It's okay, Bob, I'll get the lemonade."

"You sure you don't want to lie down, honey?"

"I'm okay, Dad."

She walked back to the house with the Old Man following.

"She'll be okay, Harold. It wasn't too bad."

But who was I kidding? I was as worried as the Old Man.

Three

The rising sun diminished my dreams like the dew, and my thoughts turned to Miss Gabriela Felipe Mendez, a student teacher on loan from Puerto Rico. I would be starting at a new school in the fall and so this would be our last class together. I had become quite fond of Gabriela over the last couple of months and she was fond of me, at least I think she was.

"Fly Me to the Moon" blasted up the stairs and I ran to beat the Rat to the bathroom. I sang along with Frank as I showered and gave my hair a second wash. Then, dressed in my best jeans and T-shirt, I trotted down the stairs. The Rat scurried past me. She was in the school play, and she'd been looking forward to it for weeks. She was still a little kid really. She still got excited over things like the school play.

That's why she was wearing her Armani dress, which she was very proud of and usually only wore on Sundays. One of the women in the Red Cross had bought it for her for collecting so much money for the African Appeal. The Rat was as good as a debt collector when it came to collecting money. Most of the volunteers would stand to one side and ask for a modest donation. Not the Rat, she'd run up to them, rattling her can in their faces. She was a proper little extortionist, and I think she embarrassed some people. But it was for a good cause, I suppose.

Breakfast was over in a flash and we were out the door and pedaling away before "My Way" was finished. We didn't sit on our seats until we reached the train tracks. But we stopped when a Northern Harrier plunged into the Indian Grass. The Northern Harrier is a hawk with a three-foot wingspan. There's a lot of wildlife in the greater Winnipeg area. It's like the Serengeti without the lions. Suddenly the hawk sprang up with two red-sided garter snakes in its talons. It looked great! "The early bird catches the early worm," I said.

"But are you the early bird who catches the early worm? Or the early worm who gets caught by the early bird?"

I just gave her a look.

"Anyway, it's a good omen," she said.

"How can you say it's a good omen after what you said about Dad?"

"Different omens mean different things. A hawk capturing two snakes is a good long-term omen. We're good for the long term," she stated.

"You're such a Rat."

"Everybody wants to be a Rat!"

"It's cat, you dummy."

She laughed. She was just winding me up.

We were out of breath by the time we reached the river. We pushed the bikes in the bushes, and firing up the *Marlin*, we blasted downriver. It was cool going to school in a boat. And no matter how tired I was when we started out, I always felt refreshed when we got there.

We rounded the Red River and continued up toward Luxton School. Me and the Rat could have gone to a school closer to home but we preferred the sophistication of Luxton. It's a great school with great teachers and it has large playing fields where we did all sorts of sports.

We docked the *Marlin* as close to the school as we could and, tying her fast, we ran up someone's driveway. We slowed to a walk when we saw a couple having breakfast on their patio. They said good morning to us and we said good morning to them, and then we kept on running.

"Harold's not here," said the Rat.

Harold always waited for the Rat at the school gate. If he wasn't there it was because his legs were giving him grief. "He's probably taking it easy," I said.

When we entered the playground we saw that some of the parents had already arrived; the last day of school was always a bit of an open day. Little Joe came over with some of the guys: Scott and his brother Steve who were so alike they looked like twins. James, the only black kid in my year, who everyone called Jazzy James because he could almost play the sax. And Fireman Fred who got that name because he burned down his garden shed when he was eight. He burned down the garden shed next door the following year but denied setting fire to the Walmart, even though he was seen in the vicinity.

Then there were the Hanson girls, Stephanie and Judy, who came with their older sister Jade and her jailbird boyfriend Bono. They really were Winnipeg white trash and proud of it. They bragged to everyone that their mother was the second-best shoplifter in Winnipeg. Second only to their other older sister Sara who was once Miss Winnipeg and whose beauty dazzled the security guards so much they wouldn't have caught her if they could. But the girls were always well dressed and fun to be around. And Judy was so smart she got a scholarship to a private school in the United States.

Then came Vernon, whose real name was Archibald but who went ballistic if you mentioned it, and Peter, who showed up with his born-again parents, who watched over him like he was the second coming. But he never wanted to be a Christian, or to have his parents follow him around. He just wanted to hang out with his best friend Fireman Fred to see what burned down next. And last but not least came the two James boys: Frank and Jessie. But their name wasn't James, it was Johnston. They were the coolest because their big brother played hockey for Colorado, and their sister had been dated and dumped by the lead singer from the Darkness. He said he'd kill her if she ever came near him again, and so right away she was in both Winnipeg newspapers.

I stood with them, boasting as boys do, while the Rat stood with the Hanson girls, no doubt getting tips on how to shoplift. All the talk was about the upcoming summer and what we were going to do. Little Joe had so many plans. There would be horseback riding on the reservation, camping around Lake Winnipeg, and hiking along the Red River. There was even talk of a trip to Toronto.

When the bell rang we made our way inside. I walked ahead of the guys, and weaving my way through the other kids, I headed straight to class. My first two lessons were with Miss Gabriela Felipe Mendez, and when I entered her classroom she was writing on the board. I took a seat without taking my eyes off her.

"Okay, everybody, take a seat and try to keep the noise down," she said, turning to face the class. "Now, today being the last day of school, I've put some easy exercises on the board; just underline what is a noun, a pronoun, and what is a verb, and then make a sentence out of each."

She had such a beautiful accent.

"When you are finished, make your way out of the class. The boys head to the gym, where I believe you are going to play games. And the girls can go help with the school play."

"Marie Claire's in the play, isn't she?" asked Little Joe turning around.

"Couldn't keep her out," I said.

"I'd like to play with Miss Gabriela Felipe Mendez," said Fireman Fred.

"That's no way to talk," said Little Joe. "Have some respect."

That's why I never told the guys how I felt. They were way too immature.

"Quiet now, and when you are finished, make your way quietly out of the class."

Everybody's head went down, but mine didn't. It's hard to describe Gabriela's beauty. She's like—she's like Miss Puerto Rico. I could just see her standing in her bathing suit, holding a scepter and wearing a diamond tiara. I saw her in a bathing suit once. I was doing backstroke at the pool, and when I got to the deep end I saw her standing above me, bathing suit on and everything. She looked great!

After a while, the kids who had finished put their papers on her desk and left. You could hear the girls giggling down the corridor and Little Joe's booming voice asking them to keep quiet. Most of the kids finished quickly to get out of the class, but I was in no rush. I looked at the page while listening to Gabriela's shoes tapping toward me and then away from me. When she was close I could smell her perfume. She smelled nice.

And when she walked away from me I watched her from behind. I don't want to be rude, because I really like Gabriela, but she had a better butt than Jennifer Lopez.

Soon there were only a few kids left in the classroom and I found myself sneaking glances at her. But then I looked up and she was looking right in my eyes. And for some reason I couldn't look away.

"Are you having trouble, Roberto?"

She calls me Roberto. "Well," I said.

Next thing I know her bronze face was inches away from mine. "You have done these so many times and you never get them wrong. Look—"

She started to explain what to do but I heard nothing. All I could feel was her breath puffing against my cheek and the smell of her perfume wafting around me. It made me kind of dizzy at first. Then it made me very dizzy. And boy was it warm! Why they never had a window open I'll never know! It was as hot as hell outside!

"You understand, Roberto?"

When I turned to look at her, I could see my whole face in her big brown eyes.

"Roberto?"

"I do."

She laughed a little and giving me a smile she walked away. I felt so exhausted my head fell into my hands. But I knew she liked me. She was always asking me to do stuff for her like carry boxes or wipe the board, and she never asked anyone else. And it's not just a schoolboy crush. If I were twenty years older than Gabriela I'd still like her. And I'll be thirteen soon. It's about time I started dating.

I worked as slowly as I could but the exercises were too easy and eventually I had to finish. Gabriela was helping some of the remaining kids. No surprise they were all guys. They never needed help. They were just after attention. I couldn't stand that. It wasn't like she asked them to carry boxes or clean the board. I put my work on her desk and made my way out of the class. And she never even saw me leave.

I headed down to the locker rooms in a bad mood, and getting changed, I entered the gym. There I joined in a game of crazy football. There were no rules. We just split into two teams and dragged a medicine ball back and forth like a tug of war. You had to get the ball to the opposite end to score a goal, but nobody did. But it was a laugh, and we all had a good time.

After lunch, the rest of the parents turned up. It was strange seeing my friends with their parents. I'd known some of them for years, and now I was seeing them in a different light. They weren't individuals anymore; they were part of a group, and they had a life after school that was more important than school. What's more, some of the kids were like clones of their parents, which was a little freaky. And they had mothers. It must have been nice to have a mother. I mean our dad's great. You couldn't ask for a better dad. But it would have been nice to have a mother as well.

Anyway, once the parents had met the teachers, we made our way into the main hall to watch the school play. I don't know what it is about school plays, but they're usually bad, and they're made even worse when you give the leading role to the Rat. She was playing Juliet from *Romeo and Juliet*. Not the whole play, thank God, just enough scenes to make you wish you hadn't come.

When everyone had taken a seat, the lights were dimmed and the curtain raised. And there was the Rat standing on this imitation balcony. I started laughing right away. She was wearing a big white dress, and she had a big white cone stuck on her head. She looked like a rocket waiting to be launched into outer space. Then Romeo—Ronny Hill was his name—ran on the stage. He was wearing women's tights with an oversized shirt and he had a big broad belt wrapped around it. He looked like a plump ballerina.

"Oh speak again, bright angel," said Ronny. "For thou art as glorious to this night being over my head as is a winged messenger of heaven—"

But the Rat hadn't said a word. What's more we were supposed to know that they had met at the Capulets' party, gotten drunk, and fallen in love. When Ronny had finished his lines, the Rat started screaming like a banshee: "Romeo, Romeo! Wherefore art thou Romeo?" What made it worse was that Romeo was standing two feet below her in plain sight. And she was staring into the audience. She looked like a bewildered blind kid.

Then she started ranting like a lunatic about him denying his father, and her not wanting to be a Capulet, and doesn't a rose smell just as sweet and all that. I'd seen the movie, but it was nowhere near as funny as this. I laughed quite a bit until I got told off. Then I had to sit there and pretend to be interested, like the parents.

The curtain closed once they were done, and when it reopened they had the scene with the sword fight. That was the only good part. It was funny as hell because this kid, Kyle Benjamin, got hit in the eye with a wooden sword. "Ah, my eye!" he cried. And collapsed on the stage holding his left eye. The Montagues and the Capulets froze. This wasn't in the script, they thought. Then Ms. Mountshaft ran on the stage, "Come on, Kyle. The show must go on." She tried to get him up and fighting again, but he wasn't having any of it. "I want to go home," he pleaded. The audience started to snigger, and so, grabbing him by one leg, she dragged him away. "Don't just stand there!" she hissed. "Get on with it!" The sword fight resumed. Only this time, there was a little more aggression because the Capulets wanted to get even with the Montagues for injuring one of their men.

When Kyle came out in the next scene he had a patch over his eye. He looked like a pirate. And so the whole play turned into a swashbuckling version of *Romeo and Juliet*, and the better it was for it. I think they should have had a theme in the first place. Romeo and Juliet in Outer Space, or Romeo and Juliet meet Hannibal the Cannibal—something that gives it spice.

The Rat refrained from shouting in the rest of her scenes and she never forgot a single line. I could even see her whispering Romeo's lines to him when he hesitated. The Rat has memory like RAM. But in her final scene, the one where she wakes up and finds Romeo dead, the Rat became deranged. She went absolutely crazy with sorrow and overacting. It's so strange to see your little sister behave like that. I felt so embarrassed for her, I could feel my own face reddening. Why she didn't stab herself I don't know. God knows she had hold of that dagger for long enough. But eventually she held up the instrument of death. She looked at it as serious as a samurai ready to commit suicide. All of a sudden she cried out "Ah!" and plunging the dagger into her belly, she collapsed on the stage. It's over, I thought. That's it. But then she got up! Who stands up after stabbing themselves? I bet that wasn't in the script. And boy did she stagger around the stage. But that was the Rat for you. Once she was in the limelight she never wanted to leave it. Finally, she hit the deck.

"Curtain. Curtain," shouted Ms. Mountshaft.

When the applause died down Father Henri came out to give his summer sermon. He reminded me of a convict somehow. He had closely cropped hair and his jaw was blue with shaving, but that wasn't it. He had an aura about him: like someone who had done a life sentence in solitary confinement. I always imagined he'd been in prison in his earlier life and he'd turned to the church when he'd got out. But it probably wasn't true.

After the sermon was over, the headmaster took to the stage. He thanked the actors and the parents and everyone who'd worked in, or been to, Luxton in the last one hundred years, which is how old it was and how long his speech seemed to last. I liked the headmaster; he was fun, but he did like the sound of his own voice. Eventually we all spilled out on to the playing fields where the teachers served us free snacks and gave us presents of pencil sets.

I was sad then. I would miss the teachers and the school a great deal. It wasn't just Gabriela, it was everyone. They were all good people. And I'd imagined my final day at Luxton being a little more of an occasion. I thought me and the guys would be standing around reminiscing about the old days. But they began to drift away quite early, as though it didn't matter, and that made me sadder.

I couldn't find Little Joe, and so I took a stroll around the inside of the school and reminisced by myself. But then I turned a corner and saw the Rat talking to Ms. Mountshaft.

"You excelled yourself, Marie Claire. I knew you'd rise to the occasion and you did."

"I couldn't have done it without you, Ms. Mountshaft. You were a real inspiration."

I wasn't going to get involved in that, so I went back the way I'd come. I walked down the Arts and Crafts corridor, and passing a display case, I saw my little balsa wood boat. I'd made it when I first came to

Luxton, and I hadn't thought about it since. Most of the kids rushed to finish theirs but I took my time with mine, and it won first prize. I was so proud. It's strange how the little things can make you proud.

The Hanson girls came by and tried to get me to go into town. I'm pretty popular with the girls. Well, I am good looking and tall for twelve. But I wasn't up for it, and so I went back to find the Rat. But she wasn't talking to Ms. Mountshaft now. She was talking to Miss Gabriela Felipe Mendez! They both turned to look at me, and I kind of froze.

"Este es mi hermano," said the Rat.

I didn't believe it. The Rat could speak Spanish. That was the Rat for you. She was always sneaking off and learning something new when you weren't looking. *"Tu le gustas,"* said the Rat.

Gabriela laughed out loud. What had that damn Rat said?

"El es simp·tico e inteligente. Y yo estoy segura de que va a ser un hombre muy guapo. Tu tienes suerte de tener un hermano asi." Gabriela looked at me and then back at the Rat. "Well, Marie Claire. I'll see you after vacation. *Hasta luego.*"

"*Hasta la proxima,* Miss Felipe Mendez."

Gabriela walked toward me. "Good luck at your new school, Roberto. I'm sure you'll do really well." She looked right in my eyes. "I just want to say, you have been a great student. It has been a pleasure to have you in my class."

She looked really sad. I'm not kidding. I couldn't believe how sad she looked. "Maybe we'll see each other around Winnipeg," I said.

"Maybe. *Adios*, Roberto."

Me and the Rat said good-bye to the rest of the teachers, and wishing them a happy vacation, we made our way down to the *Marlin*. I waited until there was no one around before I got her in a headlock. "What did you say to Gabriela, you little Rat?"

"Gabriela? Miss Felipe Mendez to you."

"You tell me or I'll pull your damn head off!"

In the end she squealed. "I just told her—"

"What? What?"

"Relax, Roberto, she's twice your age."

"She's only nineteen. Now you tell me or you're going back in the headlock!"

"I just told her you had a crush on her. That's all."

"Oh my God!"

"And she said you were nice and intelligent and would grow up to be a good-looking guy, but you're way too young for her."

I dropped down in the boat. "You drive," I said.

"It's steer, Bob, not drive."

Nice and intelligent. That's what she had said; not just nice, but nice and intelligent. And good-looking as well.

"What did you think of the play, Bob?—Bob?"

Mature even, because I'm very mature for my age. Maybe she'd let me hang out with her. And then when I'm fifteen I could ask her out. Because, when I think about it, there isn't much difference between our ages. Dad was sixteen years older than Mom when they married. I don't want to get ahead of myself, but I'm going to that swimming pool every day over summer vacation. I'll go there until I see her and then—well, I don't know. But I'll be there, so I'll find out.

Gabriela filled my thoughts all the way up the two rivers. I thought about her as I tied up the *Marlin* and as I got on my bike. The cycle home was all a blur. All I could see was her face next to mine, and my face in her big brown eyes. I was still thinking about her as I rested my bike against the house. I never thought about what the Rat had said about the Old Man dying until I found him dead on the kitchen floor. And then I thought about nothing else.

Four

He was curled up like a child. His hair was neatly combed, and he had a spatula in his hand. I was half expecting, desperately hoping, for him to jump up and say it was a joke. I would have laughed. I really would have. But he wasn't going to. His eyes were open and the life had gone out of them. Death must have come for him when we were at school. Or on the way home from school. He looked so alive it could have come for him as I laid my bike against the house. But come for him it had. I looked around the kitchen to see what he was going to do with the spatula. But there were no signs of cooking. He looked out of place on the kitchen floor. It was such a strange place for him to be lying down. But he wasn't lying down, he was dead.

Next thing I know the Rat was kneeling next to him. “Pupils are fixed and dilated. Pa’s a goner!” She closed his eyes and kissed him on his forehead. “Everything’s going to be okay, Dad. We’re going to take good care of you.” She took her cell phone from her pocket and walked up the stairs, typing a text as she went.

God could have let him live a little longer. He wasn’t doing any harm. And he wouldn’t have done any harm. All he wanted to do was look after me and the Rat. It wasn’t much to ask. But it had been taken away from him. And he had been taken away from us. “Oh Dad!” I felt the tears come into my eyes.

I heard the Rat’s cell phone ring upstairs. I could hear her muffled voice, and then I heard her coming down the stairs. “Dead as a dormouse! No, I’m fine. Okay, we’ll see you soon.” She came into the kitchen wearing her little black dress. “You seem upset, Bob, and so I better take care of the funeral arrangements. Now, I’ve spoken to the Chief and he’s coming over with Little Joe and Mary White Cloud. I told them to pick up Harold on the way. We’ll bury Dad in his prairie garden next to Mom’s ashes, and we’ll ask the Chief to perform the ceremony. We need to give him a good send-off to the other world. We don’t want his spirit hovering around here, now, do we? No, the Chief will make sure he gets off all right.”

I wiped my eyes. “We can’t just bury him! We have to inform the proper authorities!” But the words sounded strange when they came out.

"Are you out of your bleeping mind? We're not telling anyone! Look, Bob, you're bereaved! I've had a lot more time to think about this than you! We have no other family. They'll put us in a home. And them homes are all run by creeps! No, as Frank said, we'll do it my way. You get the shovels, and I'll go pick some flowers." She turned on her little black shoes and went out the door.

I couldn't understand it. The Rat wasn't upset, not even a little bit. Maybe she was in shock. Whatever the case, I could see she was right. They could put us in a home. They could even split us up. "They're not going to split us up!" I said and stormed off to get the shovels.

I followed the Rat down to the prairie garden, where she stood looking at the ground. "Here's a nice spot," she said pointing to a bare patch between the gaillardias and the purple coneflowers. "And he'll be right next to Mom. You get started and I'll move the things off the living room rug. That's what we'll wrap him in."

"This isn't right! Our dad deserves better than this!"

"No, Bob. This is exactly what he would have wanted. He loved Mom and the prairies and he loved his prairie garden. It's like burying a captain at sea. And he wouldn't want us to be sad. So try not to upset yourself too much. I'll tell you what. Why don't you come back to the house? The Chief will be here soon. He'll help you dig."

We made our way back to the house and sat quietly until the Chief's jeep pulled up outside. I looked out the window. Little Joe, his grandfather the Chief, and

Running Elk got out first. They held the door open for Harold, and following him came Mary White Cloud, my mom's old friend. The Rat opened the front door, and they made their way inside.

"Hey, brother," said Little Joe putting his hand on my shoulder. "I'm really sorry." Running Elk came in with Mary White Cloud's rocking chair; she never went anywhere without it. "I'm sorry, Bob," said Running Elk, and she sounded like she really meant it. Then Mary White Cloud came in. Mary White Cloud, who had helped deliver the Rat, never looked her seventy years. Her eyes were pale and bright and when she smiled her face glowed with warmth. "Hey, Bobby." She was the only one who ever called me that. She touched my arm and sat in her rocking chair.

The Chief helped Harold take a seat, and then, going in the kitchen, he knelt over Dad.

He looked at him for a few seconds and then he came back in the living room. "There are no signs of pain on his face. I am sure he died peacefully." The Chief was a big man with thick gray hair that he wrapped in a ponytail. He had a hard, serious face, and in all the time I'd known him, I'd never heard him laugh.

"We want to bury him in the garden next to Mom," said the Rat. "And we want you to perform the ceremony, Chief."

"I cannot do that. There has to be an autopsy."

"But it's what he wanted," said the Rat. "And it's what we want. Isn't it, Bob? The authorities can't find out. If they do they'll take us away and put us in a home."

"Come here, Wazhashnoons. Let me look at you," said Mary White Cloud. The Rat stood in front of her and Mary took hold of her hands. "My, how you've grown. How old are you now?"

"I'll be eleven soon."

"And you look more like your mother every day. Tell me child, what dreams have you had?"

"I've had many, but one keeps coming back. There's a man, and he's surrounded by tall buildings. He tells me he's going to look after me and he keeps me somewhere safe, like a castle, and he reads to me all the time. I don't know why he reads to me. I can read myself." The Rat frowned. "You know who the man is, don't you, Mary?"

Mary White Cloud looked at the Chief and then back at the Rat.

"Can we bury Dad first?" asked the Rat.

"You cannot bury him here," said the Chief. "It's breaking the law."

Mary White Cloud pulled her shawl around her. "I remember a time when my son called them white man's laws. He would talk about the way they used their laws to destroy his people. I can also remember him calling an autopsy a sacrilege to the dead."

"That was long ago, Mother," said the Chief. "The words of youth."

"The words of youth are not always foolish. You have become so involved in the day-to-day running of the reservation. You think about what is politically correct without consulting your heart. You seem to have lost your spiritual beliefs. Even though last week I told you I heard the owl call John's name. Even though you can see how gifted his daughter is."

The Chief shook his head. "I am a Native Chief. It will reflect badly on the reservation and on the First Nations people themselves. I have responsibilities, Mother."

"But you have no responsibility here. This is not the reservation, and the DeBilliers, while they have always been our friends, are not your people. You are held in high esteem by many, my son. Is it that which you fear losing?"

"And what if I am prosecuted, Mother? What then?"

"Then I will be sorry to see my son in court. But if you do not bury John according to the wishes of his children I will be ashamed."

The Chief bowed his head, a little, and then he looked at me. "We will help you dig the grave and I will perform the ceremony, if that is what you want. But make no mistake, they will exhume the body when they find out."

"His spirit will be gone by then," said the Rat. "So it won't matter."

"True," said the Chief.

"We have to put Dad in his suit," said the Rat. "And he has to be wrapped in the rug. He always liked that rug. Mom bought it in Paris."

"I'll help you," said Running Elk.

Me and Little Joe followed the Chief outside and we walked down to the prairie garden. Without so much as a word the Chief took off his jacket and picked up a shovel. Me and Joe did likewise and we began to dig. The ground was soft but it was hard work all the same. My hands ached with gripping the shovel and I was soon breathing heavily. Me and Joe took turns in taking a break but the Chief, old as he was, was big and strong and he worked without stopping. Within an hour he had the grave dug, and climbing out of the hole, he put on his jacket. "Let's collect the body," he said.

My father was no longer my father, he was the body.

When we entered the living room the furniture had been pulled back off the rug.

"Grandfather, can you bring him in?" asked Running Elk.

The Chief looked at me to see if I wanted to help but I looked out the window. When they brought Dad in the room I kept looking out the window. I could hear them straightening his legs and pushing the rug over him. I watched Little Joe go outside. He took a drum and a tambourine from the jeep. Then I heard his footsteps coming back into the house.

"Would you like to look at him, Bob?" asked the Chief. "Before we—"

I shook my head.

"He looks okay, Bob," said the Rat. "He even looks happy."

But I couldn't look at him and so they tied him up with some cord.

"When you're ready, Bob," said the Chief.

When I turned around they were waiting for me. I stood next to Little Joe at the front of the rolled-up rug and we picked him up. Running Elk and the Chief took the back while Harold and Mary White Cloud followed behind. The Rat put on her sunglasses and, holding the large silver crucifix she had taken from the mantel-piece, she led the procession.

No one spoke as we made our way out of the house to the grave. The only sound was our jeans rubbing together and our feet swishing in the grass. I couldn't believe how little he weighed. With the four of us carrying him he weighed no more than a bag of groceries.

When we reached the garden, Running Elk and Little Joe put the instruments down and helped lower Dad into his grave. Then the Chief stood at the front of the grave and we stood around it. He threw dust in the air and spoke in the old language so the ancestors would understand. Then he began to chant a song like the Indians in the old cowboy movies. The Rat, who knew all the old songs, could chant with the best of them, and she sang along. Running Elk and Little Joe joined in, beating the drum and shaking the tambourine. Mary White Cloud began to dance from side to side, and we all did the same, except for Harold who shuffled on his crutches. I moved my feet as best I could, but my heart wasn't in it. Unlike the Rat who danced like she was at a rave. When the Chief stopped singing we fell silent. He nodded to the Rat who removed her sunglasses and took his place at the front of the grave.

"Dear Lord, we ask you to look after our dad and allow his spirit to roam free and happy in the spirit world. He was a good dad who always looked after us, sang for us, and cooked for us." The Rat paused. "His pancakes were probably the best in Winnipeg, one might even say Canada, and his French toast was envied by all. Omelettes were another speciality and even though hc couldn't make mocha his regular coffee was pretty good." She paused again. "He cooked a great barbecue. His speciality was barbecued catfish, which he cooked with corn and roast potatoes. Duck was another favorite, as was his roast pig with his very own applesauce. We had it one Christmastime, and I swear it was the best meal I ever had. Dad always made Christmas special. But it wasn't just his big meals. Something simple like his oven-baked oatmeal raisin cookies could brighten the day. And whenever I was feeling down he would make me a special sandwich, and right away I felt better. And that was another speciality: making you feel better."

The Rat continued until the cookbook of Dad's life was complete, and then she finished with an Amen.

"Well done, Marie Claire," said Harold.

The Rat looked pleased with herself. "Would you like to say something, Bob?"

I shook my head. I just couldn't. She dropped a purple coneflower into the grave, and we began to fill it in. It felt strange burying my father on that sunny afternoon. He'd cooked us breakfast that very morning, and now he was dead. Tears blurred my vision as I shoveled the soil over him. I couldn't believe I wouldn't see him again, but the grave was soon filled in. The Rat pushed the crucifix into the ground and we wandered away. It was over, just like that.

"Give me your arm, Bobby," said Mary White Cloud.

I put my arm through hers and escorted her back to the house.

"We all have to leave this earth someday. I know you are very sad, but you will see him again when it's your turn."

"But I'm also worried about what will happen now, Mary. Little Rat said they'd put us in a home. She couldn't handle being put in a home. She's crazy and they'd try to make her normal."

"She only appears crazy because she does not behave like others."

"But she says strange things, Mary. She said Dad was going to die and it came true! And she says other things that come true."

"We can all see the future from time to time. But the truth is that Marie Claire is a very special child. She's received a great gift from the Great Spirit. But even if she wasn't gifted she is still a precious being and you should guard her with your life."

I looked at the Rat who walked on ahead of us. She was talking to Harold about the play. "She's not even bothered that he's dead!"

Mary stopped me. "That's not true, Bobby. Of course she's bothered! But with her insight she can see that death is only the beginning. And so she's happy for him. And if you could see what she sees, you would be happy for him too."

But I couldn't see what she sees, and I might not believe it if I did. Because even though I pray sometimes, and I try to believe in God, I'm not sure if I do. And I found it so hard to believe in an afterlife. It just didn't seem real. People floating around on clouds and being happy for eternity. It was like believing in fairies and Santa Claus. It would be nice if it were true, but I doubt it was.

When we got back to the house, Running Elk and the Rat served us coffee, sandwiches, and the last apple pie that Dad ever made. And for the first time they seemed to get along. And I was glad Mary and the Chief were there. It's good to have your friends around you when something like this happens. And they were wise. It's good to have wise friends.

Later we made our way onto the porch and watched the sunset.

"It was a nice service, Bob," said Harold, sitting down next to the Rat. "And I'm sure he's in a better place."

"Thanks, Harold."

"If anyone's going to a better place it's your father," said Running Elk. "He was a good man. I liked him a lot."

The Rat looked at Running Elk. "You liked our dad?"

Running Elk rolled her eyes. "And you're supposed to be gifted."

It was even nice to have Running Elk there. She was never friendly but I felt she was a true friend. And I was sure that one day her and the Rat would be the best of friends. One day.

When it was dark the Chief built a blazing fire. Bringing out some chairs, we sat around it. Then, in the voice of a seasoned storyteller, he told us many a Native legend. Legends you could not find in storybooks, but which had been passed down from a time before white people came to the Americas. They all had a moral about death and the afterlife, and I found them comforting to listen to. Even the crackling fire made me feel better. Maybe that's why they built it. I watched the orange sparks float up into the night sky. They made me think of tiny spirits on their way to heaven. Who knows? Maybe it is true.

When the Chief had finished, we cooked deer meat, which we ate with rice and bread. Then Mary talked about Dad's life before we were born, or too young to remember. She told us about the first time he drove a combine harvester, and how it ended up in a ditch. She told us how he bought a car to drive to Montreal, when he was accepted into university, and how it never made it out of Winnipeg. She told us that, for many years, he had been the most successful farmer around. And that much of the harvest was donated to the poorer reservations. The Chief confirmed this. Even Running Elk could remember the old folks talking about his kindness. I felt sad listening to his old friends talk about him with such affection, but I also felt happy and proud. He wasn't just a good dad, he was a great man as well.

Running Elk and the Rat served us more coffee and we drank it while looking at the stars. It was a nice evening and I enjoyed sitting outside. Harold insisted on helping the Rat do the dishes, and when they returned Mary White Cloud sat up in her rocking chair. It was time to discuss what would happen.

"You know your father was proud of you, kids. And you always did him proud. You were the only thing that kept him going after your mother died."

"What are we going to do, Mary?" I asked.

She sat forward, her face glowing in the fire. "Maybe you could go to your uncle."

"We have an uncle?" I said.

Even the Rat looked amazed.

"Your father had a brother, a bad brother by all accounts, and his name was Jerome, Jerome DeBillier. And he still lives, as far as we know, in the city of New York."

"He's the man in my dream!" said the Rat.

"Maybe," said Mary.

"Was he really bad?" I asked.

"He had some hard bark on him, that's for sure. He was twelve years younger than your father and twice his size. He went to sea at fifteen. Joined the French Foreign Legion at nineteen. When he came back he was always in some sort of trouble, fights and whatnot. There was even a rumor he'd killed a man in a bare-knuckle contest on the coast of Africa somewhere. He always had the ladies around him too. Every time I saw him he was with someone different. Your mother was in New York with him when she died in the car accident. Your father went there to bring home her body. When he returned he told us that Jerome had become a drug dealer and that he was responsible for your mother's death. He told us never to mention his name again, not to him and not to you kids." She took a photograph from her bag and handed it to me. From the light of the fire I could see a portrait of a young, mean-looking man. He had a small scar on his right cheek, like the sickle of a quarter-moon, and his eyes were as black as his hair.

"I can't see any resemblance to Dad," I said and passed the Rat the picture.

"I can!" said the Rat. "That's Dad's brother all right!"

Mary looked at me. "I've known Jerome since he was a small boy. And, bad as he was, I believe he'd look after you."

Chief White Cloud stood up and threw some logs on the fire.

"What do you say, Chief?"

"I do not agree with Mother. Maybe you could live with foster parents. We would take you in ourselves but

I am too old to adopt, and now that my daughter is dead I have to take care of Little Joe and Running Elk."

"I'm not living with foster parents and I'm not going in a home," said the Rat.

"I was thinking we could ask the authorities to locate Jerome," said the Chief. "But they would never let you live with him, not if he sold drugs for a living."

"We'll go to New York and locate him ourselves," said the Rat. "And we'll leave tomorrow. Right, Bob?"

When I looked at her she looked worried. I didn't want to go in a home and I didn't want to live with foster parents, but I could if I had to. The Rat couldn't. She needed space, at least twenty acres, to go crazy in.

"We'll leave tomorrow," I said.

The Rat looked relieved. "Thanks, brother. I knew you wouldn't let me down."

"Can you help, Chief?"

The Chief made a grim face. "I have already broken the law by helping you bury your father. But, as Mother pointed out, the law is not always right. But I'm sorry, Bob, I can help you no further."

"We can get the train to Toronto and cross the border!" said the Rat.

"Two kids traveling alone on a train will look suspicious," said Running Elk. "And you'll need money for the tickets."

"Freight trains leave every day for Toronto," said Harold. "I don't like to think of you traveling in that manner, Marie Claire, but if you want me to I'll—"

"Of course!" said the Rat. "Harold will put us on a freight train!"

Mary White Cloud rocked in her rocking chair. "I feel that someone in the spirit world watches over you, my little Marie Claire. And I believe that your destiny, like ours, was painted on the walls of caves long before you were born. And so, what will happen, will happen. But I can't help but feel that you are in danger."

Chief White Cloud looked concerned. "On that I agree. You are only children. New York can be a dangerous place. You might not find Jerome. He might not want you if you did. For all we know he may no longer be living there."

"He's there," said the Rat. "I can feel it!"

"Wait a day or two," said the Chief. "I will try to find a family to take you in."

I could see that going hobo-style to New York appealed to the Rat's sense of adventure. In her mind she was already on that train and I was on it with her. The Chief's words fell on deaf ears.

Five

When I woke the house was silent. No trumpet sounds blasted up the stairs. No crooning came from the kitchen. The smell of pancakes and coffee had been replaced by a fresh breeze. It even seemed cold in the house, as though winter had come to Winnipeg overnight. I got dressed, and making my way downstairs, I entered the kitchen. Everything was wiped clean and bare. I stood there for a moment looking at the spot where we had found him, and then, pushing open the screen door, I went outside. There I saw the Rat kicking a soccer ball in and out of the orange cones.

"It's exciting, isn't it? We might meet celebrities! My acting career could take off!" She blasted the ball into the back of the net and ran to retrieve it. "The others left early this morning, and they took Harold with them.

He said to be at the Symington Yards before midnight. That's when the train leaves." She placed the ball at the beginning of the cones and started over. "We'll have to take care in Toronto. It's a dangerous city. And the people are a bit snobbish. But don't worry about them. We'll just be our pleasant selves, and if they're not nice to us we won't speak to them." She came to the end of the cones and kicked the ball hard. She missed and it rolled off toward the garden.

"Are you okay?" I asked.

"Sure, Bob," she said looking slightly surprised. "But I haven't had breakfast yet. Can you make me some pancakes, like the way Dad makes them?"

"Dad's dead. You know that, right?"

"Of course, Bob. That's why I'm asking you to make them."

We went in the kitchen and I made her pancakes. She frowned at them at first, but she ate them quickly once she got started, and then she ran upstairs. "I'm going to get started on my packing."

I didn't like being left alone in the kitchen. It felt empty without the Old Man. But I filled up the sink and started the dishes.

"How much stuff can I take?"

I dried my hands and went upstairs. She had two suitcases open and all her clothes were laid out on her bed. She had all her shoes, soccer gear, and coats. She even had a bathing suit. It was as though she was going on vacation. I felt weary and sad, so I sat down on the bed. "We can't carry suitcases on the bikes and we'll need them to ride to the railyards. We can even use the bikes in Toronto if we can get them in the boxcar."

"You're right, Bob. Good thinking." "We'll just take our backpacks. They're not very big, so we can't bring a lot of stuff. We'll take a change of clothes and our raincoats. We can take a towel and some toiletries, and a flashlight, but that's all. We can tie our sleeping bags to the top of our backpacks and put our cell phones and their chargers in the side pockets. We'll need them in case we get separated. The only other thing we should take is our birth certificates. It's best if we have some ID."

"What about my Armani dress and my soccer gear? I might want to play soccer."

"You can put your soccer gear in my backpack. You should have enough room for your dress."

"Okay," she said. "But we have to dress the part for the journey. Let's wear our overalls."

I agreed, just to keep her happy.

We packed our backpacks, tidied our rooms, and put everything away that needed putting away. We took the $150 from the cookie jar and split it between us. And then we made ourselves sandwiches for the journey. The Rat pumped up the tires on the bikes while I took care of Dad's room. I took the sheets off his bed, packed away his things, and wiped around with a duster. Then I took his clothes from the chest of drawers and put them in a box. He never had many things, and what he did have was old and worn.

I remember bumping into him in town, this one time, when I was out with the guys. I felt ashamed of him because he was so raggedy. Now I felt ashamed of myself. He would have dressed a lot better had he not given all his money to us kids. He even got drunk on the cheap: homemade wine and homemade whiskey. Nothing was too cheap for the Old Man when he was buying for himself. And nothing was too expensive when he was buying for us.

Hidden away at the bottom of the chest of drawers I found a photograph of him and Mom. It was taken outside St. Boniface on their wedding day. Dad looked proud and Mom looked beautiful. She had long blond hair and green eyes, and she smiled like a movie star. It was a nice photograph. I wondered why he kept it hidden away.

Sometimes I imagined having conversations with my mother, especially when I was feeling down. She was kind and patient and she always gave me good advice. Then she would ruffle my hair and carry on with the ironing. I always had my imaginary mom ironing for some reason.

After I had taken care of Dad's room I helped the Rat clean downstairs. We did a lot of things around the house, just to keep busy. We vacuumed the carpets, wiped the windows, and dusted wherever it needed dusting. We even cleaned out some of the closets. When we were done we made our way down to the prairie garden, which had now become a cemetery. The silver crucifix that the Rat had used as a headstone caught the sun and blinded us as we came.

"Omens don't get much better than that!" said the Rat.

We planted a nice mixture of prairie flowers over Dad's grave and then we each said a silent prayer.

"Amen," said the Rat when my lips had stopped moving. Then she looked up at the sky. "He's not here any more. His spirit has flown the coop. Bye, Dad!" she shouted. "Have a pleasant trip! And say hello to Mom!" She looked around the sky as though expecting a voice to shout back, and then she looked at me. "What do you want to do now, Bob? You wanna play soccer? I need someone to go in goal."

"Come on, then," I said, just to keep her happy.

It was late when I turned off the lights. Stepping out onto the front porch, I locked the door and put the keys in the flowerpot. Then I looked through the window at the lifeless living room. It was dark and ghostly as though no one had ever lived there. If we never made it back, I thought, it would be like we never existed. Suddenly I felt like going back inside. I felt like turning on all the lights and the stove. I felt like cooking and baking so that warm smell would fill the house again. I felt frightened.

"It'll be okay, Bob," said the Rat.

I turned to see her sitting on her bike with her backpack on her back. I always felt I had to be brave in front of the Rat because I was her big brother. But right there and then I could have burst out crying. But I didn't. I put on my backpack and mounted my bike. "Let's ride," I said like some Western hero, and we rode off toward the river.

Everything seemed strange that night. The land was so deserted we could have been on the surface of a barren planet. And the moon was so bright it gave us shadows as we rode. What's more, it had a pink tint. The Rat kept looking at it, no doubt trying to decipher what sort of omen it meant. But I knew that pink was almost red and red would have been a bad omen according to anyone's way of thinking.

We rode until we came to the trees, and then dismounting our bikes, we made our way down to the river. We never needed our flashlights, with the moon being so bright. But it went dark as we passed through the trees, and the darkness always looks darker when you're feeling down. I was glad when we reached the river, and putting my bike in the *Marlin*, I untied the ropes.

The Rat rustling in the bushes sounded louder than it should. "Shush!" I told her. She froze as she lifted her bike into the boat and then she lowered it gently. Getting in, we pushed away from the bank and paddled downriver. I didn't want the neighbors in the nearby houses hearing the engine. We were never out on the river that late. If they heard the engine they might think the *Marlin* was being stolen and call the cops.

Once we were at a safe distance I started her up and pulled back on the throttle. The cool foamy air put goose pimples on my arms and made me shiver, but it didn't seem to bother the Rat. She looked back at me every now and again, her mousy blond hair blowing in the breeze. I swear she was smiling.

I slowed down as we passed the imitation lighthouse that lit up that part of the Forks, and we cruised toward St. Boniface. As we neared the jetty I switched off the engine, and we drifted alongside it. The Rat jumped on to the jetty and tied us fast. I got out and unloaded the bikes.

"Bye, *Marlin*," said the Rat. "The *Marlin*'s spirit is unhappy that we're leaving."

She seemed more upset over leaving the *Marlin* than she was over Dad dying.

"She'll be okay," I told her.

"It's a he, silly."

We put on our backpacks and pushed our bikes up the ramp. When we got to the road I looked at the Esplanade Riel. I thought about all the times we had gone under it on our way to school, and I thought of Miss Gabriela Felipe Mendez. I would have given all the land that Dad left us just to talk to Gabriela. To tell her how bad I was feeling and to have her put her arms around me. It would have been so nice to have her put her arms around me!

"Come on, Bob. What are you waiting for?"

We cut through St. Boniface like criminals on the run, and took every back street we could to the

Symington Yard. When we got there we lifted the bikes over a small fence and scurried behind a signal box. The place looked dismal in the moonlight and the stench of diesel wafted in the warm air. And there were so many freight trains, containers, and boxcars. How Harold was going to find us I'd never know. And the more I thought about it the more I worried. How could Harold, who had difficulty walking, leave his house in the middle of the night and make his way down here? And then find us when he got here! And to add to my worries a guard was coming toward us. His flashlight found the doors of the boxcars and the seals on the containers. It searched the wheels of the trains and the windows of the passenger cars.

"He won't come down here," whispered the Rat.

And sure enough the beam of light hit the floor and the guard returned the way he came. Then, stepping out of the shadows, we saw two familiar figures.

"Let's go," said the Rat.

I followed her out and we made our way toward Harold and Little Joe.

"There's no time to talk," said Harold. "Follow me."

We followed him in between two long freight trains. As we neared the end of the trains, an electric murmur flowed down the one to our right. Then there was a clanking sound as the engine pulled at the boxcars. Slowly the train began to move.

"Quickly! Get in this one!" said Harold pointing to a boxcar with the doors open.

Little Joe grabbed the bikes and they were soon inside. Our backpacks followed.

"Take care of yourself, brother," said Joe. "Come back safe."

We hugged each other, something we had never done before, and I knew he would always be my friend. I climbed up into the boxcar and waited for the Rat. Harold removed a backpack from his back. For a second I feared he would try and come with us. "It's food for the journey," he said, handing me the backpack.

I wanted to say something nice but the words never came.

"You overwhelmed me, Harold," said the Rat. "A girl could not ask for a better boyfriend."

"Do you think we'll still get married?" he asked. "When we're sixteen?"

"We do get married, Harold. It's our fate." She kissed Harold on the cheek and then grabbed my hand. I pulled her inside. Little Joe and Harold walked after us as the train pulled away.

"Close the doors until you're out of town," said Little Joe. "Take care, brother! Take care, Marie Claire!"

My father was dead. I was leaving home. And now I was waving good-bye to my best friends. If I felt sad before, I felt even sadder now. When we pushed the doors closed, it went dark. "Don't put your flashlight on in case someone sees it," I said. And, sliding down the boxcar, I put my head in my hands.

I stayed that way for some time, and then I looked around me. It was too dark to see anything. And it felt strange being in the boxcar. It had an oily, musty smell and there was the constant sound of creaking wood and clattering metal. I thought I saw the Rat in the opposite corner. "Where are you?"

"I'm over here."

It was then that I realized there could be someone else in the boxcar with us. The fear hit me like lead. I fumbled for my flashlight and switched it on. "Oh thank God!"

The Rat looked worried. "You okay, Bob?"

"Sure, come on—let's get these doors open."

We tugged at the doors but they wouldn't move. Then I found a hook-like catch over the handles. I tried to push it up but it was jammed.

"What if we can't get out?" said the Rat.

I felt a surge of panic. But then I saw a lever. I pushed it down, the catch rose, and I pulled them doors wide open!

The Rat looked relieved. "Well done, brother."

We had passed through Winnipeg. I couldn't say where we were because there was nothing visible, only the pitch black of the prairies. We put our backpacks near the doorway and dropped down. I lay there until my heart stopped pounding, and then I sat up and looked at the night sky. There were more stars than I'd ever seen. There were billions. We always got good stars on the prairies, but nothing like this. All the constellations were visible and all the planets were out.

Suddenly a shooting star skated across the sky and burned up in the atmosphere.

"A sign from the Old Man," said the Rat.

I turned to look at her. "You're sad about him dying, right?"

"Of course. I loved Dad and I'll miss him a lot. But he was never happy, not really. He wanted to be with Mom and now he is."

"You don't know that."

"Yes, I do. You see, Bob, when you die your spirit leaves your body and it heads for the heavens. It flies around the different solar systems and galaxies at many times the speed of light, visiting worlds we couldn't even imagine. And being dead is your ticket to the stars, but you have to die to get there. Until that happens we can only dream about them." She looked at me, her eyes glinting in the dark. "I know you think I'm crazy, Bob. But I wouldn't lie to you, not about this." She looked up at the stars. "Can you imagine Mom meeting Dad after all these years? I bet an angel brought him to her. And now she's giving him a tour of the Milky Way and he's singing to her like Frank. And he's happy and I'm happy for him."

The Rat talked some garbage at times but that wasn't one of them. I didn't really believe what she said. But, like a child being told a fairy tale, I felt better for hearing it.

We opened up our sleeping bags and got in. The Rat was soon asleep. She could sleep anywhere, but I couldn't. For a good while I gazed at those stars and imagined the Old Man and the mother I never really knew gliding around them. And the more I thought about it the better I felt. In time the rocking of the train lulled me to sleep. I slept, and the Rat slept next to me.

Six

The boxcar shuddered and I woke to the sound of metal clattering against metal. We were cruising alongside green fields, with black and white cows, and in the distance I could see hills silhouetted against the rising sun. It was a nice sunrise, but it was too bright to look at.

I opened the backpack Harold had given us. There were cookies, sandwiches, and cans of soda, as well as a large silver flask of hot water. There were packets of crisps, chocolate, and fruit.

"Any mocha?"

I turned to see the Rat sitting up in her sleeping bag. "I doubt it." But searching the bottom of the bag, I found six sachets. Only the Rat could ask for mocha on a freight train and get it.

We had a good breakfast sitting in the doorway of the boxcar. It was nice to eat and watch the land go by at the same time. There were blue lakes and turquoise rivers with fishermen wading through them. There were hills and rocky outcrops above which long-fingered buzzards seemed to float. Then there were more lakes and rivers followed by a sea of sunflowers that bathed in the sunshine.

When the train curved for a bend we could see the front of the train and the engine that was pulling us. It slowed to a walking pace as the bend narrowed and we saw hundreds of prairie plants growing wild. Their buds exploded into a supernova of seeds that drifted on the breeze like tiny parachutes, a minute version of the Big Bang that had first put the stars in the sky.

"The land in Ontario isn't as flat as Manitoba," said the Rat.

"How do you know we're in Ontario?"

"The train stopped last night and I was talking to some Native woman from Sioux Lookout."

"What? Where?"

"Just some old Native woman. I traded her some cookies for water," said the Rat, showing me the bottle of water. "She said we would find Uncle Jerome, but that we were in great danger. But I could have told you that."

I couldn't believe I had slept through the Rat talking to some Native woman. I must have been really tired.

The train moved faster and the Rat, having eaten, got up to brush her teeth. She spat the water out as far as it would go and then she sat down with her bare feet dangling out the doorway. I looked at the wheels spinning below her and I got an uneasy feeling.

"Bring your feet in," I told her.

"We're not in danger yet, Bob. Besides, the boxcar has a good spirit. It's glad we're riding with it." She took a comb from her pocket and combed her hair. "I'm having so many dreams now that I'm without my big dream catcher. I've brought a small one but it's not doing much good. I dreamed I was on the top floor of a tall building. I go to sit down in a chair but I fall. It's like I'm falling from a great height. All of a sudden I'm being carried upward by three angels. They put me on top of a skyscraper where there are hundreds more angels bathing in a silver sun. When I look around me there are hundreds of skyscrapers with hundreds of angels on top of them. They're all sunbathing or playing or gliding from one skyscraper to another. They tell me I'll stay with them until I'm better. But the funny thing is I don't feel unwell. I dreamed about the Windigo as well."

"Windigos aren't real."

"Of course they are!"

"Have you ever seen one?"

"No, but there are lots of things you can't see that are real."

"Such as?"

The Rat thought about it. "Angels!" she said. "Sometimes a person can come up and talk to you in the street. And you think they're human, but really they're an angel. There are angels everywhere. Sometimes a human being can have an angel inside them and all they do is good. They can have a demon inside them as well. Then they become Windigos or pedophiles, and all they want to do is hurt people. Do you know how to spot the difference between a Windigo and a pedophile?"

"How?"

"Well, pedophiles hiss when they talk. But you have to listen real hard. And they pretend to be nice, especially to children. Whereas Windigos are never nice to anyone, but they are harder to spot. They're not cowardly like pedophiles but they're more violent, and their heads are full of crazy voices that make them growl. Windigos are big growlers. That's how you can spot them.

"Sometimes a human being can have an angel and a demon inside them and they fight for his soul. But the angel always wins in the end because one angel is more powerful than ten demons."

The Rat bewildered me sometimes! She really did! "Where do you get this stuff from?"

"It just comes to me," she said, in a matter-of-fact sort of way.

Looks like the Windigo wasn't the only one with crazy voices in his head. I don't know why, but I never liked to talk to the Rat about her freaky ways. But now I was intrigued.

"So how do you know things are going to happen? Does a voice tell you?"

"No, silly. Sometimes I see things in a dream or I get dreamlike images when I'm awake. But mostly I get a feeling that something will happen and the feeling gets stronger, that's all."

"But you can see ghosts, right?"

The Rat laughed.

"That's it! I'm never asking you anything again!"

"You've been watching too many movies, Bob."

"Wait a minute! You told me you could see the ghosts of the Grey Nuns of Montreal in the St. Boniface Cemetery!"

The Rat laughed harder.

"You lying Rat!" I wasn't speaking to her then. But the Rat didn't care, she really didn't!

A road ran alongside the tracks and a pickup truck kept up for a time, the driver waving out the window. Houses began to appear, and they appeared more often as we neared a town. When the train slowed we closed the doors over and looked through the gap. We saw a woman push her laughing child on a swing. Then the trees blocked them out. Then we saw a farmer on a tractor holding up the traffic. We passed a blue house, as big as a barn, and a water tower with the words JESUS LOVES YOU written on it. Then there was a fire station with proud, overweight firemen having their picture taken with small children. The fire engine looked a little old-fashioned, but sometimes old-fashioned things look nicer. And the kids, who were climbing all over it, looked like they were having a good time. But the train, clanging its bell, passed through the town without stopping, and so we reopened the doors and sat in the doorway. The houses drifted away after that and we rolled on to farmland where rows of red harvesters headed into the horizon, mowing the wheat as they went.

"Hey, Bob, you see them geese up there?" said the Rat, pointing into the sky. "Did I ever tell you why they fly in a V-formation?"

I never said anything. I still wasn't speaking to her.

"Well, the son of the West Wind and the grandson of the Moon was named Nanabush. And he was always getting into trouble. One day he was really hungry. He was dying for something to eat. Then what does he spot? A flock of geese resting on a lake. I know, he thought, I'll swim underwater and tie their feet together and I'll capture them all. So he got some twine and swam underwater, tying the birds' feet together as he went. But an older smarter goose knew what was happening and she told the other geese. On her command they flew into the air dragging Nanabush with them. And to this day geese still fly in a V-formation. And the moral of this story is, just take what you need, don't be greedy. Anything else to eat?"

As the afternoon wore on, the food in Harold's bag began to diminish. I had the appetite of a Marine and the Rat wasn't far behind me. We kept on saying we'd save things for later but we'd eat them within the hour. We said we'd save the sandwiches for supper, but they were gone by noon. Food always tastes better when you're not supposed to eat it.

The train stopped twice. And when it did we closed the doors and peeped through the cracks in the boxcar. We stopped near a town called Mud River where we couldn't see anything except a brick wall. What made it worse was that the railway workers kept walking past and so we had to keep quiet. And it was so hot in the boxcar we began to sweat. We soon drank the last of the water and all the cans of soda. But it was nice when the train moved on. We opened up the doors and put our faces into the breeze.

Later we stopped at a town that had dozens of cattle pens. Guys wearing cowboy hats loaded cattle onto the front of the train. One guy, sitting on a horse, had a sidearm and he kept on shouting to the other guys to get a move on. Guess he must have been the foreman. I was scared they'd put cattle in the boxcar. But the Rat said they wouldn't, and they didn't, and the train moved on.

The land changed from prairie land to mountains, and from big towns to small towns where small children waved at us and we waved back. There were grassy plains that spread out to the horizon and blue rivers that ran into waterfalls. There were bald eagles, sheep-covered hills, and horses hovering around streams.

There were green gorges, rocky canyons, and ravines with water gushing through them.

There was desert-looking land as well. It looked like it had been beaten by the elements since prehistoric times. There were boulders lying in valleys where the rain had caused rockslides, and there were tall rocks carved into strange shapes by the wind. I could imagine you'd find dinosaur bones there if you dug up the ground.

It was my first time out of Manitoba, the Rat's too. And if things had been different I would have enjoyed traveling across Canada on a freight train. I was really impressed by our country: how big it was and how much there was to see.

Later we passed through a shabby town with more than its fair share of badly painted houses. It had lawnmowers for sale all along the tracks and it had secondhand cars adorned with bunting. If I had a choice between living in a shabby town or in a desert, I'd live in the desert. I'm not being a snob or anything, but when you've lived in a big city like Winnipeg you could never live anywhere shabby. And shabby towns have shabby people. No one likes shabby people.

I slept for a while, but every time the train slowed for a bend the boxcar shook from side to side. It was tiring trying to stay asleep, so I sat up to see what the Rat was doing. She was staring at the photograph Mary White Cloud had given us. "Suppose he doesn't want us?" I asked.

"Who wouldn't want us? Uncle Jerome will jump for joy when he sees his new niece and nephew! We're great kids!"

She made me laugh sometimes. But we were great kids. "What if he wants us to move to New York? Won't you miss Winnipeg?"

"Oh course. I'll miss my friends and Harold. And I'll miss Ms. Mountshaft and the ballet." She put the back of her hand to her forehead. "I could have been the greatest ballet dancer Winnipeg had ever seen! I'll just have to settle for being a great actress."

"You'll always be a drama queen, that's for sure."

The Rat sat up straight. "Suppose he wants us to sell drugs for him! Hey baby, you wanna get high? Come on by! Don't be shy!" she said like a seventies pimp. Then she turned into Little Lord Fauntleroy's sister. "One ought to be careful whom one sells narcotics to. Otherwise one might end up in a rather large house where one might be ridiculed for one's accent! Nevertheless, it could be a rather lucrative venture."

"So you'd sell drugs?"

"Absolutely not!" she said speaking normally. "I wouldn't be a great kid then. And I like being a great kid."

"You'd live on the profits though. If Uncle Jerome," she had me calling him that, "decided he would take us in."

"We're orphans, brother. We'd have no choice. Anyway forget about that for now. If you had a choice of meeting a big-time American celebrity, who would it be?"

I could never understand why it's such a big deal to be a celebrity. But the Rat's obsessed with them. She doesn't so much read celebrity magazines as study them. Then she analyzes what she's studied and makes her decision. She's as good as a Wall Street trader when it comes to predicting who's on their way up and who's on their way down. And when the Rat said someone was out, it was like celebrity death. They were never heard of again.

"I don't know. Jennifer Lopez, I think, or Julia Roberts or Halle Berry. I like Halle Berry!"

"You'd wanna meet bimbos with big butts. That's pathetic!"

"You can be so snotty at times! You really can! Who'd you like to meet? Go on, tell me!"

"I don't think I will if that's your attitude." Just then her cell phone beeped. "It's Harold," she said looking at the text message. "He said we should think about getting Father Henri to give Dad a proper burial, and he wants us to be careful."

"I knew he wouldn't like the Native burial."

"It's not that Harold didn't like it. He's just set in his Christian ways." The Rat crawled into her sleeping bag. "Well, I'm going to have a nap; wake me up if something interesting happens." She sank down inside and disappeared. "Halle bleeping Berry," she mumbled. "She's old enough to be your grandmother."

At dusk the train stopped in the middle of absolutely nowhere. And as far as you could see there was a sea of wheat. We pulled back the doors and looked at the far end of the train. We couldn't see anyone, not even the driver. It was like being on a ghost train. And so we sat in the doorway and watched the sun go down.

I thought about what it would be like to live there, without ever meeting another soul, just me and the Rat. Then she drank the last of her mocha, and jumping down, she snaked her way through the wheat.

"Don't blame me if you get left behind."

She just lay there. "I won't get left behind."

The sky turned the wheat from a golden color to pink, and then red as the last of the sun faded into the horizon. I think the driver only stopped to watch the sunset because as soon as it was over the train started to move.

"You think Mom ran off with him?"

"Who?" asked the Rat, climbing back in the boxcar.

"Uncle Jerome."

"Is that what happened?" Her round eyes turned beady and shifted from side to side. "Our very own family scandal! Mom runs away with Dad's very own brother! Jerome DeBillier versus Dad DeBillier! Pistols at dawn and all that!"

I was sorry I asked her.

"Jerome DeBillier barred from any further contact with the House of DeBillier! And we missed it all!" She sat back and chewed on it for a while. "Anything else to eat?"

"No."

"I'm going to sleep then."

She curled up in her sleeping bag and within a minute she was making this little rodent snoring noise. She reminded me of a hamster we used to have. It was the laziest hamster that ever lived. Not once did it ever run around in its wheel. I don't think it knew how. It ate and then it curled up in its straw and slept.

But I could never get to sleep right away. I lay there until the stars came out and thought about the Rat's crazy version of an afterlife. I looked at the stars and the moon and imagined the other worlds that lay beyond them. All those galaxies and solar systems the Rat said we could only dream about. And so that's what I did. I closed my eyes and I dreamed about them. "Good night, Dad, wherever you are."

Seven

When I opened my eyes I saw we were coming into a railyard like the one we had left in Winnipeg. I jumped up and tried to get my bearings, but we came alongside another freight train and my view was blocked. The train slowed. There was a loud clatter as one section of train locked into another. And then we bumped to a stop.

The Rat sat up. “What the bleep was that?”

“We’re here!” I said.

We rolled up our sleeping bags, attached them to the backpacks, and lowered our bikes to the ground. Within a minute of waking we were ready to ride. We were desperate to be out of the railyard, but in both directions freight trains walled us in.

“Which way?” said the Rat.

"This way!" I said.

We rode in between two freight trains, which curved around a bend. And what happened? We rode straight into the path of a big-gutted guard.

"Hey! What are you kids doing?"

We skidded to a stop and turned quickly.

"Come back here!"

We went back the way we came, pedaling like the wind. But two more guards came toward us. We braked hard.

"Follow me!" said the Rat. She dropped to the ground and scrambled under a train.

"Hey!" shouted the guards.

The Rat disappeared, dragging her bike behind her. I dropped to the ground and followed. Underneath the train's parts looked scary. The thought of being electrocuted ran through my mind. I scrambled over the tracks and got out the other side. The Rat was already on her bike. I saw a hill with a low fence and cars running along a road. "Head for the trees!" I shouted. There were no trees, only bushes, but I was panicking. We rode across a wooden ramp that crossed two sets of train tracks and, reaching the foot of the hill, we dismounted. We scrambled upwards, our sneakers sliding on the soil. The Rat dug in and passed me. She lifted her bike over the fence and it smacked on the sidewalk. Then she threw herself over headfirst like a Marine.

"You kids are going to get hurt playing around here!" shouted the guard.

When I heard his voice, I looked back. He never tried to climb up; he just stood there with his hands on his hips, breathing heavily. I lifted the bike over the fence and jumped over.

The Rat sat on her bike with her arms folded. “What kept you, Bob?”

I couldn’t speak. My heart was pounding. All this grief, and I’d just woken up. But to the Rat it was all part of the adventure. She could have fun on a battlefield. I rode away without knowing where I was going. I was shaky for a while, but the further we got from the railyard the better I felt. In the distance we saw the top of the CN Tower and cycled toward it. We had made it to Toronto.

The CN Tower never looked that far away but it was a long ride downtown, and when we got there the city had not woken up. There were only a few people on the streets, most of them homeless. The rest were the early-morning people: garbage collectors, postal workers, and groups of taxi drivers finishing the night shift. Seeing a sign for Lake Ontario, we headed toward it. I wanted to be by the water. I always found it calming, and that’s what I needed. I was a little overwhelmed by what was going on.

Passing through a small park we came to the lake, which was pale blue like the sky, and large like the sea. It even had small waves and a sea-like breeze. It was hard to believe it was just a lake. Then we headed along the waterfront while looking at the silhouettes of islands made hazy by the mist. We passed dozens of white yachts resting in rows. We passed an old-time sailing ship that had wooden masts and sails like sheets. Next to it was a bright orange boat belonging to the Canadian Coast Guard and next to that was a fireboat with a water gun like a cannon. Most of the boats had the Canadian flag fluttering above them. I love our Canadian flag. It's just a maple leaf, nothing to get excited about. But it represents more than a tree common to our country. It represents being down to earth and true, like the tree itself. And it stands for modesty and compassion, which is our Canadian way. At least that's what it means to me. I'm sure most people care about their countries, but Canada's special. It's like America without the armies and the arrogance.

We rode past a woman feeding seagulls, a deckhand mopping the decks of an idle tour boat, and we circled Molson Place, an open-air concert venue. It felt good being by the waterfront. It wasn't just the cool breeze and the quiet lake. I felt kind of proud, like a pioneer, now that we had made it to Toronto. And I think Dad would have been proud of us too.

"What do you say to a coffee, Bob?"

"I say yes."

Riding into one of the quays we saw an old boathouse that had been turned into a Second Cup coffee shop. As we neared it the doors opened and the smell of coffee wafted around the wharf. The Rat couldn't lock up her bike fast enough, she's such an addict, but I wasn't far behind her. It was either the fear of being chased or I hadn't drunk in a while because my mouth was parched.

"I'll have a mocha!" said the Rat as we went through the door. "And I'll have an orange juice and two oatmeal raisin cookies."

"I'll have an orange juice, a regular coffee, and three oatmeal raisin cookies," I said.

We had sort of startled the Asian girl behind the counter, but she never got annoyed.

She gave us our drinks, and sitting by the window, we watched the water. I felt nice and relaxed then.

"How are we going to get across the border, Bob?"

We'd only just arrived and she was putting me under pressure. "Well, we should wait until it gets dark. Then we can find a street or a path somewhere near the border crossing but not too close. Then we'll ride across. We're only a couple of kids. If we act as though we live around there they shouldn't bother us."

"But suppose they do, Bob? And suppose there are ditches and walls with armed guards? Or rows of razor wire? Or mines that explode when you step on them? Suppose they come after us in helicopters with snipers hanging out of them? What's the plan then? Quick, Bob, what's the plan?" She stared at me like a scary kid.

"Why don't you drink your mocha?"

She laughed. She was just winding me up.

* * *

We stepped out of the coffee shop with enough caffeine and sugar in us to climb the steps of the CN Tower. But we didn't. We walked up to the Greyhound bus terminal and put our backpacks in a locker. Then we went to the Eaton Centre, Toronto's biggest shopping mall. The Rat was happy then. She donned her dark sunglasses and paraded around like a millionaire. She tried on all the free samples of perfume until she reeked nauseatingly. And then she tried on all the clothes in all the shops, while being helped by all sorts of women who thought she was cute. All except one older woman with dyed hair and too much makeup. "Are you going to buy something?" she asked. "Because if not you shouldn't be trying on the clothes." She was kind of snotty and her lip curled when she spoke.

"It's not trying on the clothes," said the Rat aristocratically. "It's trying the clothes on. And in answer to your question, no. Not quite my taste, if you know what I mean."

I laughed. I always found the Rat funny when she was annoying other people.

When we came out we walked around downtown Toronto with the Rat making constant comparisons with Winnipeg. "Their Union Station is like our Union Station but ours is prettier. Their Royal York Hotel is like our Fort Garry Hotel but ours is grander and a little more refined. And the Eaton Centre was nice but our Polo Park Shopping Centre is just as good. And, yes, they have more skyscrapers but Winnipeg is catching up. And anyway, these Torontonians are nowhere near as sophisticated as us Winnipeggers. And that's all I have to say really."

Eventually we made our way back to the bus depot while dodging the homeless people who loitered like zombies. Toronto's homeless people are nowhere near as nice as Winnipeg's. I'm not just saying that. It's true. Anyway, we avoided giving them money, and collecting our backpacks, we headed back to the quay.

It was getting hot and we wanted to take a nap, so unlocking our bikes we looked for the park we had ridden through earlier that morning. There were lots of people along the waterfront by then. They strolled or sunbathed or got in our way as we rode. When we found the park we removed our backpacks and lay under a solitary tree. The grass was springy and cool and comfortable to lie on. I don't care how nice the Rat said the boxcar's spirit was. I never got a decent night's sleep. Who can sleep on floorboards?

The Rat put her head on her backpack and closed her eyes. "Wake me up if something interesting happens."

She was dreaming in Disney World if she thought I was going to stay awake. I closed my eyes and allowed the sun to create patterns like a kaleidoscope. The patterns turned into images, and the images turned into dreams. I slept while listening to the children play and the parents shout and the Rat who snored like a rodent.

When I woke she wasn't there. Her bike and backpack were there, but she wasn't. Standing up, I saw her on the boardwalk looking out at the lake. Shaking my head, I walked toward her. Just then some guy stopped to talk to her. He had cameras around his belly. The Rat's hands went to her hips, never a good sign.

"Am I lost?" I heard her say. "I'm not lost, you goddamn creep! Now beat it or I'll call the cops!"

The man staggered back and carried on going.

"Go on, bleep off!"

I ran toward her. "What did he say?"

The Rat screwed up her face and stared hard at the retreating man. "Oh, no!"

"What?"

"I thought he was a pedophile but he's not! Sorry, mister!" she shouted. "It's okay, I'm not lost! And thank you for your concern!"

The man couldn't get away fast enough.

"Are you crazy? You can't go around saying things like that!"

"Well pardon me, Bob, for making a mistake!"

She wandered over toward some bicycle couriers, and I went back to the bikes and sat there bewildered. She just didn't seem to understand certain things. Some days I thought she really *was* crazy. I watched her as she talked to the couriers, who seemed to be entertained by her. She looked normal enough, from a distance, and I couldn't see any signs of madness. But I swear the Rat was deranged in some way.

When she got bored with the couriers she wandered back toward me. "We follow the Gardener Expressway and then we follow the signs for Burlington, Hamilton, Niagara Falls, and Fort Erie—that's where the border is. They said it would take forever to cycle there, so we better get going. And they said we'll never get past the border patrol. But what do they know? They're grown men who ride around on bikes all day." She knelt down and opened her backpack. "I bought you a sandwich and some biscuits when you were asleep. You can have them when you're hungry. And I bought a large bottle of Coke. We can drink it along the way." She put on her backpack and stood up. "I'm having a good time so far, Bob. What about you?"

"Sure," I said. "Sure" was all I could think of. What else could I say: You're crazy, and you're going to get us killed?

"Well, we better get going," she said. "And as we can't ride on the expressway, we'll have to follow it as best we can."

So that's what we did. We mounted up and followed the expressway as best we could.

EIGHT

IT WAS DARK. THE ROAD WE WERE ON WAS LONG, like a freeway except it was empty of traffic. There wasn't even a house nearby. We had been riding for I don't know how many hours, and a lot of it had been off-road. My butt ached from the seat and my hands ached from gripping the handlebars. My backpack seemed to have gained weight; it stuck to my damp T-shirt. And to add to my discomfort, I was now confused. We had been following the signs for Hamilton and then we were supposed to follow the signs for Niagara Falls. But now the signs for Niagara Falls were pointing back the way we came.

I turned to see the Rat in the streetlight. The Rat was pretty tough, she never complained, but her face looked pale and her backpack looked too big for her.

"Would you like to have a rest?"

She nodded and climbed slowly from her bike. We pushed the bikes up a low hill that ran alongside the road, and laid them behind some bushes.

"We'll rest here," I told her, "in case the cops come along." I helped her take off her backpack, and I untied her sleeping bag for her. "It's a bit cold. Why don't you get in and sleep for a while?" She crawled into her sleeping bag and curled up without a word. I undid my sleeping bag and did the same. "We'll try again in the morning," I told her.

I was shivering, and the ground was damp with dew, but it wasn't so much the cold as fatigue. I wanted to sleep but I couldn't. I just lay there wishing I was in a warm bed in Winnipeg. Me and the Rat had never been so lost. We were in a dark place in the middle of nowhere and there was no one to call for help.

I remember a dark winter's night when we had ridden home from town. The wind blasted frosty snow into our eyes all the way. When we reached the house the Rat dropped her bike and ran inside, but I didn't. I looked through the kitchen window, where the snow had stuck like an arc, and I watched the Old Man take bread from the oven. Then he attached a toy snowman to the kitchen cupboard, and standing back he looked at it. The Rat came in, and taking off her coat she talked about her day. It was such a picture. It was bitterly cold but I didn't care because I knew I could be in that warmth when I wanted.

I was desperate for that warmth now. And for the first time I thought about going to the cops and giving ourselves up. It's not like we had done anything wrong, but I felt we were on the run from the proper authorities, those people who would put us in a home without a moment's hesitation.

But maybe they wouldn't be so bad. They might find us somewhere nice to live. I turned to ask the Rat what she thought. Her eyes were closed and she looked so drained, just like she did on that winter's night. The Rat would never think about giving herself up, no matter how bad things got. And when I thought about it, neither would I. If they wanted us they'd have to come and get us. And who said we'd stay where they put us.

Suddenly a car screeched to a stop below us. Another one followed. The Rat was already out of her sleeping bag and sneaking behind a bush. The car doors slammed shut and two men came toward each other. One was young and slim. The other man was large, and he had the stump of an unlit cigar in his mouth.

"Joey. How's New York treating you?" asked the large man.

"Badly, as usual. You got the merchandise?"

"I'm afraid not. I couldn't get it."

"What!"

The larger man laughed. "I'm just kidding." He opened the trunk and they looked inside.

"Okay let's make this quick," said the younger man.

They started to move packages from one car to the other. But they never went into the trunk of the second car; they went under the back seat.

"They're drug dealers!" whispered the Rat.

"Shush."

After they were done the younger man handed the larger man an envelope and he scanned the contents. "Always a pleasure, Joey." He shook hands and, getting in his car, he drove away. The younger man put a blanket over the back seat, and closing the door, he looked around him. Then, getting in the car, he started the engine. It turned over and over, but it wouldn't start. He began to swear and bang on the steering wheel with his fist. That's when I saw the Rat rolling down the hill on her bike.

"What's wrong, mister?" She pulled up at the side of the car. "Won't it start?"

The look he gave her was more than cold. He got out the car slowly and looked around him. "Where did you come from? What are you doing out here?"

I was down there as quick as I could. "She don't mean nothing, mister."

He looked even angrier when he saw me.

"We're searching for our uncle," said the Rat. "He's a drug dealer too."

"Get lost, kid!"

"Come back," I told her.

"There's no need to be mean," said the Rat. "We we're just being friendly. We only wanted to help."

The man's face seemed to soften. "Yeah, well I'm having a bad night! I'm out of gas and I have to get back to New York!"

"We passed a gas station two miles back," I told him.

"Two miles, you say?"

"If you've got a can we'll go get it for you," said the Rat. "We're pretty fast on our bikes."

"That would really help me out! And I didn't mean to snap," he said, opening the trunk. "But you gave me quite a surprise."

But then he started swearing and banging things around because there was no can in the trunk.

"Do you believe that? The only time I run out of gas and I have no—"

The Rat drank the last of the Coke from the plastic container, and burping loudly she screwed on the cap.

"Boy, am I glad I ran into you. Okay here's five dollars. That should be enough."

"We won't be long," said the Rat, taking the money.

"Hey, you kids ain't gonna ride off with my five bucks, are you?"

"Sure," said the Rat. "That's what we do. We wait in the middle of nowhere hoping that someone will break down. And when they do we ride off with their gas money."

The guy looked bewildered. "Everyone's a wise guy tonight," he said in this winning New York accent. "I don't know what it is."

We rode to the gas station where we got told by the attendant that we shouldn't be out so late or filling bottles with gas from the pumps, but who still bid us a good evening and told us to come again. Then we rode back to the guy while eating the candy bars we had bought with his change.

"Why you said we'd go for gas for him I don't know. I bet he wouldn't do it for us."

"We don't use gas, Bob. Anyway he has a good spirit. And he's going to New York!"

"He won't give us a ride."

The Rat smiled confidently. "We'll see."

When he saw us coming he looked plenty relieved.

"Oh, you kids are the best! Just let me fill her up and I'll give you a nice tip."

I looked at him as he poured the gas in the car. He had slicked-back black hair that made him look tough, and he was pretty mean to us at first. But now that he was happy, and my fear of him had gone, I could see he was only a young guy.

Throwing the empty container in the trunk, he jumped in the driver's seat and started the engine. "All right!"

"Quick give me all your change!" said the Rat.

I handed her what coins I had.

"Thanks, kids," he said getting out the car.

The Rat added some bills, and holding the money in both hands, she offered it to him.

"What's this?"

"This is all we've got," she said in a meek voice. "We really need to get to New York to find Uncle Jerome. If we don't, they'll put us in an orphanage!"

Those drama classes were really starting to pay off!

"Ah look, kid. I'd like to help, but it'd look strange if I got caught at the border with two kids I'd only just met. I can't do it. But I really appreciate your help, I really do."

"It's okay," said the Rat, her meek voice getting meeker. "We'll get there somehow."

Her sad look continued even when he gave her a twenty-dollar tip. And he looked more than a little guilty as he got in his car. "You kids look after yourselves." But he drove away all the same.

"That was a great performance," I said. "And cradling the money in your hands like that, that was a really nice touch."

But she mumbled miserably in French. She was such a bad loser, not gracious in defeat at all. But when the car stopped, the Rat's head turned toward me. She looked at me with her smug face, which was the most annoying of her faces. Then, when it began to reverse, she raised her eyebrows twice in victory. She knew I couldn't stand that. But on this occasion I didn't care.

"Put your bikes in the trunk," said the guy, "and try not to scratch the paint."

We dumped our bikes and backpacks in the trunk and jumped in the back seat.

"My name's Marie Claire DeBillier, and this is my brother Bob. And we're from Winnipeg."

"Well my name's Joey and I'm from Cloud Cuckoo Land!" said Joey driving away. "I must be out of my mind doing this!"

"It'll be okay," said the Rat.

"Yeah. Well, how am I gonna explain who you are when we get to the border?"

"We'll think of something."

"Forget that. Just pretend to be asleep, and with any luck they won't bother us."

It felt cozy being in the car, especially after cycling so much, but as we neared the border everything became tense. We got through the Canadian side with no problem, but then we came to the US side.

"I can't stand these retards. They give everyone grief except the terrorists. Them they let in with open arms. You kids get under that blanket and pretend to be asleep."

We drove into a brightly lit area and the car came to a stop.

"Identification. Step out of the car and open the trunk."

Joey switched off the engine and got out of the car. A flashlight shone in my face and then I heard the trunk pop open.

"How long have you been in Canada?"

"Just for the day."

"What's in the backpacks?"

"The backpacks—well—I don't know—they're not mine."

The man's tone became harsh. "So you're bringing bags into the U.S. but you don't know what's in them?"

My heart beat a sickening beat.

"That's my bag, officer. You can look in it if you want."

Oh my God! I opened my eyes to see the Rat leaning out the back window.

"I don't mind if I do," said the man.

"Where are we, Uncle Joey? I'm tired."

"You can sleep soon, sweetheart."

"Where are you going?" asked a woman's voice.

"We're going to New York City to see our grandma. And Uncle Joey's taking us. Aren't you, Uncle Joey? We're going to see the Empire State Building and the Statue of Liberty and everything. And our granny's taking us on a ferry ride around Manhattan! And she's going to bake us her very own apple pie so we don't get hungry."

She sounded so convincing! Some days I wondered who the Rat really was!

"What's your granny's name?" asked the woman.

That's it! The Rat's Little Red Riding Hood performance had ruined us!

"Grandma, of course."

I was relieved when I heard laughter.

"Would you like to see our birth certificates?" asked the Rat.

She always had to overdo it! She wouldn't be satisfied until we were all locked up!

A man came close to the car. "Marie Claire—what's that? Wazhashnoons?"

"It's my Native name."

"Marie Claire Wazhashnoons DeBillier and Robert DeBillier, born in Winnipeg—"

A flashlight shone in my face.

"That's my bother Bob. He's asleep."

"How do you like living in Winnipeg?"

"It's nice, but I'd sooner live in New York. It's more sophisticated, and I want to be an actress."

I heard a bit of chuckling. I didn't know if they were border control or customs but there were quite a few of them around the car.

"Okay, you can go," said the serious voice from the back of the car.

The trunk slammed shut and Joey jumped in the driver's seat.

"Bye. Bye everyone," said the Rat waving out the window.

We were quiet as we drove away and then the car slowed again.

"Drive on," said another voice.

Joey looked in the rear-view mirror. "Kids, breakfast is on me!" And for the first time that night he sounded happy. But he was nowhere near as happy as us. Smiling, I sank back and closed my eyes.

"Yo Bobby! Bobby De Niro! Wake up—it's breakfast time!" said Joey.

I opened my eyes. It was still dark. The Rat was in the front seat next to Joey and they were both looking at me.

"Come on, kid. Let's go!" said the Rat. She tried to imitate Joey's New York accent but ended up talking like a bad version of Bugs Bunny.

Dazed, I got out of the car and followed them toward a brightly lit diner that hurt my eyes.

Joey held the door open. “Come on, Bob. They do a great breakfast here.”

There weren’t many people inside, just a few couples and some guys drinking coffee at the counter. The Rat grabbed a menu and ran through a maze of red booths.

“Yo, Joey! You wanna sit here?” shouted the Rat across the restaurant.

“I don’t know, MC!” shouted Joey. “What do you think?”

“Sure!” shouted the Rat, sliding into the booth.

“It’s not *sure*,” said Joey sitting opposite her. “It’s *shewa*!”

“Why *shewa*?” asked the Rat.

“Because that’s the way a girl from an Italian neighbhorhood talks. It’s not exactly proper American. And you gotta be loud!” said Joey, raising his voice. “Italians are loud people and proud of it. We like to be noticed. Watch,” he said, seeing a waitress. “Hey! How about some service over here!” When the waitress looked over, she didn’t seem impressed. “And when you don’t understand something, or even if you do and you don’t like it, you say Whaaa?”

“Waa!” said the Rat.

“No, it’s more like a grunt. Whaaa?”

“Whaaa?”

“That’s it! What you think, Bobby? All your sister needs is big hair and gum to crack and she’s all set.”

"Sure," I said.

"It's *shewa*!" said the Rat.

I hadn't had much sleep and she was really starting to irritate! Then the waitress came to the table. She was young and pretty, but she didn't look happy. She took a pad and pen from her pocket and stood there.

"Okay, kids, what do you say to three big American breakfasts?" asked Joey looking at the menu.

"Shewa!" said the Rat. "And can I have a mocha?"

"Whaaa?"

"Uncle Joey, can I have a mocha?" asked the Rat in this loud, irritating New York accent!

"Shewa, sweetheart!" said Joey, and they both laughed.

But there wasn't anything to laugh at.

"Three big guys, regular coffee for me and Bob, and a mocha for my niece," said Joey.

The waitress scribbled it down. "Anything else?"

Joey smiled. "Depends on what you're offering, sweetheart."

"Give me a break," said the waitress, and taking the menu she walked away.

"What you think, MC? You think she's got the hots?"

"Shewa!"

They started laughing again. They just wouldn't stop. I was glad when breakfast came. At least they were quiet for a time.

We ate eggs, bacon, and hash browns drowned in ketchup, with toast and lots of orange marmalade. I must have been hungrier than I thought because I ate every bit. Joey paid the bill and told the waitress to keep the change. It must have been a big tip because it put a smile on her face and she never stopped refilling his coffee cup. Maybe she did have the hots.

Joey and the Rat were getting along like a couple of gophers. Maybe that's because Joey was a bit of a kid himself. They were praising each other on their performance at the border. Then the Rat started talking in one of her accents and Joey started talking in one of his. They were like soul mates, they really were. I was starting to feel left out. "What was in those packages?" I asked.

I swear it was like someone had ripped the needle off the record. But the question was out there now. And I couldn't take it back. Joey put his cup down. Even the Rat seemed to freeze. He looked one way and then the other. And then he indicated for us to huddle up.

"Cigars," he said.

"Cigars. That's it?"

"Not just any old cigars. Monte Cristo Cuban cigars. Thirty boxes. I get them from my Canadian contact for $400 a box. I sell them to my Coney Island contact for $700 a box. He sells them to his guy on Wall Street for I don't know how much, but I make—I make—"

"You make nine thousand dollars," said the Rat.

Joey looked impressed. "Can I adopt you?"

"I'll think about it."

"Anyway, I'm putting the price up after this shipment because I'm the one who's putting up the dough and taking the risk. Then I'm off to Atlantic City. It's not to gamble, it's to see family. Well, they're sort of family. You see this guy and his wife took me in after my mom died. They're retired now, and so I like to go down there every now and again and give them something. You know, to show my appreciation."

"Our parents died too," I said.

"Yeah, when?"

"Mom a long time ago; Dad died the other day."

Joey slumped back. "Oh kids, I'm sorry! I didn't know! So that's why you're looking for your uncle?"

"We don't want to go in a home," said the Rat.

"Of course not! Your uncle will have to take you in! Where does he live?"

"We don't know," I told him.

"You don't know. But you must have an address or a street."

"Nothing."

"A borough? The Bronx? Brooklyn? Manhattan?"

"New York City is all we know."

Joey looked amazed. "Do you know how big New York is? Kids, you'll never find him."

"We will," said the Rat. "I know we will."

"Yeah, but you don't wanna go wandering around New York City by yourselves. There are a lot of strange people there."

"Pedophiles, right? Goddamn pedophiles are all over the place!"

Joey froze. He went to say something but he burst out laughing. “You kill me, kid. You really do. Okay, look. As soon as I get back from Atlantic City I’m gonna help you find your uncle. I don’t care how long it takes. I got help when my mom died, and I’m gonna help you. No one’s gonna put you in a home. You have my word on that.”

The Rat smiled. “We’re glad we met you, Joey. Aren’t we, Bob?”

“Sure we are.”

He looked kind of bashful, but I was glad we’d met him. He might have been a big kid, but he was a nice big kid. And when he said he’d help us I knew he meant it. We’d made our first New York friend and we’d only just arrived. Things couldn’t have gone any better.

Nine

I dreamed strange dreams all night.

They began with Mary White Cloud rocking in her rocking chair whispering the name of Jerome DeBillier. Then the Old Man made an appearance and, strange as it seemed, I was lying in his grave looking up at him. "You're not going to sing, are you, Dad?" I asked. "I'm afraid I am, son," he replied. But when he sang it was silent. And then the Chief came alongside him and they sang silently together. Next, Miss Gabriela Felipe Mendez was calling to me, "I'll be your mother if you want me to be." When she spoke I could feel her breath against my cheek. She opened her arms wide and I went to hug her. Suddenly she was way in the distance. I paddled toward her as fast as I could. Why I was padding, I don't know. She was standing in the middle of a prairie and I was on dry land. I got out the boat and ran toward her. "I'm coming!" I shouted. But I bumped into Father Henri and fell to the ground. He raised his Bible and looked down at me. Then he started screaming and shouting, and when he did, fire and brimstone fell from the sky. I ran through the prairie as fast as I could while dodging the missiles that erupted around me. Suddenly I was standing at the crossroads in clear skies. A man was walking toward me. His eyes were as black as his hair and a long black coat flowed around him. "Are you the Devil?" I asked. "No," he replied, "but I used to have a demon inside me." I was terrified. I tried to run but I ran in slow motion. Then once again I fell.

"Get up, Bob. We're here!"

I saw Joey and the Rat. They were upside down. But that wasn't a dream. They stood with the back door open looking down at me. I don't know what was more frightening: the nightmare or the reality. I climbed out of the car and stood up in a garbage-filled street lined with rundown buildings. Surely this can't be it, I thought.

"Welcome to New York, Bobby boy!"

The midmorning breeze blew yesterday's newspapers around my feet, and I shivered with fear and fatigue. Joey lifted the bikes and backpacks out of the trunk, and then he looked at me and laughed. "Disappointed? Take a right at them lights and go over the Brooklyn Bridge. See how disappointed you are then." He looked at his watch. "I have to meet my Coney Island contact and get to Atlantic City. Look, why don't you kids come with me? These people are really nice, and we'll only be gone a few days."

"We'll stay," said the Rat.

"We want to start looking for him right away," I said.

"I have a trailer by the river, but you couldn't stay there by yourselves. I know. This is what you do. You go to the Central Park Youth Hostel. It's on 103rd Street between Central Park West and Manhattan Avenue. Can you remember that?"

"Sure."

"There's a girl who works there called Sexy Sandra. She's an old girlfriend of mine. You tell her Joey sent you. Tell her I'll come by in a few days to pick you up. She'll take care of you." He cringed. "But for now, kids, I have to go." He took a wad of cash from his pocket and, peeling some off, he gave it to the Rat.

"You don't have to, Joey. You're our friend."

"That's why I'm doing it, Marie Claire. Besides, Sexy Sandra's not stupid. She'll want to be paid up front." He gave the Rat and me a hug and got in his car. "You kids have my cell—call me if you need me."

As soon as the car drove away, I wished we had gone with him. It would only have been for a few days, like he said, and now we were in New York by ourselves.

"Joey's our friend," said the Rat. "We have to look after him."

"What does that mean?"

"Nothing."

But nothing always meant something with the Rat.

"Come on, Bob. Let's go find New York!"

And so that's what we did. We took a right at the lights, like Joey said, and rode down toward the Brooklyn Bridge. There was traffic roaring over the bridge, but there was a boardwalk running through its center. There were people walking and cycling on the boardwalk and there were people coming up through a gap at the end.

"There must be a staircase under the bridge," I said. "Follow me."

We made our way around the side of the bridge, with the angry drivers blaring their horns at us, and headed into the gloom of the underpass. In the center we found a set of stone steps and clambered upwards with our bikes. Once on the boardwalk we rode up toward the bridge's brown churchlike arches. There were hundreds of steel cables flowing from the arches, and there was traffic flowing underneath. You could see it through the gaps in the boardwalk. And below the bridge was a green river, twice as wide as our Red River, where ferries and barges plodded back and forth.

The farther up the bridge we went, the more we saw of New York's famous skyline. I'd seen it on television a thousand times, but it's much more impressive in real life. There were so many skyscrapers you couldn't count them. There were hundreds by the bridge and looking further up into Manhattan, there were hundreds more. It was an island of skyscrapers.

"There's the Statue of Liberty!" said the Rat.

It must have been nice for the old immigrants to see her, especially after such a long journey. Winnipeg should have had a Statue of Liberty for our immigrants because they had a long journey too. Longer. But the French never saw fit to make us one.

"Come on, Bob."

We rode up to the center of the span and stopped to take in the view. Above us a beautiful American flag fluttered in the breeze. It looked magical. But everything looked magical. What's more, the city seemed to buzz. It wasn't a sound you could hear—it was more of a vibration. Maybe it was the millions of conversations, or the cars on the streets, or the electricity that ran through the cables. Or maybe it was a force that came from the city itself. When I looked at the Rat she was smiling. "It's the Emerald City!" she said.

Suddenly I was scared. I felt like we were on the verge of something. And I knew that once we rolled down the boardwalk we'd have no control over it. "What shall we do?" I asked. I said it more to myself but the Rat's pointy ears picked it up.

"First I have to go to Ground Zero to say a prayer," she said, pushing her bike to the edge of the slope. "And then we can start our search."

I felt like I was on a high diving board and she was hurrying me to jump. But it was too late to turn back now. And when the Rat got religious there was no stopping her. So we rolled down the boardwalk and into Manhattan singing "New York, New York" as we went.

We cycled into the city, weaving in and out of the double-parked delivery vans, the slowing yellow taxis, and the cops who slapped citations on stagnant windscreens. The streets were loud with pounding jackhammers, screaming whistles, and orange-vested construction workers who shouted to each other in thick New York accents. As did the drivers who hurled insults at the cars that held them up. New York was so noisy it made me nervous. And it was as smelly as an old garage.

As we rode we sneaked glances at the high-rises and the helicopters that hovered above them. Some of the buildings were huge masses of steel and glass while others looked so old and sophisticated they might have had gargoyles at the top.

The Rat stopped her bike, and oblivious to the traffic, she frowned up at them. Then she came back down to earth and asked a guy the way to Ground Zero. He never stopped walking, but shouted street names and pointed as he went. We didn't understand his directions, but we headed off in the direction he had pointed in.

When we found it, the Rat gave me her bike and, walking toward a security fence, she looked down into what was more of a construction site than a hole. Then she clasped her hands together, and bowing her head, she prayed. A couple of construction workers stopped their hammering and looked on. It was a bit embarrassing, to tell you the truth. But the Rat didn't care, and neither did the passing New Yorkers. I would soon learn that you could act as crazy as you wanted to in New York and nobody would care. So in that sense, the Rat was in the right place.

When she came back she looked sad. But it *was* sad. I remember the Old Man crying the day it happened, and the day after. And I remember the Rat, who was really little at the time, putting her arms around him to comfort him.

Suddenly she stopped and turned her head as though she was listening to something. "There have been angels here," she said, "hundreds of them. They must have helped the people into heaven." Then she scanned the area.

I looked around as well to see what she was searching for. "Are you looking for angels?" I asked.

"No, stupid. I'm looking for a coffee shop! I'm upset, Bob. I need a mocha!"

"Okay! Okay!" I said. She's such a little mood swinger.

We wandered around until we found a place with a lot of business types inside. The Rat's mood changed when she got her mocha. She went from being sad to sarcastic in a second. "Not as sophisticated as Winnipeg people," she said, analyzing her fellow coffee drinkers.

"No," I said.

"No. Not really. And that guy can't take his eyes off that woman's legs! Every time she looks away he's staring at them!"

d over to see a big brunette in a short dress
lid have legs worth looking at. But I said noth-
Rat could be a real prude at times. Most of the
you asked me.

ook! Now he's touching them! In public as well!"

Why don't you drink your mocha?"

I have a plan, Bob!" she said, sitting up. "We'll start in the Bronx. I've heard there are a lot of drug deal-s there. One of them is bound to know Uncle Jerome. have a very good feeling about the Bronx. A great feeling, in fact!"

"Are you kidding? Do you know how dangerous the Bronx is? We could get killed."

"Call yourself a man."

"I never did. And this is your first time in New York. You don't even know where the Bronx is."

"I know what I know, Bob. And the Bronx is the place to start."

"You don't know anything."

"Ah bleep you, Bob. I'll tell you what, *you* lead the way if you're so damn smart. See how far we get. Go on. Where do you wanna start our search?"

She folded her arms and glared at me. I didn't have a clue where to start our search and she knew it. Then she sipped her mocha smugly, like she held all the cards. Some days I felt like punching her in the head. I really did.

"The last time I had a feeling as good as this was when Taija got hit by lightning."

The Rat once had a rival back in Winnipeg and her name was Terrible Taija: a kid as scary as a serial killer. Even Little Joe didn't like her and he likes everyone.

She stole the fundraising money that was meant for St. Boniface and said she had found it in the Rat's coat pocket. No one believed her, not the Luxton teachers, not the other kids, and certainly not Father Henri. I mean, there's no doubt the Rat was a closet shoplifter and I'm sure she'll be convicted of something someday. I'm surprised it hasn't happened already. But she would never steal money collected for a good cause. Never.

Anyway, she told me one morning she had a very good feeling that this was the day Terrible Taija would get her comeuppance. And sure enough Taija was struck by lightning. She never died or anything, but she stuttered for a month and she wobbled when she walked. After that, her mother moved her to Churchill—the shame of failing to frame the Rat still hanging over her. The Rat's convinced she'll be eaten by a polar bear one day, and is no doubt looking forward to hearing the news. As for the lightning, I think it was just a coincidence. But the Rat's premonitions could be pretty accurate.

"Okay. We'll start off in the Bronx."

"And we should check the Internet. Uncle Jerome might have a website."

She was still a little kid really. I smiled with satisfaction as I told her that New York drug dealers don't have internet sites. But I did check the phone book. I didn't

g dealer would have his name in the phone
er, but in New York you never know. I even
formation, but there wasn't a single DeBillier

could be the last of the DeBilliers," said the Rat.
ke the Mohicans."

e found a bank to change our Canadian dollars
American dollars, where we walked around a maze
opes and posts until we arrived at a teller.

"This is a lot of money for you kids to be carrying
round," said the teller, who looked like a stern school-
teacher. "There're a lot of crooks in this city."

"She's right, Bob. Make sure you count the money."

"Little girl, I wasn't talking about me. I'm not a crook!"

"You wouldn't tell us if you were," said the Rat.

The Rat was just winding her up. She did that some days. She took a dislike to someone and decided to wind them up. She could be a bit of a bully. Very sternly and slowly the woman counted out our money. The Rat was making us enemies and we'd only just arrived.

We found a subway, and bumping our bikes down a set of steps, we saw a guy in a glass box.

"We want to go to the Bronx," said the Rat to the guy in the glass box. "Can we have two tickets, and can you tell us how we get there?"

The guy passed her the tickets and spoke into a microphone. "Blur! Blur! Blur! Blur! Blur! Blur! Uptown Blur! Blur! Blur! The Bronx."

"Can you repeat that please?" asked the Rat.

The guy looked offended. "Blur! Blur! Blur! Blur! Blur! Blur! Uptown Blur! Blur! Blur! The Bronx!" Then he pushed the mike away to indicate that no further help would be given.

"I think we've upset him," said the Rat. "Maybe it's not his job to give out information."

"Here, kids." A tall redheaded policeman held open a black gate and we went through with our bikes.

"Thank you, officer," said the Rat.

"Go down them stairs over there and take the C train to 42nd Street. There's an underground walkway you can take to Times Square, and from there you can take a train to the Bronx." Then he looked at us, puzzled. "Why you kids wanna go the Bronx?"

Just then someone called him on his radio, and we slipped down the stairs hoping he wouldn't follow.

The New York subway was depressing. It was dirty and dismal and the floor was sticky with gum. You'd think a city as rich as New York could get the gum off the floor, or at least get the drunk off the bench so we could sit down. And the people were different from Winnipeg people. Some of them spoke different languages. But that wasn't it—they were just different.

We waited for the train to come while breathing in the stale air and watching out for muggers. There are always muggers in New York movies, especially on the subway. It's a movie mugger's paradise. And there were a few crooked-looking characters standing about. In fact the whole platform looked like a lineup for *America's Most Wanted*. I couldn't wait for the train to come.

It wasn't long before one came. It roared into the station, fanning us with a warm gust of wind, and then screeched to a halt. But we couldn't get on, it was jammed with people. Even if we never had our bikes we couldn't have got on. The people inside watched us while waiting for the doors to close. And not one of them looked happy. When it left we made our way to the end of the platform, hoping the cars would be less full on the next train.

"There's a rat!" said the Rat. "Look at the size of it. There's another!"

"They're your New York cousins."

She laughed and I laughed with her. "Here's a train," shouted the Rat to the rats. And as though they understood her they scurried away.

When the train stopped we squeezed inside with our backpacks and bikes while bumping into people. We apologized as best we could, but they didn't look impressed. And so we stood there, feeling uncomfortable until the doors closed. Then we rocked and swayed with the other passengers until we saw a station that said 42nd Street.

"We're here," said the Rat.

We got off, and along with an army of people, we followed the signs to Times Square station.

"Don't get lost," I said. It was crazy. There were thousands of people coming and going, and there were so many staircases and signs, and so many uptowns and downtowns, we were like rats in a trap, at least my sister was.

Eventually we saw a sign saying the Bronx and bumped our bikes down the steps to the platform. But it had two tracks.

"Excuse me," I said to this white-whiskered old guy. "Is this side for the Bronx?"

"What? NO! This is going downtown. Down. Town! You want to take the 2 train opposite. You have to go back up the stairs. Read the signs, kid!" And then he glared at me like I'd tried to mug him or something. Trust me to ask the grouch.

"That's the famous New York rudeness," said the Rat.

She wouldn't have thought it was so famous if he'd been rude to *her*. But we scurried to the opposite platform just in time to take the Bronx-bound No. 2 train.

As soon as we were on board, a black woman in a dirty white T-shirt swung open the door between the cars. "Hello, everybody," she shouted. "My name is Janice. I'm hungry and homeless and I haven't eaten in days. If anyone could help me out with some spare change, or something to eat, I'd appreciate it. Y'all have a nice day."

The car went quiet as she passed through with her cup. No one put money in it. In fact most of the people put their heads down. I felt bad for her because she was poor and had no front teeth, and so I put a dollar in her cup.

"Thank you, sir," she said, and passing through to the next car she closed the door behind her.

"You're such a sucker," said the Rat.

Then a black man came into the car. "My name is Joe. I'm trying to get some money together so I can sleep somewhere safe tonight. I was robbed last night. And the night before. I don't wanna get robbed again tonight. Any donation would be appreciated." And he too came through the car with a cup.

Once again the heads went down. But this time the Rat gave him a dollar. "Thank you kindly," he said, and followed Janice into the next car.

"You think Janice and Joe are friends?" asked the Rat.

Before I could answer, an older black woman came through. She never made a statement like the other two. She just gave her cup a little wave and smiled as she walked. And for some reason people put money in it. Maybe it was because she had a nice smile and she was better dressed. Or maybe she had a better technique. Either way her cup was overflowing. Then another one came! I'm not kidding! There was a never-ending parade of beggars passing through the car.

"There's a lot of money in this begging business, Bob."

I bet there was too.

The train went from being under the ground to over the street and when it did, me and the Rat attached ourselves to the windows. We waited for a station that said the Bronx, but one never came.

The Rat approached a man reading a paper. "How far to the Bronx, buddy?" asked the Rat, who had never called anyone *buddy* in her life.

The man looked around him. "We're in the Bronx. What part do you want?"

"We want the part with the drug dealers."

He looked at her strangely.

"Too much television," I said, and took her away by the arm.

As the train came to a stop, I grew nervous. I didn't like the idea of searching the Bronx, and now that we were there I liked it a lot less. All the other passengers made their way off the train and down the stairs. But I didn't. I just stood on the platform looking around me, and I didn't like what I saw. We had made it to the Bronx; I was just hoping we could make it out.

Ten

We got buzzed through another black gate and bumped our bikes down to the street below. The sky was clouding over. And the tracks overhead blocked out much of the dismal light, as did the tall tenement buildings that ran alongside it. They were the types with the fire escapes fixed to the outside and they looked really run-down. And even those that didn't look run-down didn't look nice. Neither did the stores with the people partitioned inside the reinforced glass, or the garbage mounds, or the abandoned cars. The Bronx was a gloomy place, and just when I thought it couldn't get any gloomier it started to rain. We pulled our raincoats and baseball caps from our backpacks and put them on. We're prairie kids. We're used to hot summers and freezing winters, but the rain I couldn't stand!

"Let's start right here and work our way back to the city," said the Rat. "We'll follow the elevated railway. That way we can't get lost."

And so we started with the four guys standing on the corner. "Excuse me, do you know Jerome DeBillier?" I asked.

"Que?"

"*Sabes* Jerome DeBillier?" asked the Rat.

They shook their heads. Moving down we asked another group of guys, but they didn't know either. Neither did the movers or the man sweeping the street. The Rat went into a store to ask the owner and I asked these two shaven-headed Hispanic guys sitting in a car, but they just glared at me. They were just a couple of bullies who wanted to scare me. But they didn't have to. I was scared already.

"No luck in there," said the Rat. "But I bought a guidebook with a pullout map. Now we can find things."

We pushed our bikes down the street asking people as we went. I didn't like asking people. I mean, I knew we were coming to New York to search for our uncle, but I never imagined how stupid I would feel doing it.

Then the Rat asked this stocky, bald white guy who must have been about fifty. He looked at her like he hadn't understood. Then he put his hand to his ear. "Speak up!" he shouted.

"Jerome DeBillier," shouted the Rat.

"Joe the millionaire. I know Joe. But he's no millionaire!" he snarled. "And even if he was he wouldn't give you anything!"

What a crank.

Then this tall Latino in a cream suit came out of a bar. "Who's a goddamn millionaire?"

"Joe," shouted the deaf guy. "But he wouldn't give you anything either!"

"Why the hell not? Who does this Joe think he is?"

"Don't mess with Joe!" snarled the deaf guy.

"Tall Tony messes with who he likes! Okay? Who the hell is this Joe anyway? And who the hell are *you* telling *me* I can't mess with him?" said Tall Tony prodding the deaf guy with his finger.

The deaf guy slapped his hand away. "Don't touch me, dickhead!"

"Touch you! I'll squeeze your bald head until the gum comes out!"

Suddenly the deaf guy smacked Tall Tony with a right hook. Then they both started throwing blows. I'm not kidding. They actually started fighting over this guy Joe, whoever he was. The Rat's eyes widened and she got up close like a referee.

"Get away!" I told her, but she ignored me.

"It's a fight!" shouted a guy coming out the bar. A dozen people followed him and, ignoring the rain, they cheered on the contenders. Other people came running from across the street. Some shouted for them to stop while others looked on, happy for them to fight. Within a minute there was a crowd. One guy pulled money from his pocket. "Two to one on Tall Tony to take the deaf guy!" he shouted.

I lost sight of the Rat. Then I saw her with the gambling guy. She had money in her fist and she was rooting for someone. She always got crazier when crazy things happened. Then I saw a cop car coming down the street.

"It's the police!" I shouted.

Some people scattered or piled back into the bar. Others cheered their arrival as though it added to the entertainment. The cop car pulled up with its lights flashing. But that didn't stop Tall Tony and the deaf guy going at it.

"Come on!" I shouted.

The Rat ran toward me with her bike. "Another minute and I would have won ten bucks!"

"Forget about that. Let's go."

We rode until the commotion was way behind us. More cop cars raced to the scene; we could see them pull up where the fight had been. Me and the Rat looked at each other and laughed. "Who did you have, anyway, Tall Tony?"

"Are you kidding!" said the Rat. "I had the deaf guy, he was a real meanie. That drunk wouldn't have gone the distance."

The Rat was crazy. But she was really crazy if she thought the deaf guy would have taken Tall Tony. He was twenty years younger at least.

"I'm going to ask that old couple," said the Rat, and went off to talk to them.

"Nice bikes."

I turned to see a guy taking shelter in an open doorway. He was smartly dressed in a shirt and tie, and a suit jacket hung casually over his shoulder. He looked so out of place with his surroundings.

"Yeah, they're okay," I said. "You live here?"

"Me? No I can't stand this neighborhood," he said speaking with a kind of accent. "It's my mother's house. She's lived here all her life and now she won't move. 'Come live with us,' I tell her. 'Maria and the kids would love to have you.' But she won't listen. She loves it here. I can't stand this neighborhood or this rain," he said looking around him.

"Me neither."

He laughed a little. "So, why you walking around in it?"

"I'm looking for my uncle. His name's Jerome DeBillier. You know him?"

He looked puzzled. "Jerome DeBillier. I think he's a friend of Larry's. Hang on." He went in the house, and walking down a dark hallway, he pushed open a door. I could just make out the light on his face. "Ma. Isn't Jerome DeBillier a friend of Larry's? He is. Where does he live?"

I couldn't believe it!

"What's your name, kid?" he shouted.

"Bob."

"Ma's calling Larry on the phone. Come in out the rain, Bob. I'll take you around there when she gets the address."

I was just about to step inside when the Rat's fingers clawed my arm. She glared at that guy like you wouldn't believe! When I looked back at him, the friendly look had left his face.

"Come on in. What are you waiting for?" he said.

"Get away, Bob," said the Rat.

She walked me away without letting go of my arm. And for some reason I let her.

"What are you doing?" I asked, prying her fingers away. "That guy has a friend who knows Uncle Jerome. His mother's calling him on the phone."

She looked up at me and shook her head. Then she looked at the house. "There's no one in that house except him. He uses it to trap people, kids mainly." Her face cringed like she was seeing something nasty. "Tonight a gang of men go in there. He's screaming he didn't do it. But he did do it and they know he did. I can see blood splatter on the walls—and I can see his lifeless body."

I was so freaked out I couldn't think. I didn't know what to believe, so I turned on her. "One day the men in white coats are going to scoop you up in a butterfly net and take you away!"

The guy appeared in the doorway and glared at the Rat. And then, smiling, he ran his finger across his throat.

I froze with fear and disgust.

"Ah bleep you, you goddamn demon!" shouted the Rat. "You think I couldn't recognize you! See how tough you are tonight when you get your bleeping head beat in!"

His eyes bulged with badness and silent obscenities drooled from his mouth. It was such a horrible thing to see.

"Come on, let's go!" I jumped on my bike but the Rat stayed where she was. "Leave it!" I shouted.

She got on her bike and we sped away. I looked over my shoulder to make sure he wasn't following. He wasn't. But I kept on going.

"Goddamn murderer!" said the Rat riding alongside me.

I pulled up. "He's a murderer! That's just great!" I shouted. "Now I have to worry about murderers as well as gangbangers, drug dealers, and street fights! I can't wait to see what will happen next!"

"No need to be so dramatic, Bob."

A statement like that coming from the biggest drama queen on the block brought me back to my senses.

"I know," she said, "let's break for lunch. We'll have a nice lunch and then we'll start over. We're not going to let that goddamn demon spoil our day. What do you say to pizza?"

I was so freaked out I said okay. What else was I going to say?

After pizza we continued our search. But the hours passed and we still hadn't found one person who knew our uncle. It was only then that the Chief's words turned over in my mind, *You may never find him. He might not even be in New York*. I'd let my crazy little sister talk me into coming here because she didn't want to go in a home. He could be in jail. He could be dead for all we knew. I felt so down when I thought about it. And we were so far away from home.

I stood there and watched the Rat have fun in her own little world. She sidestepped to the salsa music while asking people as they passed. There was no doubt in her mind. It was as though she expected one of them to point him out in the street or to give her directions to his home.

The rain came down harder, soaking my sneakers and dampening my jeans. I wandered down a side street, and finding an abandoned building, I stood in the doorway. It smelled a bit, but I was too tired to care. I'd have given anything to be back in Winnipeg.

The Rat followed me down. She looked puzzled. "What are you doing, Bob? You'll never find him standing here."

"We'll never bleeping find him anyway!" I said. But I never bleeped.

"What! Our dear dead father is not yet cold in his grave and you've taken to using profanity!"

"Shut up!" I told her. "You say *goddamn*!"

"So! *Goddamn* isn't swearing! You're not damning God or anything. It doesn't mean anything, not really. Now, I'm going to look for him! Are you coming?"

I felt so sad I couldn't speak.

The Rat looked worried. "Are you okay, Bob? Would you like me to go get you something?"

I thought about the Old Man, and the grief came.

"I think we've done really well so far, getting to New York and all. Lots of kids wouldn't have made it this far."

I could feel the fear and the anger growing inside me.

"We'll find him, Bob," she said. "We only have to believe."

"Don't be so stupid! We'll never find him! We should never have come here!"

She cringed. "Don't be like that. Come on. You don't want to go in a home, do you?"

"I don't know! At least I'd be away from you! Do you know how crazy you are? Do you know how much I have to put up with? If the proper authorities do catch up with us they won't put you in a home. They'll put you in a mental hospital!"

The Rat looked at me and then she walked away. I stood there for a second, my head fell into my hands, and then I started to cry. I tried to stop myself but I couldn't. I cried for myself because I was feeling so lost. And I cried for the Rat who would now have to go in a home. And I cried for our dear dead father who I loved very much.

When I managed to stop myself I popped my head out the doorway. I expected to see her but she wasn't there. I dried my eyes and went back to the corner. But she wasn't there either. And her bike had gone!

I looked around me but she was nowhere in sight. I panicked. I unlocked my bike and rode around like a madman. I rode down a dozen side streets, but nothing. I rode back on to the main street looking in the stores and restaurants as I went. Then I started asking people had they seen a little white girl on a BMX, but no one had. Seeing a train station I ran up the steps to the overhead. She wasn't there. Then I saw a police car parked on the street below. I had to tell them. She could be lost. That strange guy could have got her. But as I ran down the stairs I saw her standing alone on some vacant lot. Jumping on my bike, I sprinted around the block and skidded on to the muddy ground. She was watching the rain drip into a large puddle. She wasn't crying—the Rat never cried—but she looked pale and confused, which was even worse. "Are you okay?" I asked.

"Do you really think they'll put me in a mental hospital?"

Boy did I feel ashamed! She must have been feeling something after Dad's death even if she never showed it.

"Because my fits are getting worse and sometimes my head—"

"No! I was feeling bad and I took it out on you! I didn't mean it, I swear!"

She looked up at me. "So, I'm not even a little bit crazy?"

"Well—maybe just a little."

When she chuckled the joy and the color came back into her face. There's one thing I'll say for the Rat, she never holds a grudge. "Come on," I said. "Let's go find our uncle." I put my hand on her shoulder and we walked our bikes back to the main street.

"You think he'll have contacts in show business?" she asked. "Maybe I could enroll in a drama school while I'm here. Or get a part on Broadway."

"We'll see."

She looked up at me. "We will find him, Bob. I know we will."

"I know," I said. But I didn't know. But as I was feel ing so guilty I went back to asking people with as much enthusiasm as possible.

We asked a traffic cop, a woman out with her kids, and a painter up a ladder. We asked a taxi driver parked outside a pizzeria, a postal worker, and the women he was arguing with. We asked the store owners, the street vendors, and the boy in the candy store where the Rat bought her gum. We asked the guy in the tattoo parlor and the girl he was tattooing, and her girlfriend who said her mom would kill her. We asked the barmaid in the Irish pub, and she asked her small dog who was up on the bar, but he didn't know. We asked the black girls skipping in the rain and they asked their friend Leticia who said she didn't know and didn't care. We asked this one guy in a soiled suit who said he could find out, but it would cost us. And we asked the guy who jumped out of the car and chased the man in the soiled suit down the street, but he never answered. We asked the woman with the broken umbrella and the guy wearing the headphone set who wouldn't stop dancing. We asked the girl on the roller blades, the guy she wouldn't go out with, and his friend who told him so. We asked black people and white people, and the Korean people standing in the doorway of the take-out place. We asked a thousand Hispanic people, who seemed to be the majority in every neighborhood we went through, but nobody knew our uncle. Not a single soul.

But I have to say that, as rough as the Bronx was and as dangerous as it was supposed to be, most of the people were polite. They danced to the Latin music blasting from car stereos or shouted friendly insults to their friends. And there were no bandana-headed street gangs standing on the corners, and I didn't see anyone dealing drugs. I was relieved in a way, even if it was a drug dealer we were looking for.

"Ask Al the butcher on the next block," shouted a woman from her fire escape. "He knows everyone. And remember me if any money comes your way. I'm an old woman on welfare."

"We're on welfare too," said the Rat. "It's great, isn't it?"

The Rat had taken to talking in a New York accent and cracking her gum like a regular New Yorker. But I was glad she'd gone back to having fun.

We crossed to the next block and went into the butcher's. It had sawdust on the floor and the meat looked more brown than red.

"Hey buddy, you know Jerome DeBillier?" asked the Rat. "We think he might live around here."

The butcher, who had a few days' growth of beard on his face, took an unlit cigar from his mouth and went to the back door. "Pa! You know a Jerome DeBillier?" he asked, shouting up the stairs.

A voice came back. "He's the guy on the TV."

"No, he lives around here somewhere," shouted the butcher.

"He's the guy on the TV, I tell you. He's always on it."

"He don't know him," said the butcher.

The Rat showed the butcher the photograph, and wiping his hands on his apron he gave them a look. "I tell you, kid, I know the name from somewhere and I know this face. But for the life of me I can't put the two together. Listen, if you're back this way tomorrow, pop in. The cobwebs might have cleared by then."

"Okay, Al. Have a good one."

"Same to you, kid."

We continued following the elevated tracks, asking people as we went. But we never found anyone who knew him, and I never thought we would. Not until I came out of a store and saw the Rat's face. As soon as I saw it I knew she was on to something.

"Yes, that's Jerome DeBillier," said this old Hispanic woman looking at the photograph. "But he's a young man there. He must be in his forties by now."

I couldn't believe my ears!

"You know, my granddaughter used to clean apartments on his block. He had the penthouse, you know? It was a very important job she was doing."

"Where was that?" asked the Rat.

"It was on Fifth Avenue, somewhere. I don't know the number, and she's gone back to the Dominican Republic. But I remember her telling me it overlooked Central Park."

"Is he still a drug dealer?"

"One of the biggest in New York, some say the country." The woman put up her umbrella. "Why are you kids looking for him?"

"He's our long lost uncle," said the Rat.

"Sure he is, sweetheart," said the woman. "And I'm having tea with Donald Trump." She walked away laughing as she went.

"You think she knew him?" I asked. "She seemed a little crazy."

"She is crazy, Bob, but she did know him! How else would she have known it was an old photograph?"

The Rat was right. I should have thought of that.

She pulled her map book from her pocket. "Central Park. Fifth Avenue. There it is. We've found him! And look, we can take the 145th Street Bridge back into

Manhattan. Come on, Bob. He's not getting away from us!" She got on her bike and rode away.

Once she gets her ratty little claws into something she never lets go. Who knows, maybe he wouldn't get away from us, not with her pedaling after him.

Eleven

We rode down a broad, gray street lined with large brown houses. They had steep steps, and there were slim Roman pillars on either side of the front doors. Black women leaned out of the windows of the houses while watching their tiny kids run around in raingear. There were a lot of black people around there. They stood in doorways or huddled with jackets raised to keep out the rain or strolled around like they didn't care.

"We must be in Harlem," said the Rat, seeing a sign for Malcolm X Boulevard. "I've heard of him. And now he has his very own boulevard. Hey, Bob, there's the Empire State Building."

It was way in the distance, surrounded by mist, and lit up in the tricolor of the French flag: blue, white, and red. Every time I saw the flag, the French national anthem played in my head. They had the best anthem of any country. Somehow, it made me feel proud that I had French ancestors. One day I'd like to go to France to see the house where my mother was born. One day.

When we came to a busy intersection, I saw a Starbucks and stopped. I wasn't going any further without food and a hot drink. "Are you hungry?"

"Starving," said the Rat.

We locked up the bikes and headed inside. I went to the counter and ordered coffee, cake, and sandwiches, while the Rat collapsed on the comfy seats. She read her guidebook until I hovered over her with a tray, and then she sat up and reached for her mocha. I sat next to her and we ate while watching the people run in the rain. I hated being in the rain, but I liked watching it when I was indoors.

The Rat pulled her cell from her pocket, and finding a socket, she set it to charge. "I'm sending Harold a text message telling him we've had our first lead as to Uncle Jerome's whereabouts. And I'm telling him about our exciting day."

"Exciting?"

"Can I have another mocha, Bob?"

"Get it yourself."

She pulled the map from her guidebook. "I'm looking for the hostel."

She could be so lazy at times. I went up to the counter and didn't I get the shock of my life. I thought

Miss Gabriela Felipe Mendez had moved to New York and got a job in Starbucks!

"What can I get you?"

She even spoke like her.

"Do you want a coffee?"

She looked a little younger but that was all. She could have been her twin sister!

"A tea maybe or something to eat?"

I swear I could hear salsa music playing in my head. Then she brought her face close to mine, the way Gabriela did. "If you don't tell me what you want, I'm gonna call the cops."

"Oh, I want a mocha!"

She giggled. "I'm just kidding. Where are you from?"

"I'm from Winnipeg. Winnipeg is in—"

"I took Geography. So, what are you doing in New York?"

"I'm just visiting, but I might move here."

She laughed. "How old are you?"

"Fourteen," I said. I don't know why I lied. But I do look fourteen.

"That's too bad," said Gabriela's look-alike. "If you were a little older we could have gone out." She handed me the coffee. "Because you're real cute."

I blushed slightly as I tried to hand her the money.

"Don't worry about it." She gave me a sexy wink, and she laughed as I walked away, but I didn't mind. She said I was cute. I don't think of myself as cute, but I am good-looking, as I've said.

I gave the Rat her mocha and took a seat like nothing had happened, but I was pretty excited.

"You know, Bob, that girl would be too old for you even if you *were* fourteen," said the Rat without looking up. "She'd probably be too old for you if you were twenty-five."

"You're such a rat!"

"Well you shouldn't be flirting at twelve."

"I'll be thirteen soon, a teenager—I'll flirt if I want!"

The Rat drank her mocha like a pig, stood up, and put on her backpack. "Let's go."

But I felt comfy in the coffee shop and the girl liked me. "Let's stay until it stops raining."

"It's stopped."

I looked out the window. It had stopped. "Well—well, I'm tired!" I really was tired too. And being so relaxed I'd dropped my guard. The thought of returning to the turmoil made my heart beat faster.

The Rat folded her arms. "Look, Bob. If you don't get up I'll cause a scene. This is New York. It's expected of me!"

I knew she'd do it. She'd go crazy just for the hell of it. If I hadn't been mean to her earlier that day I would have stayed where I was. But I still felt guilty, so I got up.

"You can be so childish."

"I *am* a child, Bob."

That irritating Rat has an answer for everything.

It was dark as we rode down Malcolm X's Boulevard. And the dark made New York look more menacing. But it wasn't too bad. There were families sitting on stoops, and groups of guys joking around on the street corners. And somewhere in the distance someone was playing a trumpet. It was like being in a scene from a movie.

The map-reading Rat knew the way to the hostel, and so I followed her down Malcolm X Boulevard until we came to what she said was Central Park. It was big and gloomy with dark trees swaying around a boating lake. We never went inside. We followed it around until we came to a long avenue that ran alongside it.

"This is Central Park West," said the Rat. We rode down it, the Rat checking the street numbers as we went. After no more than ten minutes the Rat rode into a side street and pulled up. "This is it," she said.

And sure enough there was the hostel. Locking up our bikes, we went inside.

There was a guy sitting in a small office behind a glass window.

"Is Sexy Sandra here?" I asked.

He pulled open the window and gave me a look. "Sandra is off today. If you want to see her you'll have to come back tomorrow."

"We're supposed to be staying here," said the Rat. "Our Uncle Joey told us Sexy Sandra would take care of us. He used to be her boyfriend."

The guy looked old and tired. "Joey, yeah I remember him." He looked on a notice board behind him. "There's nothing here, kid. Why don't you come back tomorrow?"

"We have nowhere to go," I said. "But we have ID."

The guy shook his head. "I'm afraid not, son. You have to be at least sixteen to stay here without an adult."

"He's twenty-five," said the Rat. "He's just had an easy life."

The guy smiled but he closed the window all the same.

"Let's go to Fifth Avenue and look for Uncle Jerome. We won't need a place to stay if we find him," said the Rat. Then she tapped on the window. "Hey, buddy, what's the quickest way to Fifth Avenue?"

"Go through the gap in the park wall at the end of this street and follow the path across. Ten minutes tops."

We rode down the street to the park. The Rat started to ride in but I grabbed her by the arm. I tried to see inside, but the park was too big and dark, and there were trees everywhere. Any one of New York's many maniacs could be lying in wait, ready to pounce. "Maybe we should go around," I said.

"I think it will be okay, Bob."

"All right, but stay close to me."

We rode through the park, with the trees still dripping rain on us, and followed the path that led to the other side. Halfway through I thought about all those New York movies where muggers waited, ready to ambush the passing pedestrian. There were usually three of them, and they usually had switchblades. But all we saw were some joggers and a policeman sitting in a tiny electric tricycle. I felt a lot safer when I saw him.

We rounded a baseball field and came out on Fifth Avenue, which was wonderfully well lit after coming out of the park. A wide tree-lined sidewalk ran alongside the park, and opposite stood the apartment buildings where Uncle Jerome was supposed to live. I couldn't see any skyscrapers, like I'd feared, but the park seemed to go on for miles. Me and the Rat were quiet as we surveyed Fifth Avenue. There must have been hundreds of apartments facing the park. It was going to be a real challenge. But, that said, it looked like a well-to-do part of town and it was better than being in the Bronx.

"Let's ride up and down and see if we can see him," said the Rat.

And so that's what we did. We rode down Fifth Avenue scanning the apartment blocks from lobby to penthouse. At least that's what I did. The Rat was acting like her vacation had begun. She stopped every now and again and, pulling out her guidebook, she turned into a tour guide. "This is Museum Mile and over there is the Guggenheim. It doesn't fit in with any of the other buildings, but it's cute. And coming up is the Metropolitan Museum of Art, otherwise known as the Met. Note the architecture, Bob. It looks like a palace imported from Europe."

We continued all the way to the end of the park, and came to a place where there were horses and carriages, and hundreds of people coming and going. "This is

Central Park South and that's the Plaza," said the Rat pointing at a big square hotel. "Uncle Jerome might put us up there if he's as big a drug dealer as we've been told."

Then I started to worry about where we would spend the night. A roach motel probably. The sort of place that only wanted your money.

"Let's continue our search, Bob."

We headed back up Fifth Avenue. But about halfway the Rat cycled through a gap in the park wall. "Follow me, Bob." I'd just got out of the damn park and I didn't want to go back in. But I followed her down a dark path and around the side of a road. Then she got off her bike, and crossing a short lawn, she headed toward some bushes.

"What are you up to?"

She switched on her flashlight and fought her way through the bushes, bike and all, and, like a fool, I followed her. "He's not going to be in here."

"Very funny, Bob."

"If you have to pee you can go by yourself," I told her. "And I'm getting soaked in these bushes!"

We came out in a small clearing that was lit up a little by the lights coming from Fifth Avenue. There was a flat concrete base and, standing on it, the Rat held out her hands.

"Are you kidding?" I said. "I'm not sleeping in the park."

"Are you a man or a mouse?"

"What difference does it make? You're a rat, and I'm not sleeping in the park."

"Why not? It won't cost us anything, and we'll be close to where Uncle Jerome lives. And remember, Sexy Sandra won't be back until tomorrow. Besides, sleeping outdoors makes it more of an adventure."

I looked around at the dark trees and dismal bushes.

"Come on, Bob. It'll be like our old den."

When we were very little kids we had a den. It was just a large wooden box with hay poured over it. It looked like a miniature haystack. And if the Rat got upset—she got upset quite a bit when she was a very little kid—she'd crawl into it and fall asleep. I can still remember Dad carrying her out and putting her to bed. But how she can remember I don't know. "How did you know there was a den here?"

"I didn't. But it's just what we need."

I felt the concrete base. It was dry and there was warm air coming from a vent in its center. I didn't want to stay there, but it looked like we had no choice. "Okay. But just for tonight."

"Great!"

She emptied her backpack on the base and tied a small dream catcher to the branch of a tree. I untied my sleeping bag, took off my sneakers, and got in. It wasn't as hard as I expected.

"What are you doing?" asked the Rat. "I can't sleep yet. It's too early. And look, it's a full moon. I can never get a good night's sleep in a full moon!"

She bewildered me at times. "Well, maybe you should try and rest."

"Rest! It's our first night in New York, Bob! I wanna see the lights!"

"Well, I'm tired!"

She folded her arms. "How can you be tired at twelve? It's impossible. Oh I forgot. You're nearly thirteen, almost a teenager. What trouble-causing teenager would want to sleep his first night in New York City?"

I got up. When the Rat got it in her head to do something, she had to do it. Besides, the thought of lying there in the dark gave me the creeps.

"We'll leave the backpacks here and head to Times Square," she said. "That's where the lights are. I've already found it on my map. It's not far. Just follow me."

I could see the words on my gravestone: *Here lies Bob DeBillier who made the mistake of following his crazy little sister.* But I followed her anyway.

Twelve

As soon as we turned on to 42nd Street we could see the lights, even though we were still a good few blocks away. But when we locked up the bikes and walked onto Broadway, we were absolutely bewildered! There were lights rolling around rooftops, beaming from spotlights, and blooming on billboards. And when I turned to the Rat the lights were reflected in her large eyes.

"I'm broader than Broadway, brother!" she said in her Jamaican accent.

We walked along a sidewalk packed with people and then scurried to an island which seemed to be surrounded by a sea of yellow taxis. And there we looked around us in absolute awe.

"I need a drink, Bob."

We ran across Broadway, and buying a Coke at McDonald's, we drank it outside while soaking up the Times Square street life.

But then I noticed this guy. He was about Dad's age, but he looked strange. His mouth was curved into an unhappy face and he walked funny. He never limped but he never walked straight either. And his shoulders sloped to one side, or maybe one arm was longer than the other. Even his eyes looked a little crossed. Everything about him was crooked.

What's more, his clothes didn't seem right. He was wearing this shabby black suit that was shiny with use, and his shoes were old and worn. But his shirt and tie looked new and his graying brown hair was neatly cut and combed.

He stalked the crowd like a predator. Then suddenly his eyes widened and he pounced on a passing couple. "Sir, madam, how are you this evening? I hate to trouble you but I'm in need of help. We all need help at some stage in our lives and now is the time for me."

The couple walked faster.

"I was just hoping—excuse me. Hey I'm talking to you!"

Then he saw another couple coming toward him. "Oh God, I hope you can help me! I need to get to Chicago! It's my wife! The priest has already read her the last rites! I just hope I can make it in time! What do you say? Can you help me out?"

"Beat it, hustler," said the man without looking at him.

"Hustler! Did you hear that? I tell him my wife's dying and he calls me a hustler. How insensitive can you get?" Then he took a wallet from his pocket and pounced on another couple. "Excuse me, miss. This is a picture of my wife, and she's about to give birth. All I need is twenty dollars to get me to Washington."

"Sorry," said the woman, pushing past him.

"You're not that sorry though, are you? Not sorry enough to spare a few bucks!" Then he noticed me and the Rat watching him. "Look at all these goddamn tourists. They must be forking out two hundred dollars a night for a hotel. Two hundred dollars a night for a lousy bed. And what difference does it make when you're asleep? Suckers, every one of them. Then there're the shows, the expensive drinks, and the 'I love you present' he has to buy her to reassure her that their marriage is still good. And you'd think after all they've spent they wouldn't mind helping a guy out, but oh no."

"He's great!" said the Rat. "You think he'll let us hang out with him?"

"Why would we want to—"

"Hey, buddy. Can we hang out with you?"

The hustler looked us up and down. "Depends," he said. "You ever scammed anyone?"

"No we—"

"All the time," said the Rat.

The hustler gave us another look. "Forget about it, you're too young."

Then, spotting a well-dressed couple, he switched character. “I hate to bother you folks, but it’s my wife!”

“Sorry, buddy. No handouts today,” said the man, who was tall and broad.

The hustler concentrated on the woman, she had diamonds on her fingers. “Miss, my wife means so much to me!”

The woman, who was a little overweight, slowed down. “Well, what seems to be the trouble?”

“Come on, Mildred. He’s a hustler,” said the man.

“No, honestly,” said the hustler. “I’ve never done anything like this before.”

The man took Mildred by the arm and went to walk away. Then, who decides to step forward?

“She’s dying! Mommy is dying!”

Like our day hadn’t been hectic enough! Or maybe she thought it lacked excitement! Maybe that demon guy threatening to cut her throat wasn’t exciting enough.

“Oh, you poor thing!” said Mildred.

“Mildred!” shouted the man.

The hustler got on to the Rat’s part right away. “Don’t worry, dear! Daddy will get the money somehow!”

I was absolutely bewildered. They’d turned into a double act and they’d only just met!

“I know a scam when I see one!” said the man.

“George, how can you be so insensitive? Is this the sort of man I’m going to marry?” The woman opened her handbag and gave the Rat a twenty. “Here you go. I hope this helps.”

"Thank you, miss," said the Rat. And then she curtsied. Do you believe that? She curtsied. I don't know what movie she thought she was acting from.

"Mildred! Can't you see what they are?"

The woman shot him a bad look and walked away. George chased after her and took her by the arm. They argued.

"If she can't see what *he* is, she definitely can't see what *we* are," said the hustler.

Then George came back. "Here you go, buddy!" He said loud enough so Mildred could hear him. But when he handed the hustler a twenty he spoke softly. "You're scum! You know that?"

"I know," said the hustler. "But you're not marrying her for her good looks, are you, George? And isn't she a lot older than you?"

George looked enraged, but he turned and walked away.

"You see that, kids? The man's wearing a Rolex that she probably bought him, and he's crying like a baby over a few bucks." Then the hustler snapped his fingers at the Rat. "Okay, kid. Hand it over."

The Rat handed the hustler the twenty and he gave her back a ten. The Rat looked at the money and then at the hustler.

"Look, kid, I have expenses. And I have experience. I have expenses and experience. What have you got?"

"Are you kidding? Have you seen this face?" said the Rat pointing at her face. "This face could make more money than you've earned all month! Now you give me back that twenty or I'm walking!"

"There's no need for attitude. Tommy Mattolla always looks after his partners."

"Well, look after me now, Tommy, and give me back that twenty!"

"What's your name, kid?"

"Marie Claire."

"Forget about that twenty, Marie Claire. There's a lotta suckers out tonight. You wanna make some real money?"

"Shewa, Tommy! But don't try to hustle me! I have friends downtown!"

"What's this? Threats? I'm being threatened here?"

"I'm just making it clear, that's all!"

"You've made it crystal. Now, let's go to work."

The Rat went to follow him, but I grabbed her by the arm. "You're not hanging out with him. You don't even know the guy."

"It's okay, Bob. I'm pretty sure he has good spirit."

"I don't care what sort of spirit he's got! You're not hanging out with him!"

The Rat pushed my arm away. "I wanna have some fun! If you don't like it go back to the den and I'll catch you later!" And with that, she followed the hustler.

She knew I wouldn't leave her. She was just being a selfish little brat! I felt like slapping her face. But I didn't. I followed on behind like a dope.

And then it began. The Rat and the hustler hit Broadway with Oscar-winning performances that involved everything from train wrecks to robberies, from stock market collapses to stolen tickets. There were dying mothers, muggers, and sickness in Seattle. There were enough deaths to fill a morgue and enough births to fill a maternity ward.

Yet the hustler really did seem like he had a good spirit. I mean, I wouldn't trust him with a dime, but he was tough and streetwise and somehow I felt we were safe with him. It was even fun to watch him perform with the Rat as his little poisonous protégée. But it didn't last. A rivalry developed between them, and they started to give each other the needle.

"Stop overacting," said the hustler. I knew that wouldn't go down well but I could see his point. She looked like she was acting the part of the Little Match Girl standing barefoot in the snow. She was even shivering. Who shivers in this heat? She looked like a ten-year-old junkie. Maybe that's why the suckers were giving her so much money. But criticizing the Rat's performance in front of the suckers was not good business. I said nothing.

"I happen to be part of the Luxton drama class, Tommy! Appointed by Ms. Mountshaft herself. Don't tell me how to act."

"I did a summer at Juilliard," said Tommy. "I don't even know where Luxton is. And who the hell is Ms. Mountshaft?"

The Rat came over to me. "I'm making more than him, and he's jealous."

Then Tommy came over. "She's a good earner, your sister, but she's got a lot to learn. Tell her to calm down, Bob."

I was hoping they'd call it a night after that, but they didn't. They angled their way down Broadway like a vicious version of Fagin and the Artful Dodger. This can't be good, I thought. And it wasn't. It all came to a head on the corner of 47th and Broadway when the moon was at its highest.

"I just need to get back to Miami," said Tommy, talking to a group of tourists, "to see her for the last time!"

"Is she dying?" asked one of them.

"She's already dead," said the Rat. "But he'll make her rise again if you give him enough money."

Tommy's scowl darkened. "She wouldn't need to die if you were any good!"

"If *I* was any good!" shouted the Rat. "If *you* were any good, she wouldn't have dumped you for the clown! And he wasn't even that funny!"

"That was you! You ruined a perfectly good marriage!" Then he turned to the tourists. "She has mental problems."

"Of course I have mental problems!" shouted the Rat. "Who wouldn't with a father like you?"

A crowd soon gathered.

"She's been kicked out of so many schools," said Tommy. "Schools for delinquent children at that!"

"That's because I never got any sleep!" said the Rat appealing to the crowd. "He had me working in a sweatshop!"

"We needed the money to pay your psychiatrist."

"You needed it to pay off your bookies! And I won't even mention his drinking problem!"

When the crowd grew larger I got nervous! "Let's go," I said, but she ignored me.

"I had to drink! You were driving me insane! All that lying and stealing and setting fire to your pet poodle! Poor Pier, he never knew what cooked him!"

The Rat wiped away an imaginary tear. "He sold my sister's medicine when she was dying of leukemia!"

The crowd gasped.

"I had to do it, to buy food!"

"You did it to buy drugs!" retorted the Rat. "And he never paid the drug dealers, and now they're hunting us down! I could be killed at any minute."

People began to jostle for a better place.

"She was responsible for her mother's death!" said Tommy addressing the crowd.

"That was him! He kicked her when she was pregnant!" screamed the Rat.

A few angry jeers came from the crowd. Tommy crouched as if cowering from a blow. "You kicked her as well!" he shouted.

All eyes fell on the Rat.

"I missed! It was you I was trying to kick! To stop you from strangling her because she was having your brother's baby!"

Tommy froze with stage fright. He looked at the angry faces around him and then back at the Rat. "You're a goddamn liar!" he shouted.

"I might be a goddamn liar, Tommy Mattolla! But I'm a better goddamn liar than you'll ever be!" And with that she took a bow.

The crowd cheered and clapped. Shock turned to surprise on the hustler's face and, taking the Rat's hand, he bowed alongside her.

The Rat opened her arms. "Are you not entertained?" she shouted.

As the applause grew, Tommy pulled a hat from nowhere and worked the crowd. I couldn't believe it. People pushed into one another to put money in that hat. Then someone threw the Rat a rose and she came over all starry-eyed. Her first Broadway performance had been a success.

All of a sudden Tommy wasn't there and two cops were heading toward us! Me and the Rat merged with the crowd, and then we ran for the bikes. "Let's ride," said the Rat and we sprinted away.

My eyes felt heavy when we reached the gap in the park wall. But they opened wide as we entered the park. We rode down the dark paths and pulled up by the lawn. Then getting off our bikes we stood there in silence. We looked around us, scanning the trees and the lawns and looking deep into the dark shadows. We couldn't see anyone, not unless they were hiding. "Come on," I whispered. We ran across the lawn, pushing our bikes, and fought our way through the bushes. I switched on my flashlight as soon as we were through, and keeping it low I searched the den. I was dreading that some strange homeless person had taken our place. But there was no one there, thank God.

The Rat dumped her bike, took off her sneakers, and slid into her sleeping bag. "This is great!"

I lay down next to her. And there we were with nothing but bushes separating us from murderers, robbers, and all sorts of other creeps, and the Rat thought it was great.

"And it's been a great day as well," she whispered. "We're in New York and we've seen lots of great stuff, and we've made another friend. I bet Tommy knows a lot of people. We'll have to ask him if he knows Uncle Jerome."

"We won't see him again," I said looking around at the bushes.

"Of course we will. We're partners. He's not getting away from us—turn the flashlight off, Bob, or I'll never get to sleep."

I switched off the light and lay there. I was so jumpy. There were strange shapes in the shadows and the slightest sound made me sit up. It was only when the Rat started snoring I kind of relaxed. I put my hands behind my head and looked at the moon. Next thing I knew my eyes closed and our first day in New York City had come to an end. And boy was I exhausted.

Thirteen

In my dreams I was in Times Square and there was someone singing. Then I woke to the Rat singing in the sunshine, *"I recall Central Park in Fall—"*

"Shush, you'll give us away."

"Give us away to who?"

I looked around me. We were camouflaged by the trees and bushes. Even when I stood up I could only see the top of the Fifth Avenue apartment blocks.

"Did you sleep well, Bob?"

"Sure, but I'll sleep a lot better when we're in Sexy Sandra's hostel."

"I think we're better off here, Bob. It's rent free and there's a lot of strange types that hang around them hostels. So shall we stay here, Bob? What do you think?"

She was trying to manipulate me, and I'd only just woken up. "We'll see. But for now I need breakfast."

The Rat jumped up. "Great, and then we'll knock on all these apartment blocks until Uncle Jerome comes down and claims us."

We put our sleeping bags in their holders, tied them to our backpacks, and hung them on a low branch. Then, leaving our bikes at the den, we scurried across the lawn to the path.

There were dozens of joggers out, and most of them were girls. I had never woken up to so many girls. And they were all wearing stuff that was stretchy and tight. New York has some pretty girls. One of them jogged toward me with everything bouncing.

"Good morning," she said.

"Hi!" I said. I liked her right away! Then I turned to look at her from behind. When I looked back the Rat had her arms folded.

"Our dear dead dad is not yet cold in his grave and you've turned into a pervert!"

I could see this "not yet cold in his grave" line was going to be a constant weapon with the Rat. I was going to tell her to mind her own business. But her screwed-up face looked kind of sad and so I didn't. "It's okay to look."

"No it's not. You have to wait until you're sixteen."

"No, you don't."

"You do, you're my brother!"

I put my hand on her shoulder and walked her out of the park. She kept her arms folded until I told her I'd pay for breakfast. You could always get back in the Rat's good graces by paying for things.

We walked down Fifth Avenue until we found a street vendor selling coffee and doughnuts. The Rat ordered in Spanish, and taking our breakfast to a bench, we ate while watching the New York squirrels scurry around us. And then, as if it had only just dawned on me, I asked: "Who taught you Spanish? They don't teach it at Luxton."

"Miss Gabriela Felipe Mendez gave me some tapes. I put them on when I slept, and after a couple of months I could speak Spanish. The hardest thing is to get your hearing in tune. But once you've learned the words to a dozen Spanish songs, you're good to go."

"I think I might want to learn Spanish someday."

"She's too old for you, Bob, and she always will be."

"But do you think she likes me?"

"Of course she likes you. You're my brother."

When we had finished we put our trash in the garbage and headed to the first apartment block at the beginning of the park. And there I approached the doorman. "Does Jerome DeBillier live here?"

He looked straight ahead like a Mountie on guard duty. "We're not allowed to give out information about our tenants."

"Can't you give us a clue?" asked the Rat.

"I'm afraid not."

We moved away so he couldn't hear us. "You think we should bribe him, like they do in the movies?"

The Rat scoffed. "I'm not giving my money to a doorman."

We walked to the next building. "Does Jerome DeBillier live here?" I asked.

The doorman, who was dressed like he was out of the twenties, frowned as he thought. "I know that name. But he doesn't live in this building. Is he a relative?"

He had such a high-pitched Irish accent I almost laughed.

"He's our uncle," said the Rat. She had a big smile on her face. I could see she wanted to laugh too.

"Go see Connor in the next building over, he'll know. Tell him Sean sent you."

We thanked him and walked away, laughing as we went. He was a nice guy. You couldn't help but like him. But Connor, a short stocky Irishman, said he'd never heard of Uncle Jerome. Then he went back to arguing with some movers over the damage that he said they'd caused to one of the building's doors. "Ask Patrick on the next building over," he said. "He might know."

Patrick shook his head, "You can take it from me that Jerome DeBillier does not live within a block of this building. Because if he did I'd know about it, and I don't. But you kids have a grand day!"

I walked up Fifth Avenue with the Rat walking behind me.

"My name is Marie Claire and I'm from County Mayo. Oh to kiss the Blarney Stone!"

I stopped abruptly and she bumped into my chest. "Will you stop speaking in that irritating Irish accent?"

She looked up at me. "To be sure!"

She did stop, but she switched to rapping instead. I could see it was going to be a long day.

There were a few apartment blocks without a doorman and so we pressed the buzzers and asked the tenants themselves. One guy told us he'd call the cops if we pressed his buzzer again, and so the Rat kept her finger on it to teach him a lesson. Then she pressed another buzzer. "Hello," said a man, speaking in an effeminate tone.

"Do you know Jerome DeBillier?" asked the Rat.

"Yes, but he doesn't live here."

The Rat's eyes widened. "Where does he live?"

"I'm not telling you. And do you know why I'm not telling you?"

"No," said the Rat.

"Because you woke me up!"

The Rat kicked the wall and walked away. "What a bleep! I bet he did know our uncle! And I bet he knows where he lives!" She ran back and pressed his buzzer.

"Hello."

"We're sorry for waking you, now can you please tell us where our—"

"I'm not telling you a goddamn thing! Now stop ringing my buzzer!"

"Ah bleep you! And I'm glad I woke you up! And get a bleeping job!" shouted the Rat.

She spoke French for the next few blocks and then, as if by fate, we found the French Embassy. But they wouldn't even let us inside. The French could be quite snotty at times, and they were especially snotty at the embassy.

We continued all the way up to the Guggenheim Museum. My enthusiasm faded a little as we passed it. But it went away completely when we came to the end of the park. We were back in Harlem by the time we entered our last apartment block.

"Sorry, son. No one listed under that name," said an old black security guard.

We walked outside where once again it started to rain. "Doesn't it ever stop raining in this city?"

"I know," said the Rat. "Let's go to the Metropolitan Museum until it stops. We can look at the paintings and get cultured. They might have some Vincents."

And so that's what we did. We walked all the way back down Fifth Avenue, and giving the girl a dollar donation, we climbed the marble-looking staircase.

The Rat liked paintings. At home she had books with famous paintings in them and she'd sit and look at them for hours. Vincent Van Gogh was her favorite. No surprise there, the man cut off his ear and shot himself in the chest. Why wouldn't he be the Rat's favorite?

She started off by staring up at paintings of baby angels. "There should be fat angels and old angels and angels that aren't very good-looking. Otherwise people will think you have to be beautiful to be an angel, and you don't. You only have to be good."

I followed her around while she stood in front of every single painting in the museum. I liked a lot of the paintings, especially the seascapes by Monet. I like seascapes. But after an hour or so, my mind couldn't take in any more images. In the end it was just as nice to look at a bare wall.

It was still raining when we stepped outside. And so we took shelter at the top of the steps. Suddenly, the Rat stepped forward.

"What is it?" I asked.

"It's Ice!" She ran down the steps and hid behind a group of people. She peered around the side of them. Then she ran to another group and did the same. She was watching a black man walk up Fifth Avenue. He wore a black suit, and there was gold around his neck. I couldn't see his face at first because it was blocked by his umbrella. But when he looked toward the museum, I recognized him. It was the Iceman, the Rat's favorite rapper.

She followed him away from the museum using lampposts and cars for cover. I hate to say it, but the Rat had turned into a stalker. I ran down the steps and ran after her. I had to try and stop her from whatever it was she was going to do. I grabbed her by the arm.

"Let's introduce ourselves!" she said.

"He won't want to meet us."

"Why won't he? I bought his CD."

I wanted to meet him. I'd never met a celebrity before, not unless you count the Mayor of Winnipeg.

The Rat's eyes widened. "We'll invite him for coffee!"

"I don't think he'll want—"

"Just think how impressed Miss Gabriela Felipe Mendez will be when she finds out you had coffee with the Iceman!"

The Rat was trying to manipulate me. "Okay, then."

She sprinted away and stopped in front of him. "Hi Ice! I'm Marie Claire DeBillier and that's my brother Bob behind you. We just thought—"

But the Iceman walked past the Rat as though she didn't exist. The Rat looked puzzled and then she ran ahead of him. "We don't want to bother you, Ice. We just wanted to say that we're your biggest fans in Canada and we really like you and—"

But again he walked past her.

"Come on, he doesn't want to talk to us," I said.

But she wouldn't listen. "Ice, Iceman! Ice baby! Ice tea! Ice cube! Ice and lemon! Just plain ice with nothing in it!"

Ice stopped. "Little girl! Don't you know it's rude to shout at people in the street? Especially when you don't know them!"

"But I do know you, Ice!"

"No, you don't!"

"But I do!" said the Rat excitedly. "You're twenty-seven years old! A Virgo! An ex-boxer and a Bears fan! You like women with big butts, fast cars, and a fast lifestyle. But you're deeper than that, and I quote 'You enjoy doing things for underprivileged children from deprived backgrounds and you stand wholeheartedly behind community programs that keep kids away from drugs,' unquote. I've read everything about you Ice! And I bought your CD! And I never pirated it, even though I could!"

Ice looked angry. "So you bought my CD and you read about me in the newspapers! That does not mean you have the right to accost me in the street! Now, why don't you run along home?"

The Rat turned around and looked at the park. "I am home in a way. You see we live in the park."

"You live in the park!"

"Yes, it's not so bad, and it's only until we find our uncle. You might know him, Ice! His name's—"

"I don't know what sort of dumb parents you have! But they should teach you some manners! And they should teach you not to tell lies!"

I stepped forward. "Dumb! Our parents are dead and they were good people! You better not say another goddamn word about them!"

The Iceman took a step toward me. He was a big guy with a solid bald head. But I wasn't backing down, not after what he'd said! He looked at me for more than a few seconds and then, turning slowly, he walked away.

The Rat's hands went straight to her hips. "Yeah, you better walk away before my brother kicks your bleeping butt! Calling our dad dumb! You never even finished high school! And don't try bullying us! We have friends downtown!"

I looked at my fists. They were clenched.

"And you've never done anything for the underprivileged!" shouted the Rat. "We're underprivileged and look at the way you treated us!"

Then the fear caught up with me. My legs began to quiver and my stomach turned over. I had to sit down on the nearest bench. "Cut it out now," I said.

"Ah bleep him! He doesn't scare me!"

"Well, cut it out anyway."

The Rat glared at him until he was out of sight and then she turned her attention to me. "You were so brave, Bob!"

"Forget about it now."

"No, you were really brave! I'm proud of you! And Dad would have been proud of you too! Well done, Bob! And wait until Miss Gabriela Felipe Mendez finds out how mean he was, and how you stood up to him. She'll be so impressed."

"She won't find out."

The Rat pulled her cellphone from her pocket. "Oh yes she will. Because I'm sending Harold a text message telling him what happened. I'm also telling him to go to her house and tell her. And you know he'll do it."

All of a sudden I had energy.

"And to think I used to think Ice was an angel," said the Rat, her little fingers twiddling away. "Just goes to show you how wrong you can be. You want a coffee, Bob? I'll buy."

"Sure."

"And then we can do some more touristy stuff. We can even take a ferry ride if you want. What do you say, Bob?"

I never said anything. But I felt as high as a skyscraper at the thought of that story running around Winnipeg and landing at the feet of Miss Gabriela Felipe Mendez. I really did.

I felt nervous as I walked toward the steps of the Plaza. It would be no big deal if they never let us in. But it would be embarrassing having to walk away.

"Just act like we own the place, Bob."

"Good afternoon," said the doorman, and standing to one side he let us pass.

It felt nice inside the plush lobby. I followed the Rat alongside the lengthy reception desk where the glamorous receptionist smiled at us and we smiled back. Then we followed the smell of coffee until we came to a large room filled with comfy chairs, and people, and a guy playing a piano. And there we took a seat. At least I took a seat. The Rat bounced up and down to demonstrate how springy they were.

"Will you stop that?"

She sat up like a gopher and looked around. "It's so sophisticated in here, Bob. I wouldn't be surprised to see Spielberg sitting at the next table."

A waitress in a black waistcoat spotted us. "Can I get you kids something?" she asked while looking at our clothes and our, no doubt, dirty faces. There was no need for the look she was giving us.

"Yes, you can," said the Rat in her most superior British accent. "Mother and Father have left us to our own devices for lunch. And one must be careful where one eats. But as we're slumming it for the day we decided to eat here. I shall have a large mocha and a chocolate cake. Bartholomew, my brother, shall have the same."

The waitress wrote down our order and walked away. But the Rat called her back. "Oh, miss." The waitress returned and stood in front of her. "Doesn't matter," said the Rat. The waitress tried to smile but she looked angry as she walked away.

"Another bleeping actress!"

It was funny. And it was a buzz ordering stuff in the Plaza without paying to stay there. And if it was expensive I didn't care. The Rat was paying.

She sat with her legs crossed, acting cool, until the waitress put our order on the table. Then she waited until she was gone. "This is bleeping brilliant, Bob! Coffee in the Plaza and putting Ice in his place!"

Then she lay back in her seat. "Me tell yeh, Bob," she said speaking Jamaican. "Dis is da life for I and I, you know! None a dat sleepin in de park. Dat's for de birds."

When the coffee and cake had gone we hung around the lobby hoping to see celebrities. But we never saw any and so we stepped outside and back into reality.

"Well, I suppose we better keep on looking."

The Rat looked at the shoppers pouring down Fifth Avenue like she was desperate to go down there. "Shall we see some more stuff, Bob? What do you think? After all, it's stopped raining."

I didn't mind and so we walked down by the Rockefeller Center. Its buildings were constructed by John D. Rockefeller who I'd read about in school. He was pretty self-righteous, and ruthless when it came to money. He even put his own brother out of business. That would be like me putting the Rat out of business, if she had one.

I bought a disposable camera, because the Rat wanted some shots to send home, and she ran in front of a large statue of Atlas holding up the world. I bet John D. Rockefeller looked at himself as Atlas at one time. I bet Louis Riel did too. That's what happens when you get to become powerful. You look at yourself as someone who can move the world. "Take my picture, Bob." The Rat raised her hands in the air as though she was holding up the world. It was such a nice photograph.

I'd been on a high since the Ice incident, but then the sadness hit me. The Old Man wasn't here. Him and the Rat would have had a ball in New York. Suddenly I felt a lump in my throat.

"What was it like, Bob?"

"Good." I tried to smile. "What do you say to that ferry ride?"

"Great. Just follow me."

So we got on our bikes and rode west with the Rat singing "America" from *West Side Story.* She never stopped until we reached the river and the red and green ferries. I went to the ticket window on the pier while the Rat locked up the bikes.

The tickets were expensive and we didn't have a lot of money. If we didn't find Uncle Jerome soon we'd be hustling in Times Square for real.

Then I saw the Rat lying on a bench. "You are so lazy," I said. But she wasn't being lazy— she was having a fit. I ran toward her and lifted her head off the bench. I held her close. "It's okay. I'm here!" I could tell by the tremors that it wasn't too bad. "It's only a mild one. You'll be out of it soon." I pushed her hair away from her face. Her eyes were closed tight and she was sucking air through her clenched teeth. "Just hang in there!" After a minute or so she stopped shaking. And then the pain left her face. "It's over now. You're okay."

Slowly her eyes opened. Her face was a little white, but she didn't look too bad. "There are lights," she whispered, "flashing lights and photographers and lots of people looking at us—and then I'm in a hospital and everything is white. I'm so lonely there." Half dazed, she sat up and tried to focus on me. "If I went—if I went really crazy would you still want to be my brother?"

"You are really crazy and I *am* your brother," I said, but she stayed serious. "Look, there's no such thing as a crazy kid. You have to wait until you're older before you can go crazy."

"But would you?"

"If they put you in a padded cell, in a straitjacket, and locked you up in the maddest part of an asylum, I'd still want to be your brother."

"Thanks, Bob. I knew you wouldn't let me down." She rested her head against my shoulder and before long she was asleep.

I felt sad then, but not in a bad way. I felt sad with the feeling you get when you think about things. If someone had told me last week that I would be in New York City holding my sister by the Hudson River, I would have laughed. But here I am. And then I realized it didn't matter. Because I would sooner be here with the Rat than anywhere else by myself.

I got comfortable and, putting my arm around her, I watched the river go by. The clouds created shadows and light, turning the water from a Van Gogh green to a Monet blue. It was so nice to see. But when our boat sailed away without us I got a bad feeling. "It doesn't mean anything," I said. "Not really."

The sun was halfway below the sea when she woke. Her fit must have been worse than I thought. She seemed better as we rode back to the den. But I knew she was better when she went back to singing.

"It doesn't matter about being crazy, anyway," she said. "Because I'm happy. And I'd sooner be happy and crazy than not crazy and miserable."

"Why don't you just try being happy and normal?"

"That's being greedy, Bob."

We rode alongside Central Park until we came to the gap in the park wall. We were just about to ride in when the Rat's cell beeped.

"It's a message from Joey. He said to say hello to Sexy Sandra, and he said he's staying an extra night, as long as we're okay."

"Damn, I was hoping he'd come back tomorrow."

"Don't you like the den?" asked the Rat.

"Sure, I love living in the bushes."

It was then that we noticed a few photographers hovering outside an apartment block. Two black women came out of the lobby like they were walking on a catwalk and just behind them came Ice. I couldn't believe it. He stood there posing for the photographers with the girls hanging around his neck.

"Look at him. He's so full of poo. Boo! Boo!" shouted the Rat.

Ice looked over.

"We're not scared of you, you big bully!" Then she turned to me. "You think he lives in those apartments? Because if he does we're practically neighbors, except he pays rent and we don't."

He posed for a few more photographs and then slipped into a waiting limousine. But as he did he paused and looked me right in the eyes. It wasn't a bad look; it was just a look. I don't know why but I felt bad when he had gone.

The Rat looked a little down herself. "You think he'll want to be our friend if he sees us again? Because I do like his music. What do you think, Bob?"

"Forget about him."

We rode into that dismal park until we came to the den, and then we dragged our bikes through those damn bushes. Pushing them to one side I switched on the flashlight. The Rat undid her sleeping bag and slid inside.

"We could give him a second chance. But he has to apologize! You'd have to get him to apologize, Bob!"

"Haven't I just said to forget about him?"

The Rat slid down in her sleeping bag and pulled it over her head. I'd snapped at her again and now I felt worse. "So how are you feeling? Are you okay?"

"Sure, Bob. Why wouldn't I be?" she said from inside her sleeping bag.

"I was just making sure. Is there anything you'd like to do tomorrow?"

"I'd like to get washed."

I laughed when I realized we hadn't washed in days. "You dirty Rat."

The Rat chuckled. "Like I haven't heard that one before." Then she popped her head out. "What are we going to do about Uncle Jerome, Bob?"

"I'll think of something tomorrow. Go to sleep now."

I didn't know what we were going to do about Uncle Jerome. I was at a loss. And I dreaded to think what would happen if her fits got worse. And I was kind of sorry about Ice, even if Gabriela did hear I stood up to him. It would have been great if he was as cool as they made him out to be, but he wasn't. He was just a CD cover, an image dreamed up by some marketing people no doubt. I suppose it's better to be real people like me and the Rat living in the park than it is to be a phony living in a Fifth Avenue apartment. But what did I know? I wasn't even a teenager yet.

FOURTEEN

"I'VE ALREADY FOUND THE SWIMMING POOL ON my map. It's somewhere around the top of the park," said the Rat, pushing her way through the bushes. "And remember, no looking,"

"Who am I going to look at? You've got us up so early!"

"Didn't you say something about the early worm?"

"No I didn't! And look, we're the only people awake!"

"Ice is awake."

And sure enough, there was Ice standing on the balcony of a Fifth Avenue apartment.

"I bet he's been out all night," said the Rat. "Boogying with big-butted women. What shall we do, Bob?"

"Nothing. Just leave it."

We watched him as we made our way out of the park and he watched us. We headed up Fifth Avenue with the

Rat looking back over her shoulder. "He's still watching us!" Then she turned around and walked backwards. "If he was nice to us, would you speak to him? Would you want him to be our friend?"

"Can't you forget about him?"

"No," said the Rat. "I can't."

We walked around until we found the swimming pool and then we waited outside until it opened. The Rat asked if it was okay if we took a shower. The woman didn't seem to mind. She even gave us free packets of shampoo.

"Check them before you go inside, honey. Make sure there's no one in there."

Whether she meant cleaners or homeless people I didn't know, but I made the Rat check inside before I took my shower. "All clear!" she shouted.

The floor of the men's changing room was damp with disinfectant, and the shower walls were grimy with grunge. But the showers blasted out hot water and boy did it feel good. I soaped up and washed it off. And then I soaped up again just for the hell of it. When I stepped out of the shower, my skin was so clean it was shiny. I put on a clean T-shirt and some regular jeans, glad to be out of my overalls, and then I combed my hair in the mirror.

"Oh, I've got company this morning."

I turned to see an old black guy. "I'll be out of your way in a minute."

"Don't rush on my account!" He gave me a grouchy look. "What's your story? Folks kick you out?"

"Something like that."

"Where you sleeping?"

"The park, not far from the Metropolitan Museum."

He shook his head in disgust. "If I slept over there they'd move me on at gunpoint. You white kids can get away with anything!"

I put my stuff in the backpack. "Where are you sleeping?" I asked, hoping it wouldn't offend.

"Not that it's any of your business, but I'm over by the Harlem River. Nobody bothers me over there. It's quiet, and I've always liked being by the river," he said, the anger leaving his voice.

"Me too."

Then his face cringed. "Hey kid, you wouldn't happen to have any shampoo would you? They wouldn't give me none upstairs."

"Sure, I have a packet. You can keep it."

He smiled as he took it from me. Then he had a good sniff. "Orange. Smells nice." His face softened. "Yeah, well, you seem okay. If you get moved you can come over. Just ask for Erwin, everyone knows me."

"Thanks, Erwin."

"But listen, one night, two at the most, that's all I can do. Otherwise you get all sorts turning up—and listen, I didn't mean to shout."

"It's okay. It was good talking to you, Erwin."

I went outside to wait for the Rat. She came out wearing her French National soccer uniform and bouncing a soccer ball.

"Where did you get that?"

"I brought it with me. And I brought a small pump so I could pump it up." She kicked the ball as she came. "Let's go look for a soccer field."

"They won't have a soccer field here. Americans don't play soccer."

But the Rat roamed the park determined to find one. And to my surprise she did. It was a proper soccer field with goals and nets and good grass. She dropped her backpack on the ground and kicked the ball high into the air.

"We'll play penalties. You go in goal."

She always wanted me to go in goal, but I didn't mind. I only played to keep her happy. She put the ball on the penalty spot and blasted it as hard as she could. It went straight into the corner of the net. I never stood a chance. "Goal!" she shouted and threw her arms in the air. As I threw the ball back to her I saw him. He wasn't dressed in a suit today: he was wearing basketball shorts and sneakers.

The Rat looked at me and then she turned quickly. "Ice!"

Ice was looking at me and he didn't look happy.

The Rat's hands went to her hips. "You stay away from my brother, Ice!"

She must have thought he'd come to fight, but I could see he hadn't. He looked sad, the way the Old Man did when he felt down.

"Listen, about yesterday. I just wanted to be by myself, so I could think. I didn't mean to disrespect your parents. That was wrong. I shouldn't have said what I said."

"Are you apologizing, Ice?" asked the Rat. "Is that what you're doing?"

"Well, I guess I am. But you were—"

Ice never had a chance to finish. The Rat ran at him and threw her arms around his waist. "We're sorry too, Ice!"

The Iceman looked down at the Rat with his arms held out. "Hey, little girl. Can you let go? Hey, can you hear me?"

The Rat let go. "Sorry, Ice. I'm just so pleased you want to be our friend!"

"I never said—"

"And we weren't lying, Ice. Our dad died and we're living in the park until we find our uncle."

Ice looked down at her screwed-up face. I could see he felt bad and then I felt bad for him.

"Do you want to play soccer, Ice?" I asked.

The Rat's eyes widened. "Do you want to, Ice? Do you know how? Because if you don't, I can teach you!"

"I have to be going. I just wanted to—"

"Here, just try." The Rat dropped the ball at his feet and ran to the goal. Ice kicked the ball soft and she caught it. "That was good, Ice. Try again." Ice kicked the ball harder. The Rat pushed it away and it landed at my feet. I kicked it back to Ice and he kicked it into the goal.

"That was great, Ice," said the Rat. "Your turn in goal, Bob."

Ice and the Rat kicked the ball to one another, taking turns to shoot at the goal. Ice went through the motions at first, just to keep her happy, but then he got into it. He juggled the ball from one foot to the other before he took a shot, and he ran to retrieve it when it passed him. The sadness seemed to leave Ice as he played soccer with the Rat. After a while he looked to be enjoying himself. But he was nowhere near as happy as the Rat.

"You never got our names! My name's Marie Claire DeBillier and that's my brother Bob. We're from Winnipeg, Ice. Have you ever been to Winnipeg? You have so many fans there. But we're your biggest fans because we like you the best."

Ice shot at the goal and I saved it.

"Unlucky, Ice!" shouted the Rat.

I threw the ball back to him and he trapped it under his foot. "You know, I don't want to get involved, but you kids shouldn't be sleeping in the park. Maybe you could go to the cops. They'd put you somewhere safe." Then he kicked the ball to the Rat.

"They'd put us in a home, Ice," said the Rat showing off her soccer skills. "Them homes are full of goddamn pedophiles. You don't want the pedophiles to get us, do you, Ice?" She kicked the ball to Ice, but he froze and it went past him.

"Well—no. But you shouldn't be using words like that, Marie Claire. It's naughty."

"They're naughty people, Ice. You have to look out for them. But I've got nothing to worry about because you're here and you're an angel. No pedophile would dare come near an angel."

Ice looked at her, bewildered. That goddamn Rat had bewildered Ice and we'd only just met him!

"My mother used to say that to me all the time. 'You're an angel,' she'd tell me. 'And you're not just *my* angel.'"

"Well, that's what you are, Ice."

Ice frowned like he was thinking of the past.

"Can you get the ball, Ice?" said the Rat.

Ice looked behind him and walked off to get the ball.

"He won't want to be our friend if you bewilder him like that!"

"He already is our friend," said the Rat. "He's our very own Iceman." Ice kicked the ball and she caught it. "I think you'll be as big as Eminem one day, and so does *Rolling Stone*. And I quote, 'Ice emerged from the decay of those decadent Chicago housing projects to produce a dynamic debut album. His distinct voice and vivacious lyrics could lead one to believe we are not only listening to the new prince of rap, but to its next king,' unquote."

"The next king of rap. What a joke that is." Ice sat down on the grass and we sat next to him. "You know, kids, rap has been described as modern day poetry. But it's only poetry if it's well written. Any electro beat will get the brothers pounding on the dance floor, but only words will be remembered. When I write a great line, I get nervous: it's like I'm holding a winning hand in a poker game. And when I write a great song, I can't sleep. I showed some of my best work to the record company. But they're only interested in gangsta rap, and the more people who get blown away the better. It was always my dream to become a great artist—to write words that move people, like Langston Hughes!"

"'Hold fast to dreams, for if dreams die, life is a broken-winged bird that cannot fly.'"

Ice looked impressed. "You like poetry, Bob?"

The jealous Rat folded her arms and frowned at me.

"Some."

"Yeah, who's your favorite?"

Just then a black Range Rover blared its horn. Ice looked disappointed. "Oh I have to go, kids. But I enjoyed talking to you. And, like I say, I'm sorry about the other day."

"It's okay, Ice. Even angels get upset sometimes. And I won't accost you again. I promise. But if we see you shall we say hello? Do you think that will be okay, Ice? As long as we don't accost you, I mean."

"Of course you can say hello. In fact you better say hello or there'll be trouble."

The Rat smiled.

"See you again, Marie Claire. Bob, why don't you walk me to my vehicle?" I walked Ice toward the jeep, but he stopped before we reached it. “Listen, Bob. I don’t want to get involved, but sleeping rough like you’re on the run is no good. Believe me, I did it myself when I was kid. You have to get help.”

“Thanks, Ice. But we should be somewhere safe in the next day or so.”

“That’s no good, Bob. A kid can go missing in a minute. You have to get your sister somewhere safe. You hear me?”

“Sure, Ice.”

“Okay then.” He held out his hand and I shook it. “Look after yourself, Bob.” He waved at the Rat, and jumping in the jeep, he drove away.

As soon as he was gone the Rat came running over. “He was concerned about us, right? I knew he would be! It’s bleeping brilliant, isn’t it, Bob? We’re friends with the Iceman! And I knew he’d be great! Isn’t that what I said? I’m not saying I told you so, but I told you so—”

When we walked out on to the observation deck of the Empire State Building, I saw a view I can only describe as magical. It was nighttime and we could see all of New York’s boroughs, skyscrapers, and buildings, lit up by the lights from their own windows. We could see the lights burning bright on Broadway and the sky glowing above the downtown area. We could see cars, as small as ants, with their headlights on. They raced along the streets or headed over Manhattan's many bridges, most of which were lit up themselves.

We walked around so as to see as many views as possible, and then we stared up at the huge metal tower.

"That's where King Kong fell from," said the Rat.

"You know King Kong's not real, right?" I said, talking to her like a two-year-old.

The Rat looked up at me. "Bleep you, Bob!" Then she clasped hold of the metal bars that ran around the observation deck, and held them like an inmate. I did the same and we watched the night in silent wonder.

"It's magical," said the Rat. "No wonder the angels sit up high and the Great Spirit hovers in the sky. I think I used to be a bird in my previous life. Because in my dreams I have wings and when I beat them, I can fly."

"And now you're just a Rat."

The Rat laughed. "And you're the Rat's brother."

"It's getting late. We should make a move."

"Shall we pass by the Waldorf Astoria, Bob? It's almost on the way."

"If you like."

We went down in the elevator and crossing over to Park Avenue we strolled up to the Waldorf.

"Shall we hang out, Bob? We might see some celebrities."

"We're not hanging around the Waldorf like a couple of waifs and strays. Now come on. It's almost midnight." She followed me but she didn't look happy. "You met Ice today. What more do you want?"

"Yeah, but what's the big deal about ten more minutes? Anyone would think you were scared!"

I got her in a headlock. "Another word out of you and I'll pull your goddamn head off!" But then a cop car came by and so I let her go. It passed us and then it stopped.

"It's turning around, Bob."

We came off Park Avenue, and scurrying down the steps of a basement apartment, we crouched low. It was quiet for a few seconds. And then we heard a car engine cruising toward us. A spotlight shone overhead like a full moonbeam from a prison breakout. My heart started to pound. In my mind I could already see the cops capturing us and taking us away. But the beam slid silently along the wall and the cop car cruised away. "That was close!" said the Rat.

We scurried all the way to the beginning of the park. And then we headed into the park so the cops couldn't see us. It felt as spooky as a cemetery and the paths didn't go straight. They snaked around, taking us past the silent ponds and in between the dark trees that blocked out the moonlight. I felt uneasy. But I felt more uneasy when I saw a man sitting on a bench. He was wearing a woolly hat and what looked like a combat jacket.

"What do you think?" I whispered. But the Rat didn't answer. Never a good sign.

He watched us as we passed and we watched him. Then we walked a little quicker, wanting to be away from him. But when I looked over my shoulder he was following us. I felt a sickening fear sink into my stomach.

"This is very bad, Bob!" said the Rat. "What do we do?"

The fear pumped adrenaline into my body and it hit me from the legs upwards. I grabbed her hand. "Run!"

We bolted—and I mean bolted—off the path, across the grass, and through the trees. We sprinted across a short bridge, jumped a fence, and headed up a low hill. We ran side by side, our arms tight, our feet thumping into the ground. I was sure we'd left him standing. But when I looked behind me he was still there. And he was gaining! I saw the park wall. "This way!" With my lungs screaming for air I grabbed the Rat and we ran toward it. We threw ourselves over the top like two marines and dropped on to Fifth Avenue. Then we jumped up and stood back. "Who the hell was that?"

"What!" said the Rat gasping for air. "I'm supposed to know every lunatic in New York!"

Suddenly the guy jumped over the wall! He had a fat face and mean slits for eyes.

I was so scared I couldn't speak.

"Now I've got you!" he hissed.

"Hey, you kids find your uncle yet?"

I turned to see Sean and Connor standing outside an apartment block.

"This guy was chasing us!" shouted the Rat. "I think he was going to kidnap us!"

"What!" Suddenly Connor darted toward him. The guy started running. Then Sean threw his cap to the ground and joined the chase. "Get back here, you son of a bitch!" They chased him down Fifth Avenue and disappeared down a side street, their voices echoing behind them. It was quiet then.

"Come on, Bob. Let's get back to the den before the cops come."

I was so frightened I followed her without thinking. But when we reached the gap in the park wall, I stopped. My whole body was trembling. "I can't do this no more. We have to give ourselves up!" I walked off to find a cop. She grabbed my arm and I pushed it away. "You think everything's an adventure! What if he had got you?" I shouted. "What then?" My head fell into my hands.

"But he didn't, Bob," she said softly. "It'll be okay."

When I looked at her I could see she felt sorry for me. There's nothing worse than your kid sister feeling sorry for you. She took me by the arm. "There'll be no more danger tonight. Besides, no one can find us in the den. We have enough trouble finding it ourselves."

And so, like the fool in a horror movie who always goes where he'll get killed, I followed her. But when I tell you that New York had just got a whole lot scarier I'm not even joking.

I turned on my flashlight as soon as we were through and had a good look around. Then I sat on the concrete base with my head in my hands.

"You okay, Bob?" asked the Rat sliding into her sleeping bag.

"Yeah, I'm okay," I said, but I wasn't.

"Don't worry, Bob, we're safe here." But she didn't fall asleep the way she normally does. And so we lay there listing to the silence. Then she sat up on her elbows. "Do you like Mad Mike?"

I was absolutely goddamn bewildered! In the ten years, and I don't know how many months, since the Rat had been on this earth she must never have learned what fear was! "What in God's name has that got to do with anything?"

"I saw something the other day. But I didn't mention it because I know you don't like me mentioning things. Me and you were at the farm, and it was covered in snow. All our friends were there and hundreds of other people I don't even know. And there were cops all over the place. It was like a demonstration. And you were screaming at them. And Mad Mike was there. And he hugged you and you hugged him."

"I don't think I'm ever going to hug Mad Mike! But so what?"

"Don't you see? It hasn't happened yet, which means we make it home." And with that she sank in her sleeping bag and went to sleep.

I was so jittery I couldn't close my eyes. But the thought that we made it home soothed me. After a while my nerves settled and my eyes closed. And then, after a dozen nervous twitches, I slept.

I was woken by the rain tickling my face. I turned over hoping it would stop, but it didn't, it got heavier and the wind picked up. The Rat stayed asleep, nothing ever woke her, but the rain splashed on her face and caused her to cough. Lightning cracked and thunder rocked around the sky. I saw puddles forming around our base. We had good sleeping bags, but they weren't waterproof. Then the wind tore at the trees. I heard a cracking sound and somewhere close by a branch fell to the ground.

Then, when the lightning flashed again, I saw a sight that froze my heart! A hooded figure was standing in the bushes. He must have come back! "Oh God, no!" I searched for a brick or a branch, or for the small penknife we had brought with us. It went dark. Then there was another loud crack and the sky lit up. He was standing right in front of me. The Rat coughed and he looked her way. I jumped between him and my sister. My legs were trembling. My fists were clenched. We looked at each other through the pouring rain. Then he pulled the hood from his head.

"Get your stuff and come with me!" he shouted.

It was Ice. I was so relieved I could have cried! Lifting the Rat from her sleeping bag, he held her in his arms.

"Come on, son. Let's get you indoors."

Ice had come for us. Maybe the Rat was right. Maybe he was an angel. At least he was to us that night. And as far as I'm concerned, he always will be.

Fifteen

"Are you kids up?" shouted Ice.

I opened the bedroom door and saw Ice behind a breakfast bar. I felt shy as I walked out. "I'm glad you put us up, Ice. We got chased last night."

But Ice concentrated on the cooking. He was shuffling the frying pans frantically and there was a lot of sizzling and smoke.

"You want some help, Ice?" I said. "I'm pretty good in the kitchen."

"What, you think I can't cook? Take a seat, the Iceman has everything under control."

Just then he hit his head on the overhead pans and so I looked away like I hadn't noticed. A flat-screen TV took up one corner of the room, while a music system, which must have cost as much as a car, took up another. There were chunky brown sofas and Turkish-looking rugs, and there were puffed-up pillows for sitting on. And there was a glass case containing two silver handguns. They were the Berettas Ice used in his videos.

When I looked back at him he was still struggling. I think cooking was a new experience for Ice and there's nothing worse than having someone watch you when you're starting out. And so I took a seat on one of the sofas and looked at the city walled in glass.

"Morning, Ice!" The Rat came in wearing her Armani dress. "Lucky you come for us, Ice! We got chased by a lunatic!"

"Well, you shouldn't be getting chased!" said Ice in a cranky tone.

"You want some help, Ice?"

"No, I don't!"

But then he dropped the eggs on the floor and knocked over the orange juice. Then he started swearing like he was on stage. Even the Rat looked shocked.

"You shouldn't swear, Ice. You should bleep like they do on TV."

But Ice grumbled away like he hadn't heard her.

"Ice, there's smoke coming out the oven!"

Ice grabbed a dishcloth and opened the oven door.

"Use mitts, Ice!"

"AAAAAAH!" He smashed a burning tray of hash browns on to the breakfast bar. Then he started cursing and swearing like you wouldn't believe.

"Bleep instead, Ice! Bleep! Bleep! Bleep! Bleep! Bleep! Bleep! Bleep!" said the Rat bleeping out the bad language.

That blew Ice away and he laughed like a big kid. I laughed as well; it was funny.

"Come and sit down, Ice," said the Rat. "Bob, you take care of breakfast." She sat Ice at a dining table by the window and fetched some ice for his hand. "That pan must have been really hot!"

"It was!"

"But you never dropped it, Ice. You were so brave."

What a suck-up. I wouldn't have dropped it either, but I said nothing. Ice had napalmed most of the bacon, so I fried some eggs and salvaged what I could from the hash browns. I served it to them with fresh toast, and filling up a plate, I joined them.

"Tastes good, Bob. Where you learn to cook?"

"The Old Man, I suppose. He liked to cook."

"My mom, too. I ate everything she gave me. Never did learn myself," said Ice, drinking his coffee. "So you kids sleep well? Sleeping in the goddamn park. What am I going to do with you?"

"I don't know, Ice," said the Rat. "But thanks for coming to get us."

"Yeah well, don't get too comfortable!"

"We won't," said the Rat. "We're not the sort of kids to take advantage."

"Good. Because I wouldn't let you take advantage of me. And Mia's home tomorrow. I don't need any more problems."

"Are you going to marry Mia? Mia Moore the Magnificent. 'I don't so much do the catwalk as the black walk,' said Mia when speaking to the Parisian press. Will Mia and Ice become America's hottest black couple? Mia said, and I quote, 'My world would fall apart if Ice were not in it. He lights up my life.'"

"Is that what she said? Sounds like she swallowed an advice column. And you've been reading too much trash."

"Do you love her, Ice?"

"Stop prying!" I told her.

"I don't know, I really don't. But I do know the car will be here in five minutes."

"We have to be going, anyway," I said, "We have to look for our uncle. His name's Jerome DeBillier. You know him, Ice?"

The Rat showed Ice the photograph.

"Can't say I do. But he looks like an Italian gangster."

"He's a drug dealer, actually," said the Rat. "But we're hoping he's a nice drug dealer."

"Sure, I've met some really nice drug dealers. Great guys! And killers with character, and thieves who can tell you a great story. They're a barrel of laughs at a party. But they still sell drugs to children, murder people, and steal from the poor! Remember that, Marie Claire!" Ice shook his head. "Why would anyone want to bring kids into this world?"

Ice looked sad then, and so I gave the Rat a nod to let her know we should go.

"Well, Ice. It's been a pleasure," said the Rat standing up. "Let's do lunch sometime."

"So, you kids are going back to the park?" Ice thought about it. "I'm gonna be busy today. But if you wanna tag along I can get someone to look after you."

The Rat's eyes widened. "Can we, Ice? We wouldn't get in the way! We could go for things or fetch you coffee!"

"I don't want you fetching me anything. I just don't want you roaming around by yourselves. Besides, I don't know who I can trust these days. I need someone to watch my back. Can you do that?"

"We will, Ice!" said the Rat. "We won't let anyone sneak up on you!"

"Thanks, Ice," I said.

"Yeah well," he said looking kind of bashful. "Come on then, let's go."

We went down in the elevator and walked out toward a waiting limousine. A large white chauffeur with a bald head and a black moustache opened the door for us. He looked like a bad guy from the movies.

"Morning, Karl."

"Morning, Ice. Morning, kids."

Me and the Rat were buzzing as we lay back in the limo.

"Where are we going, Ice?" I asked.

"We're going to the Marriott Marquis on Broadway. I have to do at least thirty interviews to promote the new CD." Then he looked at us, puzzled. "Who am I going to say you are?"

"Tell them we're your godchildren," said the Rat. "Because that's what you're like, Ice. You're like our fairy godfather."

"Sounds good, but let's drop the fairy part."

We drove inside the hotel entrance canopy and pulled up by a group of people who hovered around the revolving doors. I didn't realize they were media people until Karl opened the door. I stepped out of the limo, and like a real amateur, walked straight into the hotel lobby. Ice and the Rat were a little more professional. They donned dark sunglasses and, stepping slowly from the limousine, they bathed in the flashing lights.

"Ice! Look this way!"

"Ice, over here!"

Ice posed for the paparazzi, signed some autographs, and strolled into the hotel. The Rat followed him, sashaying like she was showing off the latest fashion.

Once inside the hotel Ice introduced us to Barry, his big-bearded manager, a PA named Stephanie, and a couple of reps from his record company. We crowded into a round glass elevator and made small talk while we ascended through several ceilings in succession. We switched to another elevator that took us higher. And then we stepped out into a lot of commotion, camera crews, and guys shouting into cell phones.

"I'll get someone to take care of you," said Ice. And then he walked off with his people.

"We've crossed Canada on a freight train, sneaked across the border, and we've been sleeping rough in Central Park, and now we need looking after."

"I want someone to look after me," said the Rat. "To cater to my every whim."

Then this stylish young guy in a pink shirt shouted at us. "Marie Claire! Robert!" He waved as he came toward us. He looked happy and energetic and he had lots of streaks in his spiky blond hair. "Hi! I'm Julian and I'm going to be looking after you. I've found you a room, if you'd like to follow me."

"We'd love to follow you, Julian," said the Rat.

We followed him to a room that had no beds, only couches, and there we plunked ourselves down.

"Can I get you something from room service?"

"We'd like a mocha," said the Rat. "And we'd like to try some New York cheesecake, if it's no trouble."

"No trouble at all, Marie Claire!" Julian left to order room service while the Rat relaxed on the couch.

"This is bleeping brilliant, Bob! And did you see the paparazzi taking my picture? I suppose I'll have to get used to that when I'm an actress. Come on, Bob. Let's be difficult. It's more fun if you're being difficult. If that cheesecake isn't here in ten minutes, I'm throwing a tantrum."

The celebrity lifestyle was having its effect on the Rat. She was definitely going over to the Dark Side.

* * *

It was night when we got back into the limo.

"You kids have a good day?"

"We had a great day Ice! Julian took us to lunch and we were interviewed by journalists. But I never told them anything, Ice. I promise. And a man from your record company gave us iPods. Even the paparazzi were nice to us. It must be great being a celebrity."

"Believe me, it's not all it's cracked up to be. But I'm glad you had a nice day, Marie Claire." Ice looked tired.

"You okay, Ice?"

"Yeah, Bob. Thanks for asking. I'm just—hungry. You kids hungry? Karl, take us to that French place that sells lobster. What do you say to lobster?"

"We say yes," said the Rat. But I don't think we'd ever had it.

We pulled up outside a ground-floor restaurant on the West Side. It had large windows and we could see people sitting around candlelit tables. And didn't they all look over to see who was getting out of the limo. Karl held an umbrella over us, because the rain had come back, and, making our way inside, we were greeted by a gray-haired guy who snapped his fingers for the servers to come to attention. "A table by the window for Monsieur Ice!"

A buzz ran around the restaurant as we were led to our table. Some of the diners smiled at Ice while others looked at him wondering who he was. As we sat at our table the busboys busied themselves around us, snapping napkins and positioning plates, while the gray-haired guy looked on for any mistakes. Then a waiter appeared.

"Hey man, just bring us three lobsters," said Ice, handing him back the menus. "We'll think about dessert when we're done."

"Ice, what's your first name?" asked the Rat.

"No one's asked me that in years. Thanks, Marie Claire. It's Michael."

"Michael, that's so divine! I knew it would be something like that."

When Ice laughed, the Rat took the opportunity to ask him about his life. Nothing personal, of course: "Did you really shoot a man when you were sixteen? Were you really a gangbanger? Do women really send you their underwear in the mail?"

I would have stopped her, but for a man who'd answered questions all day, Ice didn't seem to mind. He even seemed to enjoy it.

Three giant lobsters were brought to the table. They were served with fresh bread rolls and a crispy salad. My lobster looked like it could do battle. But I picked up the nutcrackers and snapped off a claw. Well, I fell in love with lobster from the first bite. It was like a delicious cross between crab and duck and I couldn't crack it open fast enough. When the lobster was finished, we moved on to dessert. We opted for the chocolate cherry cake, spiced with orange brandy, and caked in a thick chocolate sauce. It was as close to chocolate heaven as you get.

When we were done, Ice and the Rat started joking around. But I was content to watch the rain lash against the windows.

"Coffee, sir?" asked the waiter.

I looked up to make sure he was talking to me. "Sure," I said. I needed coffee. I was feeling a little light-headed after the brandy in the cake. But then I sat bolt upright! Who stopped in front of the window? None other than Tommy "The Hustler" Mattolla.

Of all the windows he could have stopped in front of, he stopped in front of ours! He's got his suit collar up around his neck and his hands are clutched around it. He looked down the street as if wondering whether to continue. Then he turned and looked in the restaurant. I froze. The rain's running down his face pretty good. I didn't think he could see us. He looked around a bit and then he turned to go.

Go on, I'm thinking, keep going!

If I hadn't been staring at him the way I was, he would have carried on going. But that hustler instinct must have kicked in because he stopped and looked at me. Then his eyebrows rose, he had me. Then he saw the Rat, he had her. He looked around the restaurant, puzzled, as though wondering how we could afford to eat there, and then he turned his attention to Ice. A few seconds passed before his eyes widened and then he disappeared from the window.

I could already see him dripping in front of us, shaking hands with Ice and ordering a drink he couldn't pay for. But it never happened. All I heard was some commotion coming from the reception and then I heard nothing. They hadn't let him in. I watched the window waiting for him to reappear, but he didn't.

"Come on then, kids. Let's go." Ice put some bills on the table and we headed out of the restaurant.

I was even more surprised not to see Tommy outside. I was relieved in a way. I mean, I liked Tommy, he was fun to be around. But I knew he'd embarrass us in front of Ice. Still, I felt a little guilty as we drove away. But as we came alongside Central Park, the Rat's face reddened.

"Stop the car!" she screamed.

"What is it, Marie Claire?"

The limo pulled up and the Rat jumped out. She was nearly knocked down as she ran across the road. Ice jumped out and I followed. Then I saw what she saw. A group of guys had Tommy on the ground. They were kicking him.

"Get away from him!" screamed the Rat. She threw herself between the men and Tommy. One of the guys pushed her and she fell to the ground.

"Hey!" I shouted.

Ice never shouted anything. He dropped that guy with a solid right hook. "Touch her again and I'll kill you!" Suddenly one of the guys swung at Ice, but Ice ducked and dropped him with a body shot. Then this really big guy threw a wide right hook. Ice ducked again, but a follow-up punch caught him on the chin.

Ice staggered but he didn't go down. Then all the guys came at him. But Ice was on fire. He stood his ground and threw a drum-roll of clubbing left and right hooks. One guy went flat out, one fell on his butt, while another bounced off a tree. But then this slim, sneaky-looking guy jumped on Ice's back. He couldn't move. Another man started punching Ice in the stomach. Then I heard a battle-cry and Karl charged forward. He smashed into three of the guys forcing them to the ground. Ice threw the guy off his back and it turned into one big brawl. "Come on, Ice!" shouted the Rat. There were punches and kicks and people being thrown in all directions. There were snarls and shouts, cries and groans, and the sound of Ice's suit jacket ripping up his back. I was just about to get involved but the battle turned in our favor. Ice dropped two guys with a left-right combination. And Karl slugged the biggest guy putting him flat out. The remaining guys backed off.

"Hey, we don't want no trouble!" said one of the men. "But that creep was bothering us!"

"I'll bother *you* if you don't go away!" said Ice.

And of course the Rat was there to back him up. "Go on, you big bullies, before Ice really loses his temper!"

The guys helped their friends to their feet while me and Ice pulled Tommy from the ground. There was a cut over his right eye, but he wasn't too bad.

"You okay, Tommy?" asked the Rat. "Ice is here! He won't let them hit you no more!"

"I've been beat-up worse than that! You call that a beating?" shouted Tommy to the retreating men.

"I'll get the car," said Karl.

Tommy cringed with pain, but realizing what the Rat had said he sneaked a side glance at Ice. Then he stepped right back into character. "Marie Claire! Bob! Where have you kids been? I've been worried out of my mind!"

"Oh shewa, Tommy," said the Rat, doing the same.

Tommy looked at Ice with this dramatic look in his eyes. "And who's this gentleman? How can I ever repay you, good sir?"

"You know who this is, Tommy!" said the Rat.

Ice looked bewildered. Tommy and the Rat were bewildering him.

Tommy's eyes widened. "It's—it's the Iceman!"

"What happened?" asked an overweight couple crossing the street.

Tommy froze. Then it came to him. "Mugged!" he shouted. "I've just been beaten and mugged!"

"Oh my God!" said the women.

"They took my money, but they couldn't take my life! Thanks to this man!" said Tommy pointing at Ice.

"Hey, I know him!" said the guy. "He's one of those rappers!"

"You've got a camera!" said Tommy. "Take our picture!"

Tommy put his arm around Ice and the man took his picture.

"This rapper has just saved this guy's life!" shouted the woman to some passersby. More people came to the scene.

"I saw the whole thing!" said a guy pulling up in a horse-drawn carriage.

"Me too!" said the guy clicking away with his camera. "Ice saved him all right!"

"Good. I have witnesses!" said Tommy. "We'll go to the *Times*, the *Post*, and the police, in that order. And we're gonna need some cab money."

"We've got money!" said the overweight woman. "Don't worry about that!"

Ice shook his head. "Come on, kids. Let's go."

The limousine backed up to us and Ice opened the door. Just then Tommy pulled us toward him. "Listen, Marie Claire, Bob! My girlfriend kicked me out! I haven't eaten all day!"

He wasn't on the hustle now. He was really desperate.

"Here, take this," said the Rat, handing him what money she had. Tommy tried to smile but he looked sad. "You're too good to me, kid!" And he sounded like he really meant it.

"Ah forget about it. We're partners, ain't we?"

"You gonna be okay, Tommy?" I asked.

"Sure I am. Here, Bob. Take my card. Call me tomorrow and I'll buy you kids breakfast."

"But you're broke."

"Are you kidding? The Iceman has just saved my life. The papers will pay good money for that story."

"Come on, kids. You're getting wet," said Ice.

Tommy walked us to the limo. "Listen, Ice. If you ever need a chauffeur I'm an excellent driver. Or a bodyguard. I'm out of shape right now but give me a week. Or a PR guy. Tommy Mattolla has worked for some top people."

"Beat it, hustler!" said the Rat, sliding into the limo.

"Is that any way to talk to your Uncle Tommy? After everything I've done for you!" Then he turned his attention to the people. "Okay, folks, gather round. Now, who witnessed what?"

I looked back at Tommy as we drove away. And then I looked at his card: THOMAS MICHEL MATTOLLA, DISBARRED ATTORNEY AT LAW. Tommy was a hustler. But he never pretended to be anything else. And I liked that about him. I really did.

Ice sat there bewildered. "Sleeping rough in the park, street fights, and shady hustlers! I'd hang out with you kids more often if it wasn't so dangerous."

But that was the Rat for you. She'd most likely get us killed one day, she really would. But for now we'd got away with it, and so I sat back and enjoyed the ride—while it lasted.

Sixteen

After the long day and the big brawl we sat at the dining table drinking hot chocolate. I don't think Ice was speaking to us in a way. He looked at us every now and again and shook his head. Then he went back to drinking his hot chocolate. It was a little uncomfortable to tell you the truth.

"Is your hand okay, Ice?" I asked.

"Yeah, it's okay."

"How's your jaw, Ice?" asked the Rat.

"It's good."

The Rat looked at me and then back at Ice. "Did you enjoy the fight, Ice?"

Ice gave her a look. "No, I didn't!"

"They were real meanies," she mumbled. She went back to drinking her hot chocolate but she stared at Ice over the cup. "Are you sure you didn't, Ice? Because you looked like you enjoyed it." Ice tried not to laugh but he did. "But you weren't scared, Ice. You were brave. I knew you'd be brave. And it was a good fight, wasn't it? I liked the way you dropped those two guys at once. That was my favorite part."

Ice laughed out loud. "You have a favorite part already?"

"Sure, Ice. But it would be better if we had it on video. Then we could watch it over and over."

"Don't your friends come here, Ice?" I asked.

"If Mia throws a party, they do. But I don't really like people coming to my home."

"Why not?"

"Because when they do, they usually want something."

"We don't want nothing from you, Ice," said the Rat.

"No, that's because you're real friends. But other people pretend to be friends. I've done more favors for my so-called friends than I care to remember. After a while it's like they expect you to take care of them. And when I say 'no,' they turn traitor. They run off to the newspapers with stories about me that aren't true. I swear, I can't tell my friends from my enemies these days!"

The Rat frowned seriously. "Ice, would you like me to tell you the Native legend about the Bear and the Windigo?"

That's what Ice needs. He's bewildered enough and now he's going to get one of the Rat's legends to bewilder him some more.

"What's a Windigo?"

"Well, Ice, a Windigo is a monster. Some people say they used to be human, but they got trapped in the snow and turned to cannibalism. They grow as big as a house, their eyes become blood red, and their fingers turn into claws," said the Rat, arching her fingers like claws. "They become addicted to human flesh, but children are their favorite. They like their meat tender. Once upon a time a Windigo was stalking a Native village. It waited until nightfall and, pouncing, it ate five children. The next morning the villagers packed up and moved away as far as they could. In frustration the Windigo started killing the animals in the forest. Some he ate for food. But mostly he killed them for spite. Windigos are very evil. It snapped the antlers from the deer, squashed the squirrels, and ripped the fur from the rabbits. And so in desperation all the animals went to see the great grizzly bear. 'Will you help us, great grizzly bear?' asked the bunny rabbit. 'We need protecting,' said the beaver. 'The Windigo has no humans to eat and he's taking his rage out on us!' said the squirrel. 'If you fight and kill the Windigo,' said the owl, 'we will be your friends forever.' All the animals agreed with the owl. 'We will be your friends forever,' they said. The great grizzly bear agreed and the next morning, along with the rest of the animals, he charged down the mountain to fight the Windigo. They came to a clearing and drank some water from a stream. Suddenly there was a mighty roar and above the treetops they saw the head of the Windigo. All the animals ran for cover. 'Good luck, grizzly bear,' they shouted. Then the Windigo let out a horrific scream and came charging at the grizzly bear. But the bear stood his ground. The Windigo bit the bear's back and tore at his eyes. Then he got him in a headlock and started to strangle the grizzly bear to death! Suddenly the grizzly bear threw the Windigo over his shoulder and bit his throat with his sharp teeth. Blood ran into the river. The Windigo was dead. All the animals stood on the dead Windigo and cheered for the grizzly bear. 'We'll be your friends for life,' they said. But the grizzly bear had been injured in the fight. 'I have been injured,' said the grizzly bear. 'I will not be able to hunt or search for food. Will you fetch food for me?' 'Of course,' said the animals. But later that night they met in the forest. 'We could have killed that Windigo ourselves,' they said. 'We didn't need that goddamn grizzly bear. And now he wants us to feed him. Let him fend for himself,' they said. 'We are far too busy to get food for him.' So for the rest of the summer the grizzly bear went hungry. When winter came he hibernated. And the following spring he came out with his wounds healed. He ate plenty of salmon and he grew strong. One day he was taking a bath in the river when all the animals came running toward him. 'Please help us,' they said. 'There's another Windigo in the woods and he's so terrible.' 'Please help us!' said the beaver. 'Please help us!' said the little bunny rabbits. 'We'll be your friends for life!' said the owl."

Ice sat up. "What did the grizzly bear say?"

"'Bleep off! Go on, bleep off or I'll beat your bleeping brains in!' That's what he said, Ice! And do you know what the moral of this story is?" But Ice was laughing too much to listen.

"What's the point of listening to the legend if you don't hear the moral?" said the Rat.

Ice tried to control his laughter. "Sorry, Marie Claire, but I think I already know the moral."

"I made you laugh," said the Rat. "Now you have to do something for me."

"What?"

"I want you to sing me a song."

Ice laughed again. "Maybe Mia's right! Maybe we should have kids!"

The Rat gave Ice her scary kid look.

"What, you're serious? I'm more of a rapper. Would you like me to rap for you?"

"I'd like a song, please."

Ice made a grim face. "Alright, let's do this." Getting up he attached a laptop to his music system. "What would you like me to sing?"

"Sing something by the one and only Frank Sinatra," said the Rat.

"I've got thousands of songs on my karaoke system, but I only have one by Sinatra." Ice clicked on his laptop and picked up a mike. "Okay, here we go."

Me and the Rat sat on the sofa. Music oozed from the quad speakers and the words came up on Ice's laptop. "*That old black magic has me in its spell—*"

It was the funniest thing I'd ever heard! Ice, the rap star, couldn't sing a note! I laughed so hard, tears came into my eyes. He even looked serious like he was trying to do his best. I felt sorry for him in a way, but that made it funnier.

The Rat grabbed the other mike and, jumping up on the couch, she sang along. Then I jumped up and sang next to her. We went right through to the end of the song and then we gave ourselves a round of applause.

"Oh man, I haven't laughed so hard in years!"

"Why not, Ice?" asked the Rat.

"I'm not happy, I guess."

"Haven't you ever been happy, Ice?" asked the Rat.

"I was when my mother was alive. She was a great woman, strong and intelligent. You know she'd never let me hang out on the street. Church on Sunday, football on Saturday, and boxing three times a week. She took care of my education too. Every other week she gave me a book to read. When I'd finished I'd have to write an essay about it, with no spelling mistakes. By the time I was fourteen I'd read every book that Maya Angelou had ever written.

"I can still remember telling her: One day I'll make it. I'll get you out of these projects and I'll buy you a nice apartment. But she got cancer when I was fourteen, died when I was fifteen. And here I am," said Ice looking around him. "I'll be able to pay for this place with the money from the next CD. And I bought that Range Rover I always wanted. And I've got gold chains, diamond rings, and Rolex watches. They mean nothing to me. But to Mia things are everything. Having things makes you someone. Strange, the happiest time of my life was when my mother was alive and we were living in the projects. I'd go back there tomorrow if I could be as happy." When Ice had finished speaking his head went down.

"Don't be sad, Ice." The Rat got up and gave him a hug. She could be affectionate at times.

Ice smiled. "Hey, I'm sorry for wussing out on you kids like that. I don't know what came over me."

"It's okay, Ice," I said.

"Anyway, it's getting late. Look, why don't you kids go get ready for bed. I'll come and say goodnight when you're done."

We wandered into the bedroom and closed the door behind us.

"Ice is lonely," said the Rat. "But he won't be lonely if we're his friends."

"He has friends."

The Rat went in the bathroom. "Not real friends like us." She came out wearing her soccer uniform and dove under the covers.

"Everyone decent?" Ice knocked on the door and came in. "Listen, I've been thinking. Tomorrow I'm going to see what I can do about finding this uncle of yours. I don't know what I'll do. But I'll hire a private detective if I have to."

"You're too good to us, Ice," said the Rat.

"Just doing the right thing, Marie Claire. Can't go wrong doing the right thing. You kids say your prayers?"

"Sure, Ice," said the Rat. "And I said a prayer for you so you'll be happy again."

"Thanks, Marie Claire. One of the nicest things you can do is pray for someone. Right, you kids get a good night's sleep and I'll see you in the morning."

When the lights went out, we lay there thinking.

"This is nice," said the Rat. "But it's not quite the den, if you know what I mean."

"Don't tell me you miss that damn den!"

The Rat pulled the quilt over her head and laughed. She was just winding me up.

It must have been the early hours of the morning when the living room light lit up the bedroom. I kept my eyes half closed but standing in the doorway I saw the silhouette of a woman.

"Are you kidding?"

"What are you doing, Mia? You'll wake them up!" Ice closed the door and it went dark. I jumped out of bed and woke the Rat.

"Is it morning already?"

"No, but Mia's home and she's not happy!"

Sneaking over to the door, we opened it an inch. Mia and Ice were sitting on the sofa.

"Are you insane? You found two white kids sleeping in the park and you brought them home! Do you know what people will say? What they'll think! What if the media gets hold of it?"

"They were there when I was doing the interviews. I told them they were my godchildren."

"What happens when they find out they're not? Ice, you have to get rid of them. This could ruin your career. Everything you've worked for. Everything *I've* worked for."

"What a bleep!" said the Rat.

"Shush."

"They have an uncle in New York. Tomorrow I'm going to look for him."

"Fine, but get rid of them for now. Call the cops, Ice. I'll say I found them sleeping rough and I brought them home. That way it won't look so bad."

"I don't care how it looks! I did the right thing!"

"I can see that, baby. Your heart was in the right place. But you're not thinking, Ice. The press could have a field day with this."

"And what are they going to say? That I brought two kids home because I didn't want them sleeping in the street, the way I did after my mother died!"

Mia took hold of his hand. "They don't have to say anything, Ice. All they have to do is tell the facts with a few choice words and you'll spend the rest of your life trying to clear your name. You're a good man, Ice, but you're naïve. I have to protect you now. We have to call the cops. Let the proper authorities take care of them."

Ice looked sad. “Let them sleep now. They’re tired. I’ll call the cops first thing in the morning.”

“If you don’t call them, Ice, I will.”

“I will. Come on, let’s go to bed.”

I closed the door. The Rat switched on the bedside lamp and sat on the bed. She looked as sad as Ice. “We have to leave, Bob. They’ll put us in a home. I couldn’t handle it.”

The thought of leaving the apartment was scary. But I knew we had to go. Without another word we started to pack. The Rat got our stuff from the bathroom while I collected the cell phones. Then, quietly, we shoved our clothes in our backpacks.

When we were finished the Rat wrote Ice a note and read it to me. “‘Dear Ice. Thank you for your hospitality. We were very happy here. We will return when we find our uncle. Love. Bob and Marie Claire DeBillier’ What do you think?”

“It’s good. Let’s go.”

We put on our backpacks, and opening the bedroom door, we listened. It was quiet.

“I should have written something bad about that bleeping Mia!” whispered the Rat. “I’ve never liked her! And she’s nowhere near as good looking as she thinks she is!”

“Shush—come on.”

We crept through the dark living room as quietly as we could, but our clothes swished as we walked. It’s amazing how loud things sound when you don’t want them to. The Rat unlocked the front door and we crept out into the brightly lit hallway. Closing the door behind us we scurried to the elevator and tapped on the button. I kept looking back at the apartment. I was dreading that Ice would come after us, but he didn't. When the elevator came we got in.

"The doorman!" said the Rat as we descended.

"Oh, no."

When the elevator doors opened we sneaked a look around the corner. He was sitting in a chair behind his desk.

"He's asleep," whispered the Rat. "I can hear him snoring."

We sneaked past the doorman and pulled at the glass door, but it wouldn't open. "We're trapped," I said. Then I saw a button on the wall and pointed at it. The Rat pressed the button and the door unlocked. We ran out and into that dreaded park.

"Don't go to the den," I said. "Ice might follow us there."

We ran across one of the roads that ran through the park and, climbing over a small fence, we headed toward a big tree. Once there I slid down the trunk and the Rat slid down next to me. She looked up at Ice's apartment. "From the park to the penthouse and back again! Un-bleeping-believable!"

There was a loud roll of thunder, and it began to rain. I looked up at the sky. "Doesn't it ever stop raining in this city?" We pulled our plastic jackets and baseball caps from our backpacks and put them on. Then wrapping our sleeping bags around us we huddled up. The rain dripped on the branches and tapped on the leaves, but it stayed dry at the base of the tree. That was something to be thankful for. But then a cop car cruised through the park with its spotlight shining. We watched it, ready to run, but it moved away and went out of sight.

"We'll stay here until it gets light. We can't be seen from the road and I don't think even the weirdest weirdo will come out in this weather."

"That bleeping bimbo. I hope he dumps her!" The Rat shivered and mumbled miserably in French.

I felt miserable as well. I looked around at the dark and the damp, and at the rain highlighted by the streetlights. It was hard being back in the park after living in Ice's apartment. And I felt frightened. I hated being frightened.

"And I was having such a nice dream," said the Rat.

"Why don't you try and sleep? I'll stay awake, just in case that scary guy comes back."

"Ah bleep him! I bet he's in a nice cozy police cell!" Putting her head on my shoulder, she closed her eyes. And before long she was asleep.

I felt lonely then, and more afraid. Looking into the darkness I said a few silent prayers for our safety. "Everything's going to be okay," I whispered. But the fear took its toll after a while and I began to feel sorry for myself. I was desperate for the sunrise. I checked the time on my cell phone. There was a message from Little Joe. "Miss Gabriela Felipe Mendez told me that you and Marie Claire were on TV with the Iceman. All of Winnipeg is talking about it!"

It was going to be a long night. The rain still fell, and I still felt scared. But thinking about Gabriela and all our friends seeing us on the TV gave me such a boost. And then, somehow, I felt like I wasn't alone.

Seventeen

When I woke it was sunny. The Rat was standing with her back to me.

"What time is it?" I asked. She just stood there. "Hey I'm talking to you—right, that's it. I'm not telling you the news."

She wobbled and then her legs gave way. She collapsed hitting the back of her head on the ground. I jumped up and grabbed her. She began to shake uncontrollably. "Don't worry, I'm with you!" Her teeth clamped shut and saliva came out of her mouth. "You have to be brave!" Her hands clawed into fists and her feet dug at the dirt. The spasms grew more violent. Her eyes rolled back and she groaned in pain.

"Help!" I shouted.

But there was no one around. Her face turned white and then it turned blue. "Breathe! Breathe!" I shouted. But she couldn't, and she wouldn't stop shaking. I threw my arms around her and held her tight. "Come on you have to breathe! Think about the paparazzi and the prairies! Ms. Mountshaft and the ballet! Think about Ice and your acting career! Think about Tommy and Harold and Running Elk who you can never get along with! Think about finding our long lost uncle! Think about the Old Man and how good he was! And how he loved us! And how I wish he was here with us now!" She shook a little less. The groaning sound died away and the bad blue color left her face. The spasms settled down to a tremor, and then they stopped altogether.

I held her until her jaw unlocked and then I held her some more. She was wheezing a little as she breathed, but she was coming out of it. I wiped the saliva from her mouth and the tears from my eyes. Then I smoothed my hand over her forehead. When her eyes opened I rested my head against hers. "If you want a mocha, my little rodent sister, I'll buy you one. There's no need for all this." I put my jacket under her head and looked around me. We were alone.

She lay quietly for a few minutes and then she started mumbling. I couldn't understand what she was saying at first, but then the words came out right. "Take me home, Bob! Something bad is going to happen!"

"What?"

"I don't know, but I'm scared!"

"Come on, I thought you were tough."

"You're going to leave me, Bob!"

"I'll never leave you. Never!"

She tried to sit up. I helped her sit up and then I knelt behind her for support. She looked around, dazed.

"We're in the park, we left Ice's apartment last night because Mia came home. Look, I'll text Joey and tell him you're sick. He should be back soon anyway. And I'll text Tommy. They're our friends. They'll help us find Uncle Jerome. And if we can't find him in two days we'll go home. How's that?"

We sat there for a while without talking and then she sat up by herself. When she tried to stand I helped her to her feet. She looked steady enough and so I packed away our sleeping bags and picked up the backpacks.

"Promise you won't leave me here. You're my brother. You have to look after me even if you don't love me!"

"I do! I will!" She freaked me out talking like that. "Besides, I'll never leave you. Who would I have to drive me insane?"

She never said anything. I hated it when she never said anything. I brushed a dead leaf from her hair and, putting my arm around her, I walked her out of the park.

We found a coffee shop on the East Side and, sitting her in a comfy seat, I spent the last of my money buying her a mocha. I texted Joey telling him she'd had a seizure. And I asked him when he would return to New York. Then I texted Tommy and told him we were no longer with Ice. Then I looked at the Rat. It's amazing what a mocha could do for her. The color came back into her face, and she scanned the customers for any signs of sophistication.

"We'll give it two more days," I said. "Then we'll go home if you want."

"Are you kidding? We'll stay here until it's snowing in the streets, if we have to. You can't wuss out on me now, Bob."

I couldn't believe what I was hearing! It was like her fit had never happened! Then, for the first time, my phone rang. "Hello."

The Rat put one of her pointy ears next to mine.

"You lost Ice? What did he do, melt through your fingers? I can't leave you kids alone for a minute! Meet me in Dave's Diner on the corner of 70th and Third!"

Then the line went dead. Me and the Rat looked at one another. Then the Rat's phone rang. "Hello. Marie Claire DeBillier speaking—yo, Joey! What's happening, kid? I'm fine. It was nothing—he exaggerates. He's an exaggerator. Sexy Sandra said we never turned up? No, we found somewhere cheaper. Shewa. Okay, Uncle Joey, we'll see you later. Bye." She put down the phone and said to me, "Joey will be back from Atlantic City around six. He'll pick us up on the other side of the Brooklyn Bridge, where he dropped us off. And we can stay with him. Come on, let's go meet Tommy."

We walked the dozen blocks to Dave's Diner and found Tommy reading the paper. He scowled at us as we sat down. "I suppose you want breakfast. You don't deserve breakfast. Call yourself a hustler!"

The Rat smiled and folded her arms. "He was gonna call the cops, Tommy. What could we do?"

Tommy's eyes went shifty. "We could make money from that story. New York rapper turns police informant."

"We'll do nothing of the sort," said the Rat. "Ice is our friend. He had our best interests at heart, didn't he, Bob?"

"Give me a break," said Tommy. "He only cares about his career."

"How did you get along, Tommy?" I asked.

Tommy held up the *New York Post*. The headline read: Iceman Saves Elderly Man From Being Mugged. And below the headline was a picture of Tommy with his arm around Ice. And to the left of the picture was the Rat. She grabbed the paper and held it in front of her. "Fame at last!"

"You see what happens when you're acquainted with Tommy 'the Maestro' Mattolla. And the *Post* always pays." He said pulling a wad of cash from his pocket. "Two grand, all in all. And now I'm going to sue them so they can pay me some more."

"What did they do, Tommy?" I asked.

"Can't you read? They called me elderly! Elderly! I'm in my early fifties, or thereabouts. They'll settle out of court, of course. Should get another grand out of them at least."

"We were on TV as well," I said.

The Rat collapsed the paper in front of her.

"Little Joe texted me. He said Miss Gabriela Felipe Mendez saw us on TV with Ice. It must have been when we were going in the Marriott."

The Rat sat back bewildered. "The TV as well!"

A waiter came to the table. "Okay, breakfast is on me," said Tommy.

"We'll have two American breakfasts," said the Rat.

"You know Jerome DeBillier, Tommy?" I asked.

Tommy frowned. "Jerome DeBillier, I know that name from somewhere."

"He's our uncle. You think you could help us find him?"

"Sure, I'll help you find him. But for now we have to concentrate on getting you and Ice back together. That's where the money is. Always go with the money!"

Me and the Rat grabbed our bikes, which we had left at the den, and pushed them back through the bushes.

"We have to meet our friend Joey on the other side of the Brooklyn Bridge at six," said the Rat. "But we can hang out with you until then."

"Hold on a minute," said Tommy. "Who's this Joey character? Who wrote him into the script?"

"He gave us a ride to New York," I said. "And he's going to put us up until we find our uncle. He's Italian, Tommy, like you."

"I'm Sicilian, we have a little more class than those mainland mutts. And as I've got nowhere to stay, and nothing better to do, I think I'm gonna tag along with you kids. Make sure you're okay, if you know what I mean. There's a lot of strange types in this city."

We got three cups of tea from a park café and sat in the shade of an old tree. I gave Tommy my backpack, and laying it against the trunk, he got comfortable. "So what you wanna be when you grow up, Marie Claire?"

"I'm going to be an actress. I'm going to be the greatest actress ever!"

"Yeah, well don't forget your Uncle Tommy. Remember I made you money in Times Square and fed you when you were hungry. It's important to remember those things. What about you, Bob?"

"A journalist, I think, for a magazine."

"A noble profession. I'm thinking about writing myself one day."

"Did you really used to be an attorney, Tommy?" I asked.

"Sure, I was a good one too. But I ended up defending the wrong people, getting in with the wrong crowd, if you know what I mean. Then I was convicted of jury tampering. It all fell apart after that. The marriage collapsed, the kids never spoke to me again."

"You have kids, Tommy?" said the Rat.

"Sure, three girls. She turned them against me, of course. I should never have married her. She made slurping noises when she ate and she laughed like a machine gun—ah, to hell with them. One day I'll go back to Sicily and buy a small farm by the ocean. And I'll tell you something else," he said sitting up. "I think it's gonna happen! Whether it's something to do with Ice or meeting you kids, I don't know. But I think my boat is finally going to come in, and if you kids do right by me I'll let you sail on her. Yes, sir, big things are going to happen to Tommy Mattolla, big things!"

Then his cell phone rang.

"Hello—I understand. Okay, I'll be there. Sonny, I said I'll be there and I'll be there!" Tommy put his phone away and stood up. "Come on kids, let's go!"

The Rat jumped up. "Where are we going?"

"West Side. Hell's Kitchen."

We followed Tommy out of the park and on to Central Park West, where he flagged down a taxi. The first taxi wouldn't take the bikes, neither would the second. But the third taxi driver, who wore a turban, didn't mind. He even helped us put them in the trunk. The Rat sat in the front seat and looked back at us through the reinforced glass. "Is Hell's Kitchen a kitchen, Tommy?"

"No, it's not."

"Why do they call it a kitchen then?"

Tommy never answered her; he just mumbled and looked out the window. He'd turned into a proper grouch all of a sudden. And so the Rat turned her attention to the taxi driver.

"Are you a Sikh?"

"I am."

"Do you like being a Sikh?"

"Yes. I find it very fulfilling."

"We go to church sometimes, and I have Native beliefs. But I'm a bit of a Buddhist as well."

"Well it makes no difference to God whether you pray by a river or up a mountain. And so I'm sure it makes no difference to Him whether you pray in a temple or a church." He smiled at the Rat. "It's about connecting, you see, like tuning in a radio. You should find a religion that gives you the best reception."

"What if there's no reception?" said the Rat.

"Well—" said the taxi driver.

So we headed downtown with the Rat and the taxi driver talking about religion; thank God it was only a short journey. We soon pulled up outside a bar on the West Side and, taking the bikes from the trunk, we locked them to a lamp post.

"Good-bye, little one," said the Sikh taxi driver. "Have a happy life."

"I'll do my best," said the Rat, and waved at him as he drove away. "I think that taxi driver was an angel."

"Me too," said Tommy. "He's the only taxi driver I've ever met who drove off without the fare. Now, you kids, wait here. I'll be out in a minute."

The bar was dull inside, and empty except for a single barman polishing glasses.

"I want a drink," said the Rat, and followed him inside.

"You can't go in there!" But she did and so I followed her.

"Tommy, can I have a Coke?" asked the Rat sitting down next to him.

"You kids think I'm made of money?" shouted Tommy. "Can't you see I have problems?" He wrung his hands nervously and then he looked at the Rat. "Sorry, Marie Claire. I didn't mean to shout."

A big balding man with tattoos all over his forearms came out of a back room and sat at the table. He looked at me and the Rat, and then he opened a small black book.

"He'll see you in a minute," he said. "You got it all?"

"I got one thousand, nine hundred and thirty dollars," said Tommy handing him his wad of cash.

The man looked in the book. "You're short by one thousand and seventy dollars."

"Sonny, the money you've gotten from me over the years and you're making a big deal about a thousand bucks!"

"Hey, you wanna gamble, that's your business," said the tattooed man. "Now you listen to me, Tommy Mattolla! I know you from the old neighborhood. You were friends with my old man, and I've always had a fondness for you. But Big Frank, he don't like you. He's waited three weeks for his money, because I asked him as a favor, and when he sees it's short you're gonna have to suffer the consequences!"

Tommy seemed to sink in his seat. “Is it that bad, Sonny?”

“I’m afraid so.” Sonny got up and returned to the back room.

“Listen, why don’t you kids make your way back to the park?”

“Are you in trouble, Tommy?” I asked.

He tried to smile. “No, it’s just a misunderstanding. Now you run along and I’ll call you later.”

Sonny stood in the doorway of the back room. “Tommy.”

Tommy stood up.

“I’m coming with you, Tommy,” said the Rat, standing next to him. “For good luck.”

When Tommy looked down at her, he had tears in his eyes. “You kill me, kid! You really do!” Then he turned to me. “Bob, get your sister out of here!”

Tommy walked toward Sonny and they went in the back room. The Rat looked up at me and then she bolted after him. So, of course, I had to follow her!

“Get out of here!” shouted Sonny.

“No!” shouted the Rat. “We’ll leave when Tommy leaves!”

There were four mean-looking men in the back room. The biggest of them sat behind a desk. He had thick curly hair and a big face. “What’s this, Tommy?” he asked. “You bring your kids with you in the hope I’d show you some mercy. You’re pathetic!”

"Your money will be here in a couple of days, Frank," said Tommy. "I'm on to something."

"You're a small-time hustler who got his picture on the front page of the *Post* with the Iceman. That's where you got the almost two grand. But almost two grand don't pay the piper."

The man was calm when he spoke, but there was something scary about him. He was a very scary man.

"How many times can you slip in a supermarket, or step out in front of a moving car? Nobody's been knocked down more times than you, Mattolla. No, the insurance companies have bankrolled you for the last time. How are you going to get my money? You gonna tap dance in Times Square?"

Tommy looked angry. "What do you care, Frank? You always get it in the end!"

"That's true. But being made to wait by a cheap hustler like you is an insult. And I've been insulted too many times. I'm gonna break your hand, Tommy. It's for your own good. Someone get me that lump hammer. And get these kids out of here!"

Two of the men grabbed hold of Tommy.

I couldn't believe they were going to hurt him! He was an old man!

Sonny grabbed hold of me and the Rat and dragged us out the room.

"Let go!" cried the Rat.

I looked back. They were holding Tommy's arm on the desk. Big Frank was holding the lump hammer. "No."

"Ah!" cried Sonny, and looked at his hand.

The Rat had bit his finger! She ran back into the room. "You better not touch him! We have friends downtown!"

Everybody froze.

That's it. We're dead! The Rat had finally got us killed! I felt like shaking her and telling her we didn't know where downtown was!

Big Frank leaned forward on his desk. "Like who, little girl?"

"Like the Iceman! He's our godfather!"

Frank looked at the front page of the *Post*. "Yeah, you're there with him. So let's say, for now, he's your godfather. Is he going to pay me the money I'm owed, today?"

"No, but he's paying Tommy five thousand dollars for tracking down our long-lost uncle, Jerome DeBillier, and he's going to pay him another five thousand when he finds him."

"Anyone know this Jerome DeBillier?" asked Frank.

"I've heard of the name," said Sonny.

"Are you sure you ain't trying to save your friend, Sonny?"

"I'm through trying to save him, Frank. I have heard the name. I just can't remember where from."

Big Frank stared at the Rat. The Rat folded her arms and stared at Big Frank. I just stared at my life, which didn't so much flash before me as sink away.

"Even if what you say is true, I still don't have my money." Frank turned to Tommy. "I told myself I'd be lenient if you had two grand. If you can make it up right now I'll give you two more days."

"I don't have it, Frank."

"The bikes!" I said.

Me and the Rat bolted outside and came back with the bikes. "These are the best BMXs money can buy," I said. "They cost five hundred dollars each! They'll more than make up for the seventy dollars that Tommy is short."

Big Frank looked at them. "Okay, they'll do for my boys." Then he turned to Tommy. "Hustler, you have two days to get me the grand plus a hundred dollars a day in interest. Twelve hundred dollars in two days or I'll break both your hands! Now get out of my sight! Oh, and little girl, let me give you some advice. Don't ever stick your neck out for nobody, especially a scumbag like him!"

"Tommy's our friend! And you'll see, big things are going to come his way!"

I took her by the arm and walked her outside. I could have kicked her in the pants for that performance. Not that she cared; she looked pleased with herself.

"Well, Tommy. That's another fine mess we've gotten you out of."

Tommy looked a little down. "Sorry about the bikes, kids. I'll make it up to you."

"It's okay, Tommy," said the Rat. "Just remember we're sailing on your boat when it comes in."

"I'll remember. Come on, kids. It's a long walk to Brooklyn Bridge."

* * *

I didn't mind giving up the bikes to save Tommy from getting his hand broken, but New York got a lot bigger without them. And when he said we had a long walk he wasn't joking. It took us so long to get there I don't even want to talk about it! We didn't even have money to buy a drink. But eventually, after hours of plodding away, we reached the bridge and made our way up the boardwalk. Tommy developed a limp as we neared the top, not a false limp for the suckers, but a real limp. So we took a seat on a bench and looked at the river.

"When my family first came here from the old country, we used to live over there," said Tommy, pointing toward Brooklyn. "The houses have been knocked down now but we used to have an attic apartment. My brother and me had a bedroom way up in the top. It had a round window, as I remember, and some nights we'd lie awake and look out at this bridge."

"You have a brother, Tommy?" I asked.

"Not any more. He was fishing by the river one day and these kids asked him if he could swim. 'Sure,' he said, and so they threw him in. He couldn't swim. Turns out they couldn't either. He drowned. He was only eleven. Sometimes I think about what would have happened if he had lived. How my life would have been different if I had a big brother looking out for me. I remember him playing the violin. He used to play 'Three Blind Mice' over and over. I don't think he could play anything else. Who knows, he might have grown up to be a famous violinist, but he drowned instead. But that's life. We wander around like blind mice searching for whatever it is we're looking for. From mice to miserable men, from the poetry of childhood's hour to the darkness of death's goddamn dominion, we never stop searching. Why can't we just *be*?"

"Are you okay, Tommy?" asked the mice's very own relation.

"Sure, I'm just tired. Come on, kids. Let's go meet this Joey character."

So the three blind mice wandered over the Brooklyn Bridge and back to the spot where Joey had first dropped us off, which seemed like a thousand years ago.

"Here he is!" said the Rat.

Joey pulled up and jumped out of his car. "Hey, it's the original MC!" he said, giving the Rat a hug. Then he hugged me. "Hey, Bobby! So you survived without me!" But when he saw Tommy the smile left his face. "Who's this?"

"Tommy Mattolla from Manhattan."

Joey looked puzzled. "So, what can we do for you, Tommy?"

I could see Joey didn't take to Tommy, so I tried to talk him up. "Tommy's a friend, Joey. He bought us breakfast this morning when we had no money, and now he's got nowhere to stay."

"Just need a place to hang my hat for a few days. I've got plenty on the go. There'll be money coming my way pretty soon."

"Kids, I'm staying in a trailer by the river. I ain't got room for him."

"You'll hardly know I was there, kid," said Tommy.

"Believe me, I'll know!"

"Well, I don't know if I can let the kids go with you. After all, we hardly know you."

"Listen, Pops. You better be careful what you say or—"

The Rat snatched the *Post* from Tommy's pocket and showed it to Joey.

"Isn't that the Iceman?" said Joey. "You're with the Iceman, MC!" Then he looked at Tommy and back at the paper. "Who are you again?"

"Tommy's a friend, Joey," said the Rat. "He has nowhere to stay. But I told him, 'Joey will help you! He's a really good guy!'" Then she looked up at him with her big blue eyes.

Joey looked at Tommy. "Yeah, well, if you're willing to sleep outside, I've got a camp bed you can use."

"Great," said Tommy, and jumped in the car.

Joey shook his head. "Can't leave you kids alone for a minute, can I? Come on, let's head to the supermarket. I'll buy some steaks for a barbecue. Then you can tell me how you managed to befriend that rundown hustler and get your picture in the *Post* with the latest thing in rap, in the unbelievably short time that I've been away!"

Eighteen

We unlocked a set of gates, and bumping down a dirt road, we pulled up in front of a large silver trailer. The trailer was about sixty yards from the Hudson River, and alongside the river ran train tracks. As we got out of the car an Amtrak train went by, sounding its siren. Some of the people on the train waved at us, and me and the Rat waved back. One crazy guy waved both arms while a little girl, held up by her mom, twinkled her fingers.

"They'll wave at you from a train," said Tommy. "But they'll pass you in the street without a word."

When the train had gone, we looked around us. The land we were on had been cleared of anything green, but on either side of us there were lots of trees and shrubs, and across the river there were tree-covered hills. Joey told us we were way up in the Bronx but I never imagined there would be so much nature. It was like a little part of Canada.

"Is this your land, Joe?" asked the Rat.

"I wish it was. A construction company owns it. They're going to build condos here. My second cousin once removed got me the job guarding the site. So far there's nothing to guard." He pulled the grocery bags from the trunk. "Grab some of those bags." We helped Joey take the bags from the car to the trailer. It was quite roomy inside. There was a bathroom, a kitchen, and two separate rooms with double beds.

"You kids can take the spare bed. You're outside, Pops. There's a camper bed in here," said Joey opening a cupboard door. "Right I'll go fire up that barbecue."

Tommy prodded the mattress. "Looks like you kids are gonna sleep well. But what about my rheumatism?" he said rubbing his back.

"You can have the bed, Tommy," I said.

"I don't wanna put you kids out."

"You have it, Tommy," said the Rat. "Me and Bob are used to sleeping outdoors."

"Well, if you insist."

We went outside to see Joey putting burgers and steak on a sizzling grill.

"How about if I do that?" said Tommy.

"I've got it."

"I'd like to do it. To show my appreciation, so to speak."

Joey handed him a spatula. "I'll do the beans and the fries inside."

"I'll help," said the Rat.

Tommy found an apron and took control of the cooking. He turned up the heat and flipped the burgers one after the other. The smell made my mouth water.

Joey came out and gave Tommy and me Cokes.

"What, no beer?" asked Tommy.

Joey ignored him, and opening up a small table, he went back inside.

"I get the feeling I'm not wanted."

"Joey don't mean nothing."

"It's okay. I've never been popular, not even in prison. But who wants to be popular in prison?" Tommy sniggered to himself. "How you like your steak, Bob?"

"Medium, I guess. Was prison really bad?"

"No, not really. It was boring, if anything. The only thing I didn't like was bumping into my former clients. They'd always complain about the way I defended them. And what got me was that most of them were guilty, at least I hope they were. But being a prison lawyer had its benefits. People were always asking for help with their appeals and I'd always help them out. I'd charge a small fee, of course, or ask a favor in return. So it worked out okay in the end."

The Rat came out and opened out some folding chairs. "We're done."

Tommy turned one of the steaks over. "So are we."

Joey put the fries and beans on the table and we all took a seat.

I hadn't eaten since breakfast, and that's my excuse for taking a full steak and two cheeseburgers. We washed it down with a Coke while the guys had beer. And I have to say it tasted pretty good.

Joey lit up a cigarette and sat back, satisfied. "I can't believe you kids stayed with the Iceman. What was he like?"

"He was nice," I said.

"Ice was nice," said the Rat. "He's our friend. We were on TV with him as well, and we had a chauffeur and a limo and we ate in a fancy restaurant and everything. It was great."

"And now you're stuck in a trailer with old Joey."

"You're great as well, Joey," said the Rat. "And the trailer's really nice."

Joey took a long drag on his cigarette. "Yeah, the trailer's nice and there's no rent to pay. Still, I wouldn't mind living in a Fifth Avenue apartment. Or having my first CD sell a million copies."

Tommy put his plate down. "You got anything on the go?"

"Yeah, I've got something."

"Anything I could get in on?"

"Not really."

"Maybe I could help you out," said Tommy.

Joey scoffed. "*You* help *me* out! I'm the one helping *you* out, and you look like you're used to it."

"Something on your mind, kid?"

"Nothing I wanna share with you."

"How old are you, kid? Twenty, twenty-one? You've only just met me and you've got me in your pigeonhole. You look at me and you think what a broken-down bum. I'll never end up like that guy. But don't be so sure, kid. Life can turn around and bite you on the ass when you least expect it."

"You've had some bad luck, is that it?" said Joey. "It's not your fault, of course. That guy let you down or your horse never came in. Or those shares took a dive and took your savings with them. It's always easier to blame your problems on luck. But a real man blames himself for his mistakes."

Tommy looked at the ground.

I felt bad for Tommy. To some people he must have seemed like a bum but he was a good guy. They were both good guys. But they didn't like each other. And I felt awkward because me and Rat had brought them together. I tried to think of something to say that would lighten the mood. But the Rat beat me to it. "How did you get on with the cigars, Joey?"

The anger left Joey's face. "I did pretty good, Marie Claire. I sold them all. I gave some money to my step-parents and with the rest I bought watches. But now I have to get rid of the watches to get some cash flowing."

"Tommy could help you," said the Rat. "He's a great hustler."

"What's the script, Joe?"

Joey didn't answer.

"Well, if you don't wanna tell me," said Tommy.

"One hundred genuine Swiss Army watches. Got them at a bankruptcy auction in Baltimore. To break even I have to get forty dollars a watch. Figure I can double my money when I sell them, but it's selling them."

"Swiss Army, they're a good watch," said Tommy. "If we went to Times Square tonight we could sell quite a few."

"Great!" said the Rat.

"Times Square! Are you kidding? They got plain-clothes cops and Times Square security, not to mention the anti-terrorist units. I'd get the whole suitcase taken off me."

"Unless we work in teams. You take Marie Claire and I take Bob. They stay at a safe distance with the watches in their backpacks. If the cops pinch us, we only lose a few watches."

"I lose a few watches!"

"Okay, you lose a few watches, but you see my point. And me and the kids will work for peanuts, let's say fifty per cent of the net."

"Sounds good to me!" said the Rat.

"I don't like the idea of bringing the kids into it."

"It's okay, Joe. Me and Tommy have worked Times Square before."

"You took the kids hustling in Times Square."

"They were already there," said Tommy. "That's how we met. And Marie Claire here's a real star."

"We'll be great together, Joey," said the Rat. "We'll have them watches sold in a night."

Joey seemed unsure, but the Rat's enthusiasm brought a smile to his face. "Well, I have no other plans. Okay, let's do it."

So that was it. Me and Tommy put the dishes away while Joey and the Rat loaded our backpacks with watches. When we were done we locked up the trailer and jumped in the car.

"Oh, I forgot to tell you, kids!" said Joey as we drove away. "I placed an ad in the *Post* and the *Village Voice* for anyone who knows a Jerome DeBillier, and I included my phone number. They'll be in the day after tomorrow, so who knows, maybe we'll get a bite."

"Thanks, Joey," I said.

"You're the best, Joey!" said the Rat.

"I was thinking of helping out too," said Tommy. "I was going to ask Ice if he really wanted to hire a private detective."

Joey looked in the rear-view mirror. "So, your idea of helping out revolves around you making money."

"What difference does it make as long as he's found?"

"It makes a lot of difference—"

I was hoping they wouldn't argue all the way downtown. But sometimes all you can do is hope.

It was dark by the time we reached Times Square. We parked the car on the West Side and walked across

42nd Street, which was swarming with people. Me and Tommy stopped when we reached Broadway and waited for Joey and the Rat to catch up. They were laughing and joking like a couple of kids on their way to an amusement park. And Times Square had that amusement park feel about it. There were sailors and stag parties, and glamorous-looking girls. And there were lots of people in fancy dress. It was like Mardi Gras.

Then a preacher stood on a stool and shouted at the thousands of people making their way to the different bars, nightclubs, and theatres. “Repent! Repent!” he ranted.

“Repent?” said a chubby guy who’d had too much to drink. “I’ve only just got here!” Then he stood below the preacher. “Hey, Peter. Take my picture.” Some girls dressed as angels came along and stood next to him. A group of cops gathered around the angels, and a group of devils gathered around the cops. In the end there must have been about twenty people.

“What about me?” asked the guy with the camera.

“Oh give it here!” shouted the preacher. And getting off his stool he took the photograph. He gave the guy his camera back and returned to ranting. “Where’s my stool! Somebody’s stolen my stool! You thieving Babylonians, you’re all going to burn!” Then the cops came over to calm him down.

“I see the party’s in full swing,” said Joey as he reached us.

"You and Marie Claire work Broadway," said Tommy. "Me and Bob will work 42nd Street."

"Where will you be?" asked Joey.

Tommy looked around him. "By Madame Tussauds."

Joey pulled me to one side and put his arm around me. "I trust you, Bob, but I don't trust him. You take care of the money, okay?"

"Sure, Joe."

"Come on, Marie Claire. Let's go to work."

"See you later, Bob," said the Rat.

"Come here," I told her. "You stay close to Joey and don't go wandering off!"

"I won't."

"And don't be acting like a spaz!"

"Me! Acting like a spaz?! I think not. What would Ms. Mountshaft and the ballet say?"

"Well, be careful."

She stared up at me. "I can remember you carrying me in the rain because you didn't want my feet to get wet."

The Rat could come out with the strangest things! "What's that got to do with anything?"

"You've always looked after me, Bob, even when we were very little kids."

I punched her on the arm. "Someone's got to keep you out of trouble."

"Come on, MC!" shouted Joey.

The Rat ran after him.

"She'll be okay, Bob," said Tommy. "That Joey's an arrogant little wop, but he'll look after her." Tommy fixed two watches to each wrist and, pulling down his sleeve, he brushed the lapels of his suit. "Come on, Bob. Let's sell these suckers a watch."

I stood against a wall and watched Tommy at work; it was a real education. He would ask a question, "How are you this evening?" or, "Excuse me, sir, where are you from?", and depending on their answer he would either step forward or let them go.

The suckers would always ask the same questions. "How do we know they're genuine? How do we know they won't fall apart? Are you a licensed retailer?" Tommy hadn't made a single sale until a group of sailors walked by.

"Hey, boys! I've got something you might be interested in." Tommy looked around him and then he pulled up his sleeves. "Top-of-the-range Swiss Army watches. They sell at six hundred dollars retail. You can have one for a hundred and fifty dollars and they're still in their boxes."

"Yeah," said this large-jawed sailor. "Let's take a look."

Tommy brought the sailors toward me and I opened up my backpack. He pulled out a few boxes and passed them around.

"They're hot, right?" asked one of the sailors.

"Let's just say, they're a little warm," said Tommy.

The large-jawed sailor had a quick talk with his shipmates. "Okay, they look genuine enough. And I should know, I've had a few. We were all going to get a tattoo but a watch will do. We'll take one each and, since we're taking six, you'll take a hundred bucks a watch."

"Are you kidding? That's a third off!"

"Forget about it, boys, he doesn't want our business."

"Okay, you win," said Tommy.

They handed Tommy $600 and wandered away while looking at their wrists.

"Why did you give them the impression they were stolen, Tommy?"

"People prefer buying stolen stuff. They think they're getting a better deal. Tells you something about human nature, don't it?"

I cringed but I had to ask him. "Shall I hold on to the money, Tommy?"

"What, your friend don't trust me? Here, take it."

I felt bad taking the money but I was glad he handed it over without a fuss.

Anyway, after making his first sale Tommy made one sale after another. And the more he sold the happier he seemed. My only problem was the money. Sometimes he would give it to me and other times it would go in his pocket. I was hoping he would hand it over when the time came, but I could see there being a problem.

Then a guy came and stood next to me. His face was pale and his eyes were red, and greasy blond hair dangled from his head.

"What's in the backpack?" he asked.

"Oh nothing."

"Give it to me!"

"I can't."

The man's teeth clenched. "You can't or you won't?"

"He won't," said Tommy.

The man straightened up. "Suppose I take it!"

Tommy pulled out a small black baton and slapped it in his hand. "This is Harry. He's leather on the outside, but inside, he's lead. Now you move away or Harry goes over your head!"

The guy moved away, glaring at Tommy as he went.

"You okay, Bob?"

"He was kind of scary."

"Full moon always brings them out. Don't worry kid. Shout if you need me."

As the night wore on the bright lights began hurting my eyes. I was hoping we wouldn't be out there much longer. Times Square is a strange place when you're tired. But when I saw Joey running toward us I knew it was about to get stranger.

"Is she here?" he shouted. "Marie Claire, is she here?"

"No," I said.

"I turned my back for a minute and she was gone! I've looked everywhere for her! I can't find her!"

"Okay, calm down," said Tommy. "Where was the last place you saw her?"

"Around 47th and Broadway. I thought she might have gone to the bathroom or something, so I waited. Then I had a good look around. I can't find her anywhere."

"How long since you last seen her?"

"Half an hour, maybe more."

"Bob and me will head up Broadway. You get the car and cruise the area."

"I'm so sorry, Bob!" said Joey, and ran off to get the car.

The fear hit me hard. "We have to find her, Tommy! We have to find my sister!"

"What? Is that panic I hear? Come on, Bob, she's probably just wandered off. If that idiot had stayed put, she would have wandered back again." Tommy put his hand on my shoulder. "Come on, kid, we'll find her."

We walked up Broadway and waded through thousands of people. Then, crossing to the other side of the street, we doubled back. Tommy stopped every now and again to speak to various people. They stood in doorways or leaned against walls or hid in the shadows of Times Square. I wouldn't have noticed they were there if Tommy hadn't spoken to them. "Fair-haired girl, selling watches, you seen her? There's a hundred in it for you if you spot her, answers to the name of Marie Claire." His tone was serious when he spoke to the street people, but when he saw me watching him he smiled. "When we find her, Bob, we'll make her pay for supper." But when he went back to scanning the street, he looked worried. I'd only known Tommy for a short time but I knew he wasn't the sort of person to worry. That look frightened me more than anything.

I scanned the crowd until my eyes hurt. I looked in the corners of the buildings and down the dark alleys. I looked at every person who passed me. I looked at hundreds of faces and then I looked at thousands. I looked in restaurant windows. I even looked in the bars. I checked the coffee shops hoping to see her. I looked into the passing cars desperate not to see her. I turned and turned until the lights and the buildings went around me like a merry-go-round, but I couldn't see her anywhere.

Then Joey cruised along, looking around him as he came. He pulled up by us. Tommy put his hand on the roof of the car and they exchanged a few words. They never looked at each other as they spoke; their dark eyes scanned the streets. And for the first time I saw they were like father and son.

"Keep looking," said Tommy and the car cruised away.

Then the Rat's words ran around in my head like the plague *Take me home, Bob! Something bad is going to happen!* But I hadn't taken her home! And it must have been half an hour since Joey told us he couldn't find her. That means she had been missing for at least an hour.

"You have to find her, Tommy!"

Tommy made no attempt to smile now. His face was as grim as an undertaker's. I stopped looking for her. I only watched him. Only Tommy with his hustler's instinct could find her. He moved slowly. He stopped.

His head turned from side to side. He moved on. He mumbled something to himself. Then he crossed Broadway and stood on the center island where me and the Rat had stood that first night. I followed him across. He turned 360 degrees. But then he froze. Something had caught his eye!

"There she is!" he shouted and pointed across the street.

I looked but I couldn't see her! "Where?"

He pointed in a different direction. "There!"

A police car was weaving its way through the Times Square traffic. Her small face appeared in the back window. My eyes locked on to hers. She held my glance for a second. And then she was gone.

Nineteen

When I woke up it was daylight. I reached for my phone, but it wasn't there. I jumped up and went outside. Tommy and Joey were sitting in the sunshine.

"It's okay, Bob. I've got it here," said Tommy handing me the phone. "You were sleeping pretty good. I was scared she'd send you a message and you wouldn't hear it."

"I tried calling her, Bob," said Joey. "But her phone's switched off."

"She'll have done that to stop the cops from taking it off her. But she'll send me a text message as soon as she gets a chance."

"The kids said you used to be a lawyer," said Joey. "What will happen now?"

"They'll call Social Services and they'll take her to a children's home. They'll keep her there until they figure out what to do with her."

"When she contacts you, Bob, we'll go get her," said Joey. "Then I'll take you kids back to Canada. I'll keep on looking for your uncle, don't worry about that, but I think it would be best if you went home."

"There could be implications if you take her out of the home," said Tommy. "They could throw a dozen charges at you. They could even charge you with kidnapping."

"Like I told you, Pops, I stand by my friends. What do you say, Bob?"

"We have to get her back!"

"Okay, then it's settled. Now how about a late breakfast?"

"I'm not hungry."

"I know it's bad, Bob. But not eating won't help."

"Joey's right," said Tommy. "I'll fire up the barbecue and we'll have a good breakfast. Come on, kid. You can help. It'll keep your mind off things."

Tommy put bacon and eggs on the barbecue while Joey made the coffee and toast inside. When it was done we ate outdoors, while watching the trains go by. A woman waved at me from one train. She looked kind of sad when I didn't wave back. When the train had gone I felt bad for not waving, but I felt bad anyway.

We drank more coffee, and Joey smoked one cigarette after another. A lot more trains went by. I paced back and forth between the trailer and the train tracks, and then I crossed the train tracks and walked down by the river. I couldn't stop thinking about where she could be. I wondered if she was frightened or feeling lonely like me. I thought about her in the police station joking around with the cops. The guys were right. She would be safe with the cops.

But what if she escaped? She might try and find her way back here. She'd have such a long journey. No, she wouldn't do that. She couldn't find her way back here. She would probably go back to the den. She might even go to Ice. But I don't think she could escape from the cops, not by herself. So they would take her to a home. I wondered what sort of home they would take her to. What if she had a fit? I should give myself up. But they might put me in a boys' home and keep her in one for girls. I looked at my cellphone for the thousandth time and then I wandered back to the guys.

They played cards outdoors while asking each other did they know various people, most of whom sounded like gangsters. Pete the Performer and Frank the Fence. Sal and Moe, and do you know Sonny the Saint? What about his brother Joe the Boxer who killed Silent Steve in Havana's that night because he was looking at his girlfriend? Or what about Crazy Carl and those Bensonhurst boys? You hear about the fallout with the Russians?

Turns out they knew a lot of the same people but they disagreed over the stories that surround them, mostly because Tommy was older than Joey and had been around a lot more. And he let Joey know this in a not-so-subtle way. Joey slapped the cards on the table and came toward me. "I'm going to the store. That guy gets on my goddamn nerves!" And, jumping in his car, he sped away.

I took a seat at the table and watched Tommy play solitaire. "Youth, they know nothing but act like they know everything. But not you, Bob. You are wise beyond your years."

"I'm worried, Tommy."

"It ain't time to worry yet. I'll let you know when it is."

The sun was almost setting and she still hadn't contacted me. I was just about to suggest we go to the cops when my phone gave out a high-pitched beep.

"Told cops nothing. In Don Children's Home. Don't know address. The kids here are very quiet. Guys who run it seem strange. Don't leave me here, brother!"

"The Don Children's home is in New Jersey off the New Jersey Turnpike," said Tommy. "They keep a lot of the immigrant kids there."

Joey made his way into the trailer. "Text her back, Bob. Tell her we're on our way." When he came out he was carrying a crowbar.

"What's the plan, Joe?" asked Tommy.

"When we get there we text Marie Claire, telling her we're outside. She gives us a signal like flashing a light on and off. We crack open a window or a door," said Joey holding up the crowbar. "We get Marie Claire and head for the border."

Tommy stood up. "Head to the George Washington Bridge. We'll cross from there."

Joey looked surprised. "You want in on this?"

"You're not the only one who stands by his friends."

We piled into the car and, driving up the dirt road, we headed out on to the main road. I was so happy I found myself smiling. I could already see her telling us the story of how she got caught. And I could see her asleep in the car as we drove back to Canada. I didn't know what would happen after that. But I was so glad we'd met Tommy and Joey. They were great guys and I'd never forget them for helping us.

But as we neared the George Washington Bridge my phone beeped again.

"They're pedophiles, Bob. Kids are really small and they're hurting them. One of them has a gun. I've seen it. Don't come alone. Bring Ice."

I could feel the fear sink into my soul.

"Let's get the cops!" said Joey. "Let's get them right now!"

"It's too late for that!" said Tommy. "The cops are too slow. They'll send a couple of rookies to investigate what's no more than an allegation. They'll talk to whoever's in charge, make a report, and send it to Social Services. In a few days, if we're lucky, they'll send someone to investigate. It's a slow process, believe me.

And I've dealt with these goddamn pedophiles before. You don't know how slippery they can be!"

"What are we going to do?" asked Joey.

"Head to Fifth Avenue. We'll pick up Ice."

"You think Ice will come?" I asked.

"Of course he'll come! The kid's in trouble!" Tommy took a pen from his pocket and wrote on a piece of paper. "I'm writing down the address of the home and I'm telling Ice what's happened. If he's out, we'll leave it with the doorman."

The car weaved in and out of the traffic like a video game played to the max. Joey ran red lights and took corners so fast I slid in my seat. Then, when we were held up in traffic, he banged on the steering wheel. He kept his hand on the horn for large parts of the journey and he cursed the other drivers for being in his way. How he never got pulled over I'll never know, but we soon reached Ice's building.

"Just here!" I said.

The car screeched to a halt. Me and Tommy jumped out and ran inside.

"Can I help you, gentlemen?" asked the doorman.

"We need to see Ice!" I said.

The doorman picked up a phone. "What's your name?"

"Bob."

"He's having a party and Miss Moore said there should be no uninvited guests. But I remember seeing you with him—We have a gentleman here by the name of Bob. He has a friend with him. Very good, sir. Okay, you can go up."

I tapped on the button until the elevator came. When we reached Ice's floor I saw the door open and people standing outside.

I rushed into the apartment. There was music playing, and there were smartly dressed people drinking in the hallway. I made my way into the packed living room, which was noisy with loud talk, and laughter, and the clinking of cocktails. Then I saw Ice and Mia. I pushed through the partiers, knocking past a fat man smoking a cigar and a waitress serving snacks. "Ice, you have to help us! My sister's in trouble!"

The party people looked us up and down like we were peasants.

Ice looked embarrassed. "We'll talk outside."

We followed him out into the hallway while Mia apologized for our behavior.

"Can I have a minute?" said Ice. The hallway guests drifted back into the apartment. "What's the problem, Bob?"

"The Rat—my sister—has been put in a home, and it's run by pedophiles!"

"How do you know this?" said Ice.

"She sent me a text message."

"I like Marie Claire, she's a really nice kid. But she has a strange imagination."

"What are you saying, Ice?"

"Come on, Ice, we've got a car outside! Let's go!" said Tommy.

"Ice isn't going anywhere!" said Mia. "I don't know what your game is but you're not playing it here!"

"It's not a game," I said. "One of them has a gun!"

"Sure he does, little boy," said Mia. "Ice, they've probably got a TV crew waiting around the corner. It sounds like a setup to me."

Ice's manager, Barry, came out into the hall. "What's going on, Ice? The head of the company is asking for you."

"Some white trash kids that Ice befriended have got themselves in trouble, or so they say."

"Don't call them that, Mia!"

"Okay, Ice. But remember, I'm a little older than you and—"

"You're a lot older than me, Mia. Now shut up!"

"You have to help her, Ice!" I said.

Ice looked torn to the point of pain. "It's not a good time for me, Bob."

"When *would* be a good time?" said Tommy. "When they find her body?"

Everyone froze with those words. And my mind froze with the image.

"Ice!"

He looked away from me.

Tommy looked disgusted. "What? Your fancy party means more to you than a child in trouble?"

"Marie Claire could be lying."

"She could," said Tommy. "But my instinct tells me different. Either way I'm not willing to take the chance. Are you?"

Ice just stood there looking uncomfortable.

"I think you people should leave," said Mia. "Now."

"Give me the address, Tommy." I said. He gave me the address and I threw it at Ice's feet. "In case you change your mind. Come on, Tommy. Let's go."

Tommy stepped toward Ice. "I'm a lousy hustler, but I'll never be as low as you!"

"Tommy, come on!"

We dropped down to the street and went outside. Joey flicked his cigarette away and jumped in the car. "Where's Ice?"

"He's not coming," said Tommy. "It's just us."

I jumped in the back and Joey started the engine.

"Take the Lincoln Tunnel," said Tommy. "I'll direct you once we get to the other side."

The car screeched away.

I was sick about Ice. He was the Rat's hero and I thought he cared about her. But I was wrong and Tommy was right. Ice only cared about his career. And I hated him for it.

Joey cut through Central Park, screeched around a traffic circle, and headed downtown at high speed. We were lucky with green lights all the way to the Lincoln Tunnel. But once there we got held up in traffic. Tommy rattled his fingers on the side of the door while Joey put his hand on the horn.

"That won't do any good," said Tommy.

Joey cursed under his breath.

I rolled down the window and had a look. We were way deep in traffic and more was piling up behind us. I felt like yelling. I felt like getting out of the car and running as fast as I could. But I didn't. I sank down in the seat and started to feel sick. It was like we were never going to make it. Like we were already too late.

Twenty

We rolled through the tunnel, and following the road to the other side, we spiraled upwards. The sun had sunk by then, and the night was on its way. I watched the West Side of New York slide into view twice, and then slide away as the car headed into New Jersey. Then Joey went back to driving crazy. Tommy gave him directions while steadying himself in his seat, but he never told Joey to slow down. As far as I was concerned he couldn't drive fast enough.

"Oh no," said Joey looking at a dial on the dashboard. "We're way into the red. I think we'll make it but I can't be sure."

"There's a gas station up ahead," said Tommy.

Joey looked in the rearview mirror. "Your call, Bob."

My mind went blank.

"Stop for gas," said Tommy. "Best to be safe."

We pulled into the gas station. All the pumps were taken and the driver in front of us was talking on her phone.

"Goddamn New Jersey drivers." Joey honked the horn. "Come on, either fill up or move on!"

"Don't be so rude!" said the woman looking back. And carried on talking.

Joey revved the engine and came as close to her as he could. "Move your car or I'll ram you off the road!"

The flustered woman moved on, and we took her place. Joey jumped out and stuck the pump in the tank. I watched the digits crawl higher, the smell of gasoline seeping through the window. When it reached $20 Joey got back in the car and started the engine.

He screeched out of the gas station like a Ferrari from a pit stop. No one said anything about not paying. Paying wasn't important.

The car jerked as Joey changed gears. We were soon flying and everything whizzed past us in a blur. Tommy looked uncomfortable, but I felt better driving at high speed.

I went back to staring at my phone. An hour had passed since we had arrived at the tunnel. Eleven minutes since we'd left the gas station. But no messages had come.

Tommy sat forward. "Slow down. We're gonna turn soon."

The car slowed.

"Take the next right."

We drove off the turnpike and down a side road.

"At the end of this road take a left—now take a right."

We drove into a long wide road lined with huge houses set on spacious grounds.

"Slow down," said Tommy. "I think this is it."

The car ran alongside a stone wall, and pulling up by some iron-barred gates, we looked inside. A long driveway wound up toward a big stone mansion. It had rows of square windows that were three deep and a dozen wide. And at the top was a crow's nest. How we were going to find her in there I did not know.

"Send her a message, Bob. Tell her the cavalry's here," said Tommy. He got out the car and pushed the gates. "Locked." Then he got back in. "Drive away from the gate. We'll climb over the wall."

Joey drove away from the gate, and parking the car, he switched off the engine. We all sat in silence and stared at my phone. I was desperate for it to beep, but no message came back.

"That's it," said Tommy. "We're going in."

As we got out the car, I could feel the butterflies fluttering.

Joey opened the trunk, taking out the crowbar and two aluminum baseball bats. "We might need these."

"We might at that," said Tommy.

For an old man with bad legs, Tommy moved quickly. He climbed up on the wall, and taking the bats from Joey he dropped them on the other side. We heard a soft clunk. Then he disappeared over the wall.

With a short leap I gripped the top of the wall and I was up and over. I dropped into the darkness and crouched next to Tommy. Then Joey knelt next to me and handed me the crowbar. I've never been a violent kid but I felt violent then. We peered over a flower bed, watching the home and waiting.

"What are we waiting for, Tommy?" I asked.

He looked at me, and then back at the home. Most of the upstairs lights were out, and only a few of the ground floor lights were on. He was just about to speak when a car horn sounded at the gate. A light shone from the entranceway, and a slim blond woman came out of the home. She walked down the driveway and opened the gates. A car crept inside and two large men got out.

"If they knew we were coming they could have sent for backup," said Joey.

"How could they know we were coming?" said Tommy.

Locking the gates she greeted the men and they talked together in excited whispers. Then the light from the doorway darkened and another man appeared. The others stopped talking. They walked toward the entranceway, and passing him without a word, they made their way inside. The man came forward. It was too dark to see his face, but I could see he was wearing glasses. And he had something in his hand. His head turned left and right as he scanned the grounds. Then he went inside, closed the door, and the light disappeared.

"That guy looked like he had a gun. Suppose it was a gun?" asked Joey in a jittery voice.

"Then he's gonna have to shoot me," said Tommy. "Because I'm going in there to get her out."

"Maybe we should call the cops."

Tommy spoke softly. "It's too late for that, Joe. I know you're scared. Me too. But you don't want to let Marie Claire down now, do you? Come on, Joey! We're Italians from the old neighborhood. I bet you've slugged a few guys in your day, right? Because you know there's a time when you have to stand up and fight. And for me and you, kid, now is one of those times. Are you with me, Joe?"

"Sure, Tommy. I'm with you."

"What about you, Bob?"

I could feel the hairs stand up on the back of my neck. "Ready when you are, Tommy."

Tommy gripped the baseball bat. "Come on then, boys. Let's show these jerks how we do it on the West Side!"

We ran across the lawn and crouched below a window on the left of the entranceway. Tommy rose slowly and looked inside. Then he went around the side of the building and looked through another window. "It's a storage room," he whispered. "Pass me the crowbar."

I swapped Tommy the crowbar for the baseball bat, and sliding it beneath the window, he pushed it down. There was a lot of creaking and groaning. Then something sprang in the air and the window opened. We froze. All I could hear was my heart pounding.

Tommy exhaled. "Take this," he said and handed me the crowbar. He pushed the window up carefully and went to climb inside.

"I'll go," whispered Joey. "I'm a little—younger."

Tommy put his hand on Joey's shoulder. "It's all yours, kid."

Joey climbed in the window, as nimble as a cat burglar, and disappeared into the darkness. He soon climbed out again. "The door's locked," he whispered.

Then we heard voices and footsteps coming from inside.

"Over here," said Tommy.

We scurried to a wall and hid behind the tall shrubs that were growing in front of it. We heard keys in a lock and a light came on. It lit up the ground in front of the window but it stayed dark where we were.

The man wearing glasses entered the room. "Who left this window open?" He turned to the woman behind him. "Do a head count, and do it quick." He came forward and looked straight ahead to where we were standing. "Anyone out there?"

It was like he was looking straight at me. I pushed back against the wall. He put his head out the window and looked left and right. Then slowly he closed it. The light went out and the door closed.

We stepped out from behind the shrubs.

"You think he saw us?" said Joey.

"I doubt it," said Tommy. "But either way we're still going in."

We followed Tommy back toward the front of the home. He checked one window, and then another, and then he looked inside. "This one opens into a hall." He slid the crowbar into the window and pushed it down. There was the sound of wood pushing against wood and the window popped open. There wasn't much noise, but we froze all the same. Then very slowly, and carefully, Tommy pushed it up.

He took the bat from me and gave me the crowbar. "Listen," he whispered. "What we need is stealth and surprise. We'll sneak in, grab Marie Claire, and sneak out. We'll be halfway to Canada before they know she's gone."

Out on the road a car screeched to a halt. It was a long hard screech that echoed around the grounds. We all turned to the main gate. Slowly it crept toward the gate, its headlights lighting up the path. We watched, mesmerized by the murmur of its engine. Was this more of them? But the car backed away and the grounds of the home grew dark. I was just about to say something when once again its tires screeched. We heard the car roaring back toward us. Suddenly it rammed the gates with an almighty crash!

Tommy held out his hand. "Or we can let everyone know we're here, the way Ice has just done."

The gates hung off their hinges while the Range Rover, steam pouring from its engine, stopped at the entrance. In all my young life I have never been so glad to see anyone! "Ice!"

Ice jumped out of the Range Rover and marched toward the main entrance, mumbling as he went. "Telling me what I can and can't do! Goddamn phonies!"

"Be careful, Ice!" said Tommy.

"They could be armed!" shouted Joey.

Without stopping, Ice gave the front door one hard kick. Then he kicked it again. Then stepping back he smashed it open with his shoulder. We followed him inside, and walking past a dozen children's drawings we entered a large lobby, stale with that school-dinner smell. There was a reception area with several computers, to the right of a wide wooden staircase, and there was a large open room on the left. The room was dark, lit only by what little moonlight came through its windows. And above the entrance were the words COMMON ROOM.

We heard the sound of feet on floorboards, and a young stocky man appeared at the top of the stairs. "They've rammed the gates, Mr. Joshua!" he shouted, and rushed down the stairs.

The guy wearing glasses followed, pulling on his bathrobe as he came. The blond woman came after him, and they stood at the bottom of the stairs staring at us in disbelief.

When Mr. Joshua got over the shock of us standing there, he looked angry. "Call the police, Ben!"

The stocky guy went behind the reception desk and picked up the phone.

"Go ahead. Call the police," said Joey. "Goddamn pedophiles."

Mr. Joshua looked absolutely bewildered. "What did you say?"

"You heard me."

"I heard you. But I don't understand."

"We're friends of Marie Claire's," said Tommy.

Mr. Joshua looked hurt. "Is that what she told you? And you came here with baseball bats?" He turned to the woman. "Do you believe this?"

"I don't care what she believes. I wanna see my sister!"

The woman came toward me. She had eyes as big and as blue as the Rat's. "I think I understand. You thought Marie Claire was in danger and you were frightened for her." She smiled. "She misses you, that's all. I think she was scared she wouldn't see you again. You're Bob, right?"

I never said anything. She touched my shoulder. "I have three girls of my own, Bob. I would never allow anyone to harm a child!"

Mr. Joshua looked at the woman. "This is the girl who was brought in last night? She spent the whole day running around. And then she taught the smaller kids how to play soccer. I've never seen a happier kid!"

"No," said the woman. "I think she was a little sad toward the end of the day. Is that when she called you?"

I looked at Mr. Joshua's hand. What we had thought was a gun was an old-fashioned phone. But the Rat had got us so wound up.

The woman smiled warmly. "Don't worry," she said. "I've worked in childcare for fifteen years and I know a good kid when I see one. She must have gotten lonely, that's all."

Could the Rat have made up the whole thing? The woman seemed really nice. And I couldn't imagine these guys hurting kids. I didn't know what to believe.

I turned to Ice and Joey. Ice looked embarrassed and Joey was edging toward the door. It was like they'd already made up their minds.

But when I turned to Tommy he didn't look happy. "Can we see her?" he asked.

The woman frowned. "Well, the children are in bed now." Then she thought about it. "I know. Why don't you come back in the morning? You can have breakfast with her if you like. And then we can sort things out."

"What shall I do, Mr. Joshua?" said the stocky guy from behind the reception desk. He still had the phone in his hand.

The woman looked at Mr. Joshua. "I don't think we want the police here this time of night. Do we?"

Mr. Joshua looked undecided. "What about the gate? It's going to need repairing."

"I'll pay for it," said Ice.

"We might not see you again. You might not even have the money."

The young stocky guy came from behind the reception desk. "I think he's good for it, Mr. Joshua. Right, Ice?"

Mr. Joshua looked more amazed. "Ben, you know this guy?"

"This is Ice, the rap star. Love your music, Ice." Ben shook hands heartily. "If you're coming for breakfast, Ice, you could sign some autographs for the kids."

"I'd be more impressed if he'd sign a check for the gate."

"Sure, he will," said Ben.

"Okay," said Mr. Joshua. "As long as he comes back in the morning there'll be no need to call the police. But if you don't turn up—"

"I'll be here. First thing."

"When you come tomorrow don't be too hard on her," said the woman. "She's so young."

And so that was it. We all started heading toward the entrance. Ice looked like he couldn't wait to get away. I couldn't blame him after what the Rat had done. I'd punch her in her pointy ears when I saw her. But as we neared the door I started to feel bad. I didn't want to leave her there. And I knew she'd want to see me. And she wasn't a liar, not really. And she'd never told a lie as big as that. No. I wanna see my sister! Even if they have to wake her up. I turned to Tommy.

As I did so, Mr. Joshua looked in the Common Room. It happened so quickly but I thought I saw him wink. I tried to see inside but it was too dark. But the moon must have moved from behind a cloud because the room became brighter. And there, lurking by the window, was the silhouette of a man.

"Tommy."

"I see him," said Tommy. "Come out of there," he shouted.

There was a short pause and a guy came out of the darkness. He was pale and wide-eyed, and he was shaking like a junkie. Then I saw the glow of a cigarette light up someone's lips. "There's someone else in there!" I said. "They're sitting in a chair."

"Come on out," said Joey.

But whoever it was just calmly smoked their cigarette.

"Who is that?" said Tommy.

Mr. Joshua looked at the floor. "I don't know."

Tommy looked amazed. "You run this place and you don't know who that is?"

Joey looked angry. "What the hell's going on here?"

I looked at the woman. She stared at me with this cold blank stare. Then I turned to see Ben with his back to a wall. His fists were clenched like he was ready to fight.

The rage took my breath away at first. Then I found my voice. "Where's my goddamn sister?" I screamed.

Before I knew it Ice had pulled two silver Berettas from their side holsters. He aimed them at Mr. Joshua. "Tell him. Or you won't believe what happens next!"

The life drained from Mr. Joshua's face and he swallowed hard. "I'm sorry, but she ran away," he said almost choking on his words. "I didn't want to tell you in case you got upset."

"You honestly expect us to believe that?" said Tommy.

I turned to Ice. "She's here, Ice. I know she is."

Ice cocked the Berettas. Once again he aimed the guns at Mr. Joshua. "Where is she?"

He looked scared but he tried to smile. "You're not going to shoot."

"Don't be so sure!" said Ice. Then he aimed his guns at the junkie. "Where is she?"

"Think about the consequences, Ice," said the woman in a harsh tone. "If that gun goes off you could be looking at life."

"I won't ask you again!" said Ice.

The junkie's shaking got worse.

Ice's face hardened. There was a loud bang and a bullet exploded in the banister. The junkie cried out and covered his head.

The woman cringed and covered her ears. Mr. Joshua looked faint. And when I turned to see Ben, his hands were almost raised.

"We didn't do anything to her," said the woman lowering her hands. "She caused trouble and so we locked her in a closet. That's all."

I felt so relieved, my eyes closed. If the Rat had caused trouble, she must be okay. And if she was locked in a closet, she was out of harm's way.

"Okay," said Mr. Joshua, breathing heavily. "She's upstairs. You can take her. We'll just say she ran away."

Ice glared at Mr. Joshua. "If she's been hurt, there'll be hell to pay! And you're the one who'll pay it! Go get her, boys."

"I'll call the cops," said Joey.

Tommy followed me up the stairs. But he stopped by Mr. Joshua, who was staring shamefaced at the floor. "I don't like you!" he said showing him the baseball bat. "And if she's not up there, I'm going to like you a lot less!" He followed me up the stairs, which led into two separate wings. "You go that way, Bob, and I'll go this. Shout if you need me."

I shook with fear and rage as I walked down the corridor. My palms were sweating but I raised the crowbar and opened the first door I came to. The room was empty. I opened another—that was empty too. But when I opened the third door there were all these little kids standing in the dark. They were fully dressed, some of them holding small suitcases. They looked really scared.

"Is Ice here?" asked a little girl. "Marie Claire said Ice was coming to rescue us!"

"He's here! Go down the stairs, he's waiting!" They ran down the corridor toward the stairs. I opened another door and there were more little kids dressed and ready to go. "Quick, down the stairs!" I said. Before I got to the next door, the kids were coming out.

Then I heard someone banging and kicking at the far end of the corridor. I ran toward the door it was coming from. "Is that you?"

"What kept you, brother?" shouted the Rat from the other side.

I slotted the crowbar into the door and pushed. But it wouldn't budge.

"Come on, Bob! You're taking all bleeping day!"

I moved the crowbar by the lock and pushed with all my strength. Suddenly it cracked open and there was the Rat. "Free at last!"

"Are you okay? Did they hurt you?"

"Are you kidding? I told them crooks I had friends downtown who were on their way. Then they took my cell and locked me in this goddamn closet!"

I laughed and went to hug her, but she pushed past me.

"Where are you going? Ice is here! We have to leave!"

"First we have to rescue Felicia."

I grabbed hold of her. "Felicia's dead! You know that!"

The Rat gave me a look. "There's more than one Felicia in the world, Bob." And then she ran off down the corridor.

I felt stupid then, and annoyed, and glad I never hugged her.

"Here," she said stopping at a door. "We'll have to break it in."

I pushed the crowbar into the door and we both pushed. But nothing happened. "Move," I said. I went back and, running at the door, I gave it one hard kick. It never opened, but it cracked around the lock. Sliding the crowbar into the crack I pushed. There was a crunching sound and the lock sprang off.

"My brother the burglar!" said the Rat. Then she ran in the room.

It was dark inside. I could hardly see anything. But I could hear her speaking softly: "Ice is here. He'll protect you now."

I knew Tommy was on the landing and Ice was downstairs, but I still felt shaky. "Come on, we have to go!"

When she came out she had her arm around a small, frizzy-haired black girl. "This is my brother Bob. He'll protect you as well."

The girl cringed as she looked up at me, as though wondering whether to trust me. And so I smiled at her and she sort of smiled back.

Tommy came toward us. "There she is! Marie Claire DeBillier!"

"It's okay, Felicia. He's with us," said the Rat. "Hey, Tommy!"

"Come on, kid. You can't dawdle on a jail break, let's go!"

We walked back down the corridor and went down the stairs. Ice had gathered Mr. Joshua and the rest of them in front of the reception. They stared up at us as we came down the stairs. Ice still had them covered with his Berettas but when Felicia saw them she froze.

"Don't look at them. It'll be okay," said the Rat. And we kept moving.

When Ice saw the Rat he looked relieved. "You okay, Marie Claire?"

"Sure, Ice. Thanks for coming."

"Who's this?" asked Ice. And trying to hide his guns he knelt in front of Felicia. But she wouldn't look at him. She only looked at the floor.

"This is Felicia, but she's not speaking because he hurt her!" shouted the Rat and pointed at Mr. Joshua.

Sweat was pouring down Mr. Joshua's face. He looked around like he wanted to run. Then he looked pleadingly into the Common Room.

Ice's face darkened. He never took his eyes off Mr. Joshua as he rose to his feet.

The woman started to cry, but no tears came from her eyes. "I swear I had nothing to do with it. You have to believe me!"

"You liar!" said the Rat and ran at her.

Me and Joey restrained the Rat while Ice raised his Berettas. "Bob, get your sister out of here. And take these kids with you!"

There was something sinister in Ice's voice. And in the way he glared at the four people he held at gunpoint. It was like he wanted a fight.

"Come on, Ice. Let's go," said Tommy. "I don't trust these reptiles."

"Leave it, Ice!" I said. It was an evil place. I didn't want to leave him there. But Ice gave us a look as cold as death.

"Leave!" he said. So we went.

When I released the Rat she was seething. "Goddamn pedophiles!" she said.

And, putting her arm around Felicia, she walked her outside.

"Come on, kids!" said Tommy, gathering the kids around him. "We'll take you somewhere safe."

I wanted to warn Ice again about the creep in the dark. But I knew he wouldn't listen. And so taking some of the kids by the hand I followed Tommy outside.

The lights from the home faded as we passed Ice's wrecked Range Rover. And so we moved in the moonlight like a silent herd. The only sound was our clothes swishing and our shoes tapping against the tarmac. But I was relieved now that we'd rescued the Rat. And I felt good about freeing the kids. "Come on, kids. Everything's gonna be okay."

As soon as I said it I felt uplifted. Everything really was going to be okay. But then a gunshot cracked the silence.

Some of the kids started to cry. Others took it to be a starting pistol. They dropped their suitcases and sprinted down the drive. I looked at the Rat. She looked at me. Tommy turned to me. He went to say something. But a horrific scream came from the home. Then there was a lot of shouting.

"Kill him!" someone shouted.

Then gunfire erupted like you wouldn't believe! Bright flashes lit up the doorways and windows, while the ground seemed to tremble with the noise. "Run!" shouted Tommy.

I grabbed the Rat and Felicia and we ran for the gate. Next thing I know, Joey was tearing past us. Ignoring the driveway, he ran on the lawn.

"Get to the car!" he shouted, his voice echoing around the grounds.

As we went through the gate, the kids scattered in different directions. Some of them ran into a small park but most of them disappeared down a side street. I looked over my shoulder. Tommy was gritting his teeth and straining with the pain. But he wasn't far behind. Up ahead the lights of the car came on. Joey opened the door. I jumped in the back with the Rat.

Tommy staggered toward us. "What happened?"

"Ice got shot and he went down!" said Joey.

"Ice!" said Felicia, and ran back to the home.

"No!" shouted Tommy. He slammed the car door. "Get Marie Claire out of here!"

"Tommy!" shouted the Rat, and tried to follow. I grabbed hold of her to stop her from getting out the car.

"No!" screamed thc Rat as the car screeched away.

And all the time we could hear gunfire coming from the home. They must have had Ice surrounded.

The home faded behind us. I fought to keep hold of the Rat. There was no way she was going back there. No way!

Twenty-One

Boy was I exhausted. I wished I could have slept more. I put on my jeans and T-shirt and stepped outside with the last night's mayhem running through my mind. And then I saw the Rat, or the silhouette of the Rat, playing soccer in a hazy sun. I sat heavily in a chair and squinted at the river. How could she play soccer after what had happened last night? She went to kick the ball but she missed. And it was so close, too. Then she stood back and tried again, but she fell on her butt.

I shielded my eyes. "Are you okay?"

Slowly she turned her head toward the trailer. She was saying something but I couldn't hear what it was. I stood up and walked toward her. She was straining to speak but no words came out.

I ran toward her. "What is it?" I helped her to her feet.

She gagged a little and then she spluttered it out. “Nothing. I’m okay.”

I put my arm through hers and walked her back to the trailer. “You look so pale!”

She looked up at me. “You don’t look so good yourself, Bob.”

She smiled, but she held my arm like she was holding on to life itself. I sat her in the sunshine and sat close by. She was a bit dazed and her eyes were slightly out of focus, but that wasn’t what worried me. She looked straight ahead in such a strange way. It was like she was watching something. All of a sudden I felt frightened. “What’s wrong with you?”

As close as I was, she had to look around to find me.

She laughed. “There’s nothing—wrong with me—Bab.”

But she spoke so slowly and she slurred her words like a drunk. “You’re freaking me out!” I shouted. “You better take it easy.”

Startled, she sat up and fought to refocus. “I’m okay, Bob, relax!” Then she rubbed the side of her head soothingly.

I felt bad then. “Sorry, I didn’t mean to shout. I was just worried.”

I heard the car before I saw it. Then Joey jumped out, holding up a stack of newspapers. “Ice, he’s not dead!” he shouted, and gave me half the stack. “He was hit three times but he’s still alive!”

The Rat jumped up. “I told you he was an angel! Isn’t that what I said? I knew he wasn’t dead, not really! You can't kill an angel! It's impossible! They're protected by the Great Spirit!"

"Don't excite yourself!" I told her. "You're not well!"

But she wouldn't listen. She looked up at the sky, and extending her arms, she spun as fast as she could. "I can see the whole universe! And—and I can see—I can see—" But then she hit the ground hard.

"You okay, MC?" asked Joey.

She sat up on her butt. "Shewa, Joe."

Joey laughed. But I was so angry. "I've got no sympathy for you! I told you not to overdo it." I gave her a look that told her to take it easy. Then, taking a seat, I turned my attention to the papers. I could hardly believe what had happened last night. And what was more bewildering was reading about it.

"What about Tommy?" I asked.

Joey pulled up a chair. "He got stabbed! How he managed to get stabbed in that gunfight I'll never know. But he's still alive. Listen to this: 'Bloodbath at Children's Home. The story coming out of the Don Children's Home is one of abuse. Allegedly, rap star the Iceman, who shot to fame with the release of his first CD *The Iceman Cometh*, arrived at the home to rescue his goddaughter. We can only speculate at what sparked it off, but a horrific gun battle followed. One employee from the home is dead. Two are seriously injured. The Iceman himself was shot three times.'"

I was so relieved that Ice and Tommy were going to be okay. And that being the case I felt excited at having been involved in a front-page story. Because, in many ways, it was our story: mine and the Rat's. I took the *Post* from the stack.

"The *Post* says his wounds are not fatal," I said. "And he's expected to make a full recovery. And it says, 'The police are still looking for a girl by the name of Marie Claire DeBillier. Unconfirmed reports say she organized the breakout, telling the other children to be ready, that the Iceman was on his way.'" I expected the Rat to be buzzing, but she didn't say anything.

"Listen to this," said Joey. "The FBI has taken over the case. All the staff from the Don Children's Home are being questioned over the disappearance of three girls who went missing last summer. Originally it was thought that they had run away. But now they are treating the case as suspicious—goddamn pedophiles! I should have picked up a gun and—"

Then I saw my name. "'Police are also looking for a Robert DeBillier, who is allegedly the brother of the missing girl.' How could they find out so soon?"

"Are you kidding?" said Joey. "I flicked through the channels in a diner this morning. It was on every single channel. And you should have seen the footage. The street outside that home looked like a police parking lot."

"They'll see it in Winnipeg. My phone!" I searched my pockets but it wasn't there. "I must have dropped it when we were running away."

"Now you know how they know," said Joey. "If the FBI is involved they'll have traced it back to you. And listen to this: 'Ice was accompanied by a man of Italian origin. He was stabbed several times in the scuffle while allegedly saving a girl from being kidnapped.'"

"You think that was Felicia?" I asked. But the Rat never answered.

"It is also rumored that he is the Iceman's bodyguard. I wonder where they got that from? But he did more than I did, that's for sure!" said Joey scanning the papers. "That's why there's no mention of me. God, I wish I had done more!"

"What happened back there?" I asked. "Ice had everything under control when we left."

"Oh man! That woman went to stab Ice and he shot her. Then someone shot at Ice from the top of the stairs. Then that big guy in the dark started blazing away. I can still see the flashes of gunfire lighting up his face. But you should have seen Ice. He never took a step back. Not even when he was reloading."

When I looked at the Rat she was still sitting on the ground. "You're lucky Tommy and Joey were here. I never would have found that place by myself."

She tried to smile, but her mouth twisted. She looked so strange.

"Way're heroes, brader. Way safed all de liddle kids."

Joey put the paper down. "You okay, MC?"

"Stop talking like that!" I said.

"I—I can't halp et, Bab!"

I knew then that the thing that had plagued her all these years had finally come for her.

"Dant lave may, Bab! I nade yo now!"

Standing slowly, I knelt in front of her. "You never have to worry about me leaving you, Marie Claire! Because you're my sister and I love you very much!" I put my arms around her.

I could feel her tears on my face. "Me brader luvs me! Me luvs hem!"

"Are you in pain?"

She shook her head. "Tiyerd need slip."

I picked her up and, holding her in my arms, I carried her into the trailer. Joey helped me. We laid her on the bed and wrapped some blankets around her. I put a chair next to the bed and took her hand. "I'll sit here with you until you fall asleep," I said, my voice breaking up. "And when you wake up, I'll take you to see a doctor!" She tried to speak but I shushed her. "Don't worry. I'll find a nice doctor, someone you'll like!"

The Old Man once told me: "The day may come, Bob, when she deteriorates." I had dreaded that day would ever come. But when I thought about it there was always me and him at the hospital. I never thought I would be by myself.

When her eyes closed I begged God for it to be a bad dream. I wasn't even sure I believed in God but I begged anyway.

As she slept, I sat there thinking about all the crazy things that had happened since we were little kids, like the time she'd nearly drowned in the Red River and I'd saved her. Or when I'd broken my foot and she'd ridden for help. We had always been there for each other. But now I felt powerless to help her.

I went outside. Joey put out his cigarette and stood up. "How often does she get like that, Bob?"

I wiped my eyes. "She's never had trouble speaking before. When she wakes up, I'm gonna take her to a hospital. But I'm not sure they'll be able to help her."

Joey held out a newspaper. "Maybe you can take her to your Uncle Jerome."

Beneath a picture of Ice was a picture of another man. His hair and eyes were dark and on his right cheek there was a small scar. I read the headline. "Will Exocome Pharmaceuticals Swallow Its Biggest Rival?" Then I saw the name that had haunted me since the day I'd heard it. "Exocome will become North America's third largest pharmaceutical company if its major shareholder and managing director Jerome DeBillier can pull off the biggest deal of his life. In less than ten years DeBillier has taken Exocome from being an overweight giant that lost money to a lean profit-making global enterprise. Its biggest rival, the Hughes Corporation, located in Canada, is up for grabs after a shaky start to the year. And DeBillier is looking to pounce. The major players from each company will meet this evening at the Exocome Building. The meeting is expected to go on until late into the night."

Joey looked amazed. "Is there ever a dull moment around you kids?" He almost laughed. "Jerome the drug dealer turns out to own a pharmaceutical company!"

I could hardly believe it myself. But there he was. After all our searching we'd stumbled across him in a newspaper. If it had been yesterday morning I would have jumped for joy. But now I couldn't care less. There was even a part of me that felt bitter about it. But Uncle Jerome would have money. The least he could do was find my sister a doctor.

"Where's the Exocome Building?"

"It's not far from Central Park—56th or 57th, somewhere around there."

"I'm going to take her to him."

Joey put his hand on my shoulder. "Not without me you're not. I'm with you, Bob. All the way to the end."

I waited until dark before waking her. I'd never known her to sleep for so long, or so deeply. But I had to wake her. I couldn't take the chance of the meeting being over. I put the light on, so she could see where she was, and then I pushed her gently. "We've found Uncle Jerome and we're taking you to him. I think he's going to be very pleased to see you. And, it's okay, he's not a drug dealer, not really." She looked dazed. I wasn't sure she understood. I helped her sit up. Then I gave her a hug, to let her know I was with her. "How are you? Are you feeling okay?" But she never answered, or couldn't.

"How's Marie Claire?" asked Joey coming in the trailer.

"She doesn't feel like talking yet, Joe."

"That's okay. Whenever she's ready. Whenever you're ready, Marie Claire. But for now shall we go see your new uncle?"

I put her jacket on her, because she was shivering, and we walked her out to the car. I helped her into the back seat and sat beside her.

"Just a short ride, Marie Claire," said Joey. "We'll soon be there."

We drove slowly down the dirt road, and getting back on to the main road, we drove slowly toward Manhattan. There was no rush now. He'd either accept us or he wouldn't.

But in my head I was praying that Uncle Jerome would be nice the way his brother was. I was praying he'd look after me and my sister and make her well again. If he didn't want us they'd put us in a home. And now that she was getting worse they'd definitely put her somewhere different. I wouldn't let that happen! I couldn't! If he wouldn't take us both I would ask him to take my sister. At least she would be with family.

We passed some Hispanic guys standing on the corner, just like they were that first day in the Bronx. That was the day I took my anger out on Marie Claire because I was frightened and didn't want to admit it. I looked at her, and kissing her on the head I held her a little tighter. We crossed a bridge, and heading into Manhattan, we made our way through Harlem. We passed the Starbucks where the girl liked me. She was a nice girl and she looked like Gabriela. I thought about Gabriela and wondered if she thought about me.

We rounded the park, and I looked over toward the swimming pool where we got showered. We were happy then. It seemed like such a long time ago. I thought about Erwin who had offered to put us up, but only for a few nights. I liked Erwin. I hoped he was sleeping somewhere safe.

When we got to Fifth Avenue there wasn't much traffic. We were soon passing the den, and Ice's apartment, and the spot where I shouted at Ice for calling our dad dumb. He hadn't meant it. He'd been upset. And now he was in hospital recovering from his wounds. I wondered if they put him in a bed next to Tommy.

When we neared the end of the park Joey drove off Fifth Avenue and parked down a side street. Then he turned around and looked at us. "Ready?"

I got out of the car. "Come on, Marie Claire." She never moved, so I reached in and took her hand. She looked exhausted, the way she did after she'd had a fit. "It's going to be okay." She came out, and putting my arm around her, I closed the door. Joey put his arm around her too, and we went to look for the Exocome building.

We soon found it, and walking past a group of cops and a large chunk of granite with the words EXOCOME CORPORATION written on it, we climbed the steps. We walked through the revolving doors and headed toward a reception desk, our feet echoing around the deserted foyer. A security guard stood at the desk. He was a large man with a black moustache, and he watched us as we came.

"Where can we find Jerome DeBillier?" asked Joey.

"You could find him in the meeting on the top floor if you were going up there, but you're not."

"We really need to see him. It's important."

"Believe me, it's not as important as the meeting that's taking place. Now, why don't you kids run along?"

"These are his brother's children. His brother is dead. We really need to see him!"

"I've heard it all before. Next thing you know the little girl will need money for an operation or you'll need ten thousand dollars to get back on your feet. You think I don't know hustlers when I see them?"

"Bob, you want to give us a minute?"

I took Marie Claire's arm and we walked over by the door. But I could still hear them.

"Look, buddy, no one's on the hustle here. I swear to you those kids are his niece and his nephew. Marie Claire doesn't need an operation but she's not well!"

"Then take her to a doctor. What are you bringing her here for?"

"Because their uncle's got money. He can get her the help that she needs."

The security guard looked smug. "I knew you were here for money. The second I saw you."

"No! Look! Why don't you call him and ask him to come down?"

"I'll tell you why. Because I've worked for Mr. DeBillier for five years and I've never heard of him having a brother. But let's say they are his niece and nephew. He might not want to see them. So you call his secretary in the morning and work it out with her. Conversation over!"

Joey came back toward me looking downcast. "I don't know what to do, Bob."

"Ah!" Marie Claire's face cringed with pain.

I put my arms around her. "It's okay. I'm here!"

Joey's face hardened. "To hell with him! We're going in, Bob! Even if we have to fight our way in!"

We got on either side of my sister and walked toward the security guard.

"We're going up to see Mr. DeBillier," said Joey. "Don't try and stop us."

The security guard came from behind his desk. He looked amused. "Kid, I'm twice your size."

"You got a gun?"

The security guard stopped. "No."

Joey pulled a gun from his waistband. "Well, I do!"

The shock hit me. Then I got a very bad feeling. But when I thought about Marie Claire I didn't care.

The guard raised his hands. "You see them cops out there? How close to Mr. DeBillier do you think you'll get?"

"Close enough to get this mess sorted out. Now put your hands down and take a seat—now stay that way. Come on, kids."

The alarm bells were ringing in my head as we walked toward the elevator. But then they rang for real. The noise hurt my ears and made my heart shudder. They were so loud you could hear them in Winnipeg.

"Run!" shouted Joey.

I ran toward two rows of elevators and pushed a button so hard my finger hurt. I looked back to see the security guard running for cover. "He's got a gun!" he shouted.

"Who was he talking to?" I said.

But Joey never heard me. He tapped a button and looked up at the numbers. Then he kicked the door. "Come on, for God's sake!"

An elevator opened behind me. I grabbed my sister's hand. But I heard someone shout. I turned to see a cop standing on the other side of the elevators. He was glaring at us down the sight of his gun.

"Drop your weapon!" he shouted.

He was tall and mean-looking and his blue eyes looked fierce below his peaked cap. I was so frightened I felt faint.

"It's just a toy," said Joey and threw it away.

"Get your hands in the air!" he shouted.

Me and Joey raised our hands.

"You. Get your hands in the air!"

"She can't!" I shouted.

Joey gave me a look. Then he indicated the elevators. I grabbed my sister and dragged her inside.

"Don't move!" shouted the cop.

I heard a crack as Joey rushed into the elevator. I tapped desperately on the top button. The cop edged his way into view. But the doors closed and the sound of the alarms faded. Joey slid down in a corner. His chest was bleeding.

I held my head in my hands. "Oh no!"

The color drained from Joey's face as rapidly as the elevator was rising. Tears came into his eyes and dark patches appeared below them. "I'm frightened, kids!"

Marie Claire knelt down in front of him. She put her arms around his neck and gave him a hug.

"What would I do without you, MC?" His head flopped to one side and he fell unconscious. I helped my sister to her feet. There was blood on her shirt. I turned her toward me. It was Joey's blood.

The elevator chimed.

He'd done so much for us. And he looked so helpless. But I knew we had to leave him. "Come on! The cops will take care of him!"

We stepped out on to the top floor with the alarm bells blasting. There was a sign saying EXECUTIVE BOARDROOM and an arrow pointing down a long corridor lined with plaques and photographs. At the end I saw an opening.

"Come on," I said.

But she didn't move. She leaned against a wall, holding her head with her hand. Then I saw the numbers above one of the elevators were glowing red and rising. I went to help her but she backed away.

I was desperate for her to come with me but I didn't want to force her. "Please. The cops are coming. We have to go."

She bit down with the pain and then struggled to force the words out. "Am not gong ta make it, Bab—But yo aways be ma brader!"

I threw my arms around her. "You are going to make it. You have to!" I felt like crying, but I didn't. I put her arm around my neck and walked her down the corridor.

By the time we reached the end I was almost carrying her.

We came to a wide area with a water fountain in its center. There was a woman behind a reception desk shouting into a phone. "Security? What's happening? Do we have to evacuate the building?—what? I can't hear you!" Then she saw us. "Security, do you know there are children up here? One of them looks hurt!"

I saw a set of double doors with a sign saying BOARDROOM above it. I passed the reception desk and headed toward it.

The receptionist came after us. "No, you can't go in there! If she's hurt bring her to me!"

As I turned, a couple of cops came out an elevator. They came quickly down the corridor with their guns out.

"Hey!" One of them called. And then they ran toward us.

I supported my sister, and charging toward the doors, I burst in. There were a dozen people standing or sitting around a long table. Some gathered their belongings ready to leave. One guy was shouting above the alarms.

"Everyone stay calm. There's no need to panic!" But he panicked when he saw me and my sister, and the blood on her shirt. "Oh my God!"

At the other end of the room sat a large man with thick black hair. He was looking at a file while drumming his fingers on the table. I sat Marie Claire in a chair and ran toward him. One woman clutched her bag. A guy went to grab me but I pushed him away. I tripped over something. I got up and ran in front of him. "Uncle Jerome!" When the man looked up I saw the scar on his cheek.

Then the boardroom doors blew open and the cops burst in. There was a lot of shouting and commotion. Everyone was trying to calm everyone else down. Then the cop that shot Joey saw me. "There he is!" They came toward me on either side of the table. The other one, a big, broad, cop aimed his gun at me. "Don't move, kid!"

A man and a woman ducked for cover.

I looked at Uncle Jerome. "My name's—I'm your—"

Uncle Jerome sat back in his seat. He looked bewildered. I couldn't find the words. I took a deep breath.

"Jerome DeBillier! You're our uncle!" I shouted. "John—your brother—our father—is dead! If you don't want to take us both then please take Marie Claire! Because she's not well!"

Uncle Jerome looked from me to Marie Claire like we'd fallen from the sky. "You're John's kids?"

A cop grabbed my arm aggressively. He shoved it up my back and took out his handcuffs. I was crying. "Don't let them separate us! You're our uncle! You have to stand up for us!"

And stand up he did.

"Take your hands off him! That's my nephew! And put those guns away!"

The cops did as they were told. More cops and security came in the room. There was more shouting. Uncle Jerome stood on a chair. "There is no need to panic! These children are my niece and nephew!" he shouted. "Now I want everyone to keep quiet!" Suddenly the alarms stopped and everyone stopped talking. "Now everyone stay quiet while I sort things out!"

It was silent except for some commotion. My uncle looked for the person who had not obeyed his command. When a group of people cleared from his line of vision I saw Marie Claire on the floor. She wasn't moving. "Call an ambulance!" I shouted. I ran toward her and took her hand. "I'm with you, and you're going to be okay! Call an ambulance!"

Twenty-Two

And that was, as they say, a long, long time ago. I'm sixteen, now, and six feet tall. And I've really broadened out. I live with my Uncle Jerome, who has become my legal guardian. We move between his house in the Hamptons and his place downtown. Sometimes we stay at his apartment on Fifth Avenue, the apartment we had searched for but could never find. Uncle Jerome used to have me attend a private school, one of the best in New York. But now I come here to the Marymount Manhattan College, just a short walk from where we live. I like living in New York; it's become a second home, but I still miss Winnipeg.

Anyway, my classes are finished for the day, and so is my writing, and now I have to go to New Jersey.

I leave the library as quietly as I can and head to the main entrance. Students are stomping snow off their feet as they come into the building. New York never gets as cold as Winnipeg, but it's making a real effort this winter. And so I wrap up warm before going outside.

"Hi, Bob!"

I turn to see Ashley going into class. "Hey, Ashley!" She makes that sign with her fingers telling me to call her and, smiling, she drifts away. I will call her too. She's the prettiest girl in Harlem. We had a dinner date there last week. She took me to this soul food place on 125th Street. I thought it was low-rent at first because it was so rundown and they microwave the meals. But the food tasted so good you'd never know it. And the people who ran the place were really nice. I'm going to take her somewhere next week, but where I don't know.

I can't get a cab on Third Avenue now that the snow is coming down, so I walk over to Fifth to see if I can do any better. I throw some nuts to the squirrels scavenging in Central Park and then I look around me. I'm not far from the old den. It seems like a dream, now, that me and the Rat had once lived in the park. But a lot of things seem like a dream from around that time, like Joey getting shot.

I thought he'd definitely die, but he was out of the hospital in a matter of weeks. The cops never brought charges against him as long as he never brought charges against them. And that was the end of it as far as all parties were concerned. He went to live with Sexy

Sandra in Queens. He said he was only staying until his wound healed. But now they have a girl named Sydney, and another one on the way. They're even talking about getting married and moving to Venezuela, where Sandra is originally from. But I hope they don't; I'd miss them if they went.

A cab whizzes by without stopping. I can't stand that. It didn't even have anyone in it! I blow into my hands to warm them up, and then I look at my watch. I'm already late. I want to be there and gone before Uncle Jerome arrives. He can be stern in many ways. But he can be kind too. For example, he had his lawyers exhume Dad's body, when he found out we'd buried him without an autopsy—turns out Dad died of a heart attack—then he had him reburied, in the same spot, with Father Henri performing the burial rites. He also ordered a beautifully sculptured angel from Paris and had it placed over Dad's grave. I know all this happened because Harold kept me informed by e-mail. I was angry that Uncle Jerome never told me about the service. I was even more angry when I found out he had gone. But Uncle Jerome can be quite secretive.

The second cab I flag down stops, and I get in the back, glad to be in the warmth. "Take me to New Jersey."

When I first heard they were charging Ice with murder I could hardly believe it. Ice was up on one count of murder, two counts of attempted murder, and countless other charges. They were even charging him with driving recklessly. One count of murder and driving recklessly. They didn't go together, not unless you ran your victim down.

Ice's lawyers postponed the trial on more than one occasion, mainly because the pedophiles at the Don Children's Home gave up so many of their so-called friends. And they, in turn, would give up their friends. What's more, the FBI scoured the country for the three girls who had gone missing from the home. And in doing so they uncovered a pedophile network that had tentacles across the country. They started arresting pedophiles from New York to Miami and as far west as San Francisco. They were even charging pedophiles who had committed crimes twenty years earlier. No one was walking away from this one. The last I heard they'd arrested fifty of these criminals, and they were charging more everyday. And that's why they kept postponing the trial, so it would go better for Ice. But when the FBI found the bodies of the three girls they were looking for, the lawyers postponed the trial no longer.

I watch a bicycle courier in bright gear riding up Fifth Avenue the wrong way. He ignores the horns of the frustrated drivers. He even gives some of them the finger. He brings back memories of our great journey on our BMXs. I've only ridden a bike once since we gave ours to Big Frank. But I have to say it wasn't the same riding by myself.

The trial was televised and the circus was soon underway. The media wanted to talk to everyone we'd met in New York, and there was no shortage of people coming forward. They spoke to Sean and Connor, who told them how we'd been chased that night. And how they'd chased the guy who had chased us, but he got away. They talked to people in the Bronx who told them how we'd searched for our uncle in the pouring rain. It was amazing how many of them remembered us. Even the likes of Tall Tony and the bald guy he was fighting with, who both wanted to know if there was a reward or any chance of bail. Al the butcher told them if we had come back five minutes later he would have told us who our uncle was.

They talked to Karl the chauffeur, the guys him and Ice were fighting with, and the media people at the Marriott. They talked to the cops who turned up at the Exocome Building, the security guard, and Sonny, Tommy's tattooed friend. The only person they didn't speak to was Big Frank, who threatened them with physical violence.

I turned on the TV one time and they were showing dozens of clips of me and Marie Claire captured on the security video. I couldn't believe how many cameras we were on. When I changed the channel they were talking to Erwin. How they found Erwin I'll never know, but they did. He told them that white kids could get away with anything, but we weren't so bad. And we could still come over if we wanted. That's when they found out we had slept in the park. They took pictures of our den and put them with their stories.

The cab passes Rockefeller Center. I still have the photographs I took there that summer. I keep them in an album under my bed but I enlarged the one of the Rat holding up the world like Atlas. I framed it and put it on my wall. It's a great photograph, even Uncle Jerome made a copy.

The worst thing about going to court was seeing Ice handcuffed. They never gave him bail because they said he was a flight risk, and so every day they'd bring him out in handcuffs. It was so sickening to hear those slimeballs from the Children's home give evidence against him, and the lies they told! The child care worker, the woman who Ice shot, told the court that Ice went insane. "He's a gun-crazy killer! We tried to calm him down, but he started shooting at us for no reason!" And the prosecution went along with it. They were trying to paint Ice as a vigilante. If there's one thing the court hates, it's someone taking the law into their own hands.

The cab swerves on the corner and cuts across to the West Side. I move back to where I'd been sitting. Riding in New York cabs can be a life-threatening experience. But they usually get you there in one piece.

I enjoyed going to court only once. That was when Tommy took the stand. He looked so smart in his new suit, and he was a big hero to everyone. You see, when Ice went down that night, he kept up the fight from the floor. That was the gunfire we could hear. But when Tommy ran into the home, Ice was out of bullets. That creep had come out of the dark by then. He was just about to stab Ice when Tommy jumped on him. He fought with the man, a monster twice his size, and got stabbed in his stomach for his trouble. Then the jerk tried to leave and take Felicia with him. But Tommy wasn't having any of it. He got up off the floor and fought like a lion until the creep had let her go. Then he chased him outside.

The cops searched with a vengeance for him, and anyone else who had worked at the home, especially Mr. Joshua. One day they found him. He had been shot in the back of the head and his body had been dumped in a dumpster. A woman journalist asked me, did I think Uncle Jerome was involved? "He has the contacts," she said. I could never imagine him killing anyone, not like that, but I never looked at him the same way again.

Tommy gave dozens of TV interviews and the *New Yorker* did a piece on him. "From Hustler to Hero," they called it. What's more, when Tommy turned up at court he was accompanied by his ex-wife and three daughters, who came along to offer their support. Not that he needed it. He defended Ice with all the cunning of a seasoned attorney. He answered the questions clearly and stated his points with precision. When the prosecution asked him, "Was it not Ice's intention to commit murder when he learned that the girl Felicia Johnston had been abused?" Tommy grew cold. "Murder! How can you use that word? Sir, it is a dishonor to our legal system that this man should be charged with anything!

Ice defended innocent children from evil men without any thought for his own life! What is wrong with our society that we punish the brave? And yet we cower to creatures like those!" shouted Tommy pointing at the pedophiles. The people in the court rose to their feet and applauded. The prosecutor was seething, but he sat down. "No more questions," he said.

The cab passes Times Square, where the Rat and Tommy had performed, and heads toward the Hudson River, where we had almost taken a ferry ride. Then we swerve hard and drive alongside the river, which is so misty with snow you can't see New Jersey.

I never stopped getting messages and e-mails from Winnipeg throughout the trial. Everyone offered their support: Little Joe and Harold and all my old classmates. They all stood by me. Even the Mayor of Winnipeg wrote and asked if there was anything he could do. So I suppose he was a bit of a celebrity after all.

But the night before I was to testify, I felt nervous. I wanted to tell the truth, and I wanted those goddamn pedophiles to pay for what they'd done! But I never wanted to say anything that would harm Ice's defense. And I'd seen the prosecutor put Joey under pressure. He was like the Prince of Darkness in the courtroom, and the thought of facing him frightened me.

I went to bed early that night hoping to sleep, but I just lay there worrying. Then the phone rang. "Is that you, Roberto?" If I ever needed to hear the voice of an angel it was then! Whether it was the joy of Gabriela calling me, or the stress of having to give evidence, I almost cried. Thank God, I didn't. But I told her how bad I was feeling and how worried I was, and, like an angel, she listened.

"You have to be brave, Roberto! I'll tell you what. When the time comes for you to take the stand, remember, I'll be watching. It will be like I'm there with you."

I talked to her for ages. I told her I thought she was the best teacher that Luxton ever had and that I liked her more than any girl I had ever met. She never laughed or anything. She said I was a nice boy and she was glad I was safe and well. She said she would pray for me and told me to get a good night's sleep, and so that's what I did.

The flashbulbs started flashing as soon I walked out of Uncle Jerome's apartment the next morning. They continued when I stepped from the limousine, and they followed me up the courthouse steps. Uncle Jerome and his security pushed the media out of the way, so it wasn't too bad. But other people came forward as well. Some of them patted me on the back, while some of them asked for my autograph. Why? I don't know.

Ice's defense lawyer, Amber, was a redheaded woman with a serious frown. She asked me the same questions we had rehearsed in her office. It went really well, I thought, but then the Prince of Darkness stood up. He glared at me like the whole thing was my fault. I was so nervous my hands started to shake. But when I thought about Gabriela watching me, it gave me courage. He asked me a few trivial questions, and then he got serious.

"On the night that Ice broke into the home, the resident child care worker, a Ms. Hanes, was pleading with him. Is that not correct?"

"Yes."

"Tell me, what did she say to Ice?"

"She said she had nothing to do with it."

The Prince of Darkness turned to the jury. "But he shot her anyway!"

"She tried to stab Ice! He had no choice!"

"Hearsay, your honor! Move to strike!"

The judge looked at me. "Just answer the questions you're asked, son. Strike that from the record." Then he asked the jury to disregard my last remark. But I don't think they did disregard it. I really don't.

I spent the whole day giving evidence. We broke at noon and I was recalled to the stand after lunch. I can't remember half the questions they asked me. I can only remember how relieved I was when it was over. Ice's defense team said I did a good job, and I should be proud. Then Ice and all the lawyers went into the judge's chambers. Everyone seemed to be on Ice's side. I thought they would let him go.

All of a sudden the judge and the lawyers came back. Everything became tense. The word went around the courtroom that Ice had taken a plea bargain. Thanking the jury for their time and diligence, the judge dismissed them. He recommended that the Don Children's Home be closed down and that it should never be reopened. He commended me and the other witnesses for giving evidence, and he ordered the remaining pedophiles to be taken back to prison. He said that Ice was a brave and decent man who had stood up for children who could not stand up for themselves. But he had gone too far, and that no citizen should be allowed to take the law into their own hands.

He sentenced Ice to six years in prison. I turned to Amber. "Six years! What sort of bargain is that?" She told me that it was my testimony that helped secure Ice such a lenient sentence. She said it was part of the agreement that Ice would be eligible for parole in three years, and that he was being sent to a minimum security prison. Ice's defense team looked happy; even Ice looked relieved. He gave me the thumbs-up. But I still felt sick when they took him away.

"Backup ahead," says the cabbie. I wipe the steamy window and look out. There always seems to be traffic around the Lincoln Tunnel. But today there are traffic cops and a crashed car and a guy on a cell phone. As we crawl past him, I see his face. He reminds me of Tommy.

Tommy made a lot of money from his new celebrity status, and so in the end his boat really did come in. He sailed it all the way back to Sicily where he bought a small farm by the ocean. He produced olive oil and he was so successful within the first year of business that he asked his wife to come out and help him run things.

One of his daughters followed the following year, and now it's a family business. A bottle arrived the other day with the words "Mattolla's Sicilian Olive Oil" written on the box. And there was a photograph of Tommy wading through turquoise water. He looked so happy I couldn't help but laugh.

The cab picks up pace and we come out of the tunnel. "'Bout time!" says the cabbie. I'm always glad when we get to the other side of the Lincoln Tunnel. No more backups, not until we're coming back into the city. The cab climbs the same spiraling roadway we had climbed the night we rescued the Rat. Normally I get a great view of the city, but not today. The snow is coming down so thick there's not much to see.

I visit Ice every couple of months. It's funny, because he seems happier in prison than he was in his penthouse. The last time I went, he was ecstatic. He'd just become prison chess champion. I was amazed. How could a man who'd won so many awards for his music be satisfied winning a silver cup? But he was. He even told me that jail was a nice break from the insanity of the outside world. He'll have to get used to it when he gets out; the sales of his CDs have tripled.

Within thirty minutes we roll off the turnpike and pull up outside St. Vincent's Psychiatric Hospital. Howard, the security guard, raises the barrier and gives me a short wave as the cab passes through. It's a nice place. It has a great grassy lawn that surrounds the main building. There are cherry trees surrounding the lawn and pine trees surrounding the cherry trees. It looks like a well-kept park in the summertime, and just as nice now that it's covered in snow.

It's not a psychiatric hospital, not really, because the patients pay a lot of money to come here, or someone pays for them. They even have celebrities stay here. But I'm not allowed to say who they are, and so I won't. Besides, everyone has a right to privacy, especially if they are recuperating from an illness, or something.

I pay the driver, and heading into the reception, I check the register. I sign in, glad that I can't see Uncle Jerome's name, and then I head down the west-wing corridor. As I do, a nurse named Nina comes toward me. "If you're going to take her out, Bob, make sure you're not long. Mr. DeBillier will be coming this evening."

"I'm a Mr. DeBillier as well. Doesn't that count for anything?"

She gave me a big smile. "In my opinion it does."

She's nice, Nina, and I think she likes me. I want to look back at her, but there are more nurses coming toward me and they have patients with them. I keep going until I come to the last door on the left-hand side, and then I give it a gentle knock. And there, sitting by the window is my little sister Marie Claire DeBillier.

"Hey, sis!" I kiss her on the top of her head and kneel down in front of her. "You want to go for a walk? It's a bit cold out there. But it's nothing to a couple of Winnipeggers like us." I coax her to stand up, and putting on her coat, I fasten the buttons. "Look at you. You're nearly fourteen and I'm still helping you get dressed." I look in her vacant eyes and pull her hair out from her collar. "I'm doing well at my new college. I've joined the drama club and my writing is coming along. Uncle Jerome wants me to study hard. He's determined that I go to a good graduate school. I don't know why he never went. What else? Oh yeah, my driving lessons are going well. Soon I'll be able to drive you all the way home."

As I put my scarf around her I give her a hug. I can't help it. I never gave her enough hugs when we were kids. I suppose I found it embarrassing. But I try and make up for it now. And I'm sure she appreciates it in her own way. "Come on then, let's go." Linking my arm through hers, I escort her down the corridor.

"You should see the way that Nina looks at me. I think she has the hots for me. A lot of girls look at me these days. What do you say, sis? You think your big brother's a babe magnet or what?" But she doesn't say anything. She's never said a word since the night she collapsed. Most of the time she doesn't even know you're there.

Uncle Jerome has had specialists fly in from all over the world. So many specialists and they all say the same thing: She's had a psychological shock. She needs rest and tranquility. And then only time will tell. One doctor recommended electric shock treatment. Uncle Jerome threw him out of his office.

I think Marie Claire should come off the medication and return to Winnipeg, or at least live at home with us. She might start to remember the good times and who she was. I've said this to Uncle Jerome a thousand times, and we argue about it quite a bit, but he won't listen. Uncle Jerome is a stubborn, arrogant man. But don't let me give you the wrong impression. He comes here every chance he gets. And when he does, he sits and reads to her for hours. Kids' stories mainly. Stories of knights who fight evil goblins to save the princess, of lowly knaves who fall on the battlefield, or who live to become heroes, and there's always the boy who remains to tell the story. He reads stories with happy endings. But in the real world you don't always get a happy ending, no matter how much you want one. Anyway, I can see he loves her, but that doesn't make him right.

Outside, we walk down the path toward our favorite bench. The cold wind blows snow into our eyes and it sticks to our coats, but I like to get her out into the fresh air. They always have the heat on too high in the hospital, and it gets really stuffy. I brush the snow off the bench and, sitting her down, I put my arm around her. "Ice will be out soon. You remember Ice, don't you? And Joey asks about you all the time. And I'm always getting letters and e-mails from Winnipeg. No one's forgotten you. And Father Henri has mass said for you twice a year. And Ms. Mountshaft is putting on a play and dedicating it to you. Do you remember you were in a play? Do you remember you wanted to be a ballerina and an actress?"

She doesn't respond; she never responds. But I've often seen her facial expressions change. It's like she's listening to someone tell her a story. Sometimes she almost smiles and looks happy. Other times her face clouds over and she looks scared. But something always soothes her, because her bad spells never last that long. I asked one of the doctors what it was. He said she had separated herself from reality and found her own little world. She never was realistic, but I hope she's happy wherever she is.

I dream about her sometimes. I dream I'm at the top of a tall building and opposite me is a skyscraper with angels hovering around it. They're sunning themselves in the silver sunlight or gliding from one skyscraper to another. Then I see Marie Claire sitting with them. She has small wings on her back, and she's laughing. I bang on the glass as hard as I can but she can't hear me. So I rush down in the elevator and run toward the building. I search desperately for a door, but there isn't one. She's in a place I'm not allowed to go to.

"Christmas soon. Maybe this year you'll tell me what you want." I brush the snow from her coat. "You remember that old French love song Dad used to sing us? He used to sing that line about unhooking the moon. And you'd always tell him he got the translation wrong. And he'd always say, 'It doesn't matter. I'd do anything for you kids. I'd even unhook the moon.'" I turn her face toward me. "I know you're in there. I'll unhook the moon to get you to come back. They say you can't hear me but I know you can. You're just hibernating, that's all." I fix her collar to keep her warm.

"I have a letter here from Harold. I've read it to you before but I'll read it again." I pull the letter from my pocket.

"Dear Marie Claire,

I hope you are well and in good spirits. I am still studying at school but I have been promised a job at the train station when I graduate. It's not a difficult job and I get to sit down all day. I worked on your prairie garden over the summer to keep it in good condition for when you return. But now the winter is upon us. The plants are resting, ready to bloom again in the spring. One day you will bloom again because you are like a prairie plant. You are beautiful and you are tough. Bob said you are still not well, but when your winter is over you will return to us, hopefully before next summer. If not, I have spoken with my mother and Father Henri and we will soon have the money to take you to Lourdes in France, but we have to get your uncle's permission. I know he has the money to take you anywhere in the world. But we want to take you ourselves, because you are special to us. I pray for you every night and—"

"You should bring her in, Bob! It's getting cold!"

I turn to see Nina and two male nurses standing at the entryway.

"You want to go inside, Marie Claire? You don't have to if you don't want to. All you have to do is say no—okay, I'll take you in." I help her to her feet and escort her back to the entryway. "Next time I come, I'll sneak you in a mocha. I don't care what they say! Why they don't let you have coffee I'll never know. I'll bring you in a big cup of magic mocha, and who knows, it might make you well again."

Nina takes her from me, and putting her in a wheelchair, she wraps a blanket around her legs.

"Why do you do that? She's not an invalid! She can walk!"

"She can fall as well, Bob, hospital policy."

I always feel bad when the visit is over. On the way here I'm always a little optimistic. This could be the day she talks. This could be the day I say something that sparks something in her mind, and she comes back. But it never happens. I kiss her on the head. "I'll see you in a few days, my sister."

Nina doesn't smile at me. She knows I'm angry. They push Marie Claire inside, and I watch them disappear around a corner. Pulling my collar up around my neck, I walk down the driveway. But then I stop and look back. It's getting dark and the lights from the hospital are glowing yellow.

"I'll never give up on you!" I shout.

And I never will. See, my sister's the greatest kid in Canada. And one day I'll take her back there. Back to Winnipeg and the prairies and the Forks and all her friends who love her so much. And before that dog reaches the horizon, she'll be back to her old self again. One day I'll take her back. One day soon. You see if I don't!

Acknowledgments

Writing a book is hard business. Trying to get published is just as hard. And just when you think it will never happen, someone comes along who believes in your work. They show it to other people, who in turn show it to others. All of a sudden there's a campaign to get you published. And so I would like to thank some of the people involved. Sarah Manson, my agent, and Roisin Heycock, and all the lovely people at Quercus who can never do enough for you.